THE JASMINE ISLE

Ioanna Karystiani

THE JASMINE ISLE

Translated from the Modern Greek
by Michael Eleftheriou

Europa
editions

Europa Editions
116 East 16th Street
12th floor
New York, N.Y. 10003
www.europaeditions.com
info@europaeditions.com

Copyright © 1997 by Ioanna Karystiani – Thanassis Kastaniotis
First Publication 2006 by Europa Editions

Translation by Michael Eleftheriou
Original Title: Μικρά Αγγλία
Translation copyright © 2006 by Europa Editions

Library of Congress Cataloging in Publication Data is available
ISBN 1-933372-10-9

Karystiani, Ioanna
Μικρά Αγγλία

Book design by Emanuele Ragnisco
www.mekkanografici.com

Printed in Italy
Arti Grafiche La Moderna – Rome

CONTENTS

THE JASMINE ISLE

PART ONE
THE EYE OF GOD

I t could have been the fumes, the wheat starts to rot in the damp and the stevedores play silly buggers loading up, it might have been the corned beef too, Savvas Saltaferos had heartburn but wasn't about to leave Nicephoros alone in the hold, he roped his godson and Stelios into it, muscles and shoulders on the pair of them, "grab hold, let's lay him in the head, a ten-minute job."

Cigarette in hand, wrapped in oilcloth for the hoarfrost, he spent the night beside the corpse.

Scudding along, the Atlantic silent as a grave.

He chucked him his butt, "have a drag yourself," endless life-sucking whirlpool, no way they could have made port in time, a three-day sail from Caripito to Paramaribo and Nicephoros dead and gone from something like pneumonia.

Leaden-mouthed from the cigarettes, some Peruvian crap, two packets he'd smoked, Saltaferos laid the carton on the dead man's legs at dawn, four still in it, went to his cabin and left his Radio alone to gape at the dawn one last time, we're all of us alone, quite alone in this life, the captain thought, Nicephoros kaput and the rest of them here, front and center in Paramaribo with dough in their pockets; as for the miserable bitch, fifteen years with a sour mug on her, and just because life doesn't split nicely down the middle she'd chew on the pension till her ass was twice the size while Nicephoros the uncomplaining, the ablest seaman, a heart of gold, the most sought-after wireless operator in the company, who the port girls would treat to a fuck on the house, garlicky as he was, over and out at forty-one.

Three years before, in '26, Saltaferos had received a letter from Andros with a photograph, Mina with the girls, Orsa and Mosca, on the wide steps up to the Church of the Megalochari, neighboring Tinos's Virgin Full of Grace, a few words dry as dust on the back, "suffer the hardships for the sake of getting Orsalia and Mosca settled" and "the Virgin has no complaints about your absence."

The Aden-Bombay it was back then, saltpeter, the Indian Ocean had whipped itself into a frenzy, standing the *Theomitor* on its end, four days and nights bartering with Charon, goners for sure, twenty-two men heading for the bottom, and God knows, with the fury spent and the steamer on an even keel again, the captain was out of his mind, desperate to get the secret off his chest. More than half the crew from back home, but Saltaferos kept his distance at sea for the sake of discipline. He couldn't find the way, the courage—"go on, Christos, fry me up a couple of eggs sunny-side up"—to tell the cook, who had a similar story himself in Chile, dipping into the yolk to tell the tale, every gross detail, someone should know, to cover every eventuality, so why not Christos, a good man, not wanting to put himself out, the card, and softhearted to boot, mother and daughters, the Chilean women in Valparaiso, he called Frosso, Tassoula, Vangelio, just like the others back in the Aegean.

No, he could only have confessed another love to Nicephoros, there was something motherly in his eyes, brown and ordinary, they'd take anyone with a secret weighing on them to one side, "lay it on me," they'd whisper, "and worry not." Picking at a slice of Andros cheese, "want to know something," the captain said to Christos, but then at the last minute, like his tongue went numb, "when we hit a typhoon it's my godson I care about most, I've been dragging him, fatherless and an only child, over the seven seas since he was twelve, and his mother loving him close to death," he'd blurt out something else that wasn't, anyhow, a lie.

The dead man didn't fall for it, he could tune into *las señales del alma*, the radio signals of the soul, he stared him straight in the eye till Saltaferos looked down at the plate with the cheese, and then, leisurely scanning the horizon, so calm now, the captain started softly singing, *blow, blow my little mistral, blow maistralaki mou, and bring me my love*, heavy cigarette in hand all the while.

July 9th, Wednesday, Spyros Maltambes touched her hand, on the 17th, the following Thursday, he squeezed it too, not the right hand this time, the other one, he caressed it gently, squeezed it again, rubbed it where the fingers fork two by two. And she curled like a snail, felt her whole body flush and then her heart, without a sound, bursting open like a pomegranate and the little rubies sketching arcs in the air, tumbling back over her shoulders and him, up onto the saint's roof tiles, like fireflies. I must be dead, she thought without fear or regret.

On the twenty-first of the month, a Monday, he parted her curls, "to see your eyes, Orsa," before darkness fell, but his hand lingered in her hair for the longest time, his finger piercing her thick braid, patting and cupping he laid his rough fingertips on her temples, her neck, the length of her throat, traced the half moons of her ears, the half moons of her eyebrows, the straight line of her nose, the oval of her chin.

A man's fingers are heavy. You turn to stone at their touch.

Now for the where.

The first meeting down at the little bridge, behind the platans and wild figs, afternoon, melon skins and cucumber peels, Orsa's excuse, needed taking to the chicken run, the grave digger gave them his spare eggs, another time she'd have taken care not to step on the slime in the rapids and fall flat on her ass in the water, scared stiff she was of water snakes, adders, vine vipers, even the good grey house snake made her faint. She went to the first rendezvous without the stick she crashed about with to frighten off reptiles, the sun baking roofs, steps, hot houses, yards, piercing the canopy as if it were nothing but a sieve, but not so much as a headache, soaked in sweat and bliss, tumbling towards the stream, the gravedigger far from her thoughts, she showed up for their first date grasping the roasting pan in both hands, leftovers, peelings, seeds, fat and gristle.

The second date elsewhere, behind the church of Saint Dimitrios, dusk, and her on the way to her godmother's for the evening, the poor woman eaten up by loneliness out there in the dust, without neighbors, with a nameless, barkless dog. The bushes huge and the wall still hot, Saint Dimitrios dazed, a late autumn saint he, October. In the heat it was the summer saints, Peter and Paul first and foremost, Cosmas and Damianos the Anargyri, Elijah the prophet, saints Paraskevi and Panteleimon, to whom they all ran to pay their respects. Not a soul in the fields further out, the city's two thousand inhabitants unaware of their romance. The only witnesses some fluttering swallows darting into their nest beneath the corrugated sheet over the door.

Later, up at her godmother's, Orsa's thoughts were elsewhere, she'd come to keep the older woman company but did not breath a word, just stared into the night sky. She got bored, too, might even have been angry the girl wouldn't trust her with her secrets, loaded up her apron with green beans, spent an hour stringing them in the gloom leaving her godchild undisturbed in her world, until she dozed off on the divan under the crape myrtle.

Tryst number three, nightfall not far off, the moon already risen, Spyros Maltambes climbed down to the seashore first and waited for her, in the little cave where the capers dangled down like a young girl's bangs, them too, over the brow.

They took off their shoes, tepid water up to their ankles, he lunged for her knee, she let out a strangled "Spyros, no," an unearthly power in his gaze that paralyzed her and another in his arms that set her alight, charcoal in the incense burner.

Trying to breath normally, she pressed her ear to his chest, echoing with the sounds of distant oceans, and where hadn't he been, picking out the hard passages, falling in love with the most hellish ports. The girl dressed in deep coral silk. The color went for naught at night. But its touch did not.

Date number four, Sunday, July 27th, all of them invited out to celebrate with some Pandelis or other, comings and goings, toings and froings, the perfect alibi for slipping out to some other, any other, saint; they were on the best of terms with them all.

For the first kiss Orsa wore her russet silk, her father would send her bolts of it when sailing the Calcutta-Bombay, she'd bound the stems of jasmine flowers and pinned the bouquet to her strap, freshened her arms, her décolleté, her ears with cologne, sprinkled her hair as well; her finery wouldn't arouse suspicions on a day like this, no need to secretly bathe in fountains and streams before going home.

Spyros Maltambes honored the russet silk duly and creased it deeply. He held his girl tight and kissed her and scratched her with his rough palms, and Orsa would have had it no other way, she'd loved him seven long years, since she was twelve going on thirteen, since an endless, torrential November day, nineteen years old at the time he'd stripped and dived into the sea for a bet with some others, and she'd dreamed his kisses exactly like this, a little rough, like waves, so sure, indelibly stamping her lips with his.

The following morning, "go on," insisted Nana Bourada-Negropiperi, schoolgirl by disposition, literature teacher by profession, "tell me who it is." But Orsa kept her lips tight shut; she didn't want to share her secret, not for the present at least. Everything had worked out just as she'd wished. Secret trysts, deserted spots, confidential words, complex subterfuge, passion, and a touch of panic. Every love, first loves most of all, ought to keep themselves to themselves for a longish time.

The teacher's light green house, its trademark rose, Japanese by extraction, white and climbing, crowning balconies and windows and looking like snow in high summer. Sipping coffee the two of them. Madame Nana had enjoyed girlish relationships with her former students even before she was widowed.

Orsa would stop in occasionally, usually the day after in search of inner calm, to retouch her customary, unflappable image; she didn't want her mother getting wind of anything.

She shot Nana a more clement glance, her coiffeured hair, lips well-reddened, two yellowed fingers, sitting cross-legged in her new spotted skirt with the permanent pleats, available; yes, that more than anything else, available at the drop of a hat. Flattered by the girls' trust, she never let their secrets slip, kept colleagues, parents, and guardians in the dark, even when she shouldn't.

"I spent the day before yesterday thinking about this town's mismatched couples, did a bit of a reshuffle, and remarried the half of them. The headmaster's made for Glynou, and his wife's just perfect for the printer. And Father Philippos would be much better off with Francesca."

"And the priest's wife with Saint Fanourios." Orsa heard her calling round other folk's houses in search of her husband every day, twice a day, often more, "with the saint's help, she'd always know where to find him."

"The photographer goes well with Nota, the confectioner's wife," Nana went on.

"And Nota's husband with his chocolates," Orsa piped up to her teacher's pleasure, it was only natural her twenty-year-old former student would see all of this as a joke, a parlor game to kill the time that passed more slowly on the island than anywhere else, but her experience of life and countless afternoons dedicated to reflection and telling observation brooked no dispute.

"Yes, my dear, the conceit of youth is life's most wonderful mistake, matches often fail to match, and it would be a thousand times better if the confectioner had married a cake and left Nota alone"; another of her students, from many years back, she'd bring her sweets on a tray, bowed and wrapped in cellophane, and the nothingness at the heart of her married life in another spectacular and no less transparent wrapping; a hawk that Nana, fishing up all life's little disappointments from beneath the routine pleasantries and mundane reassurances.

"I'm planning a trip to Athens," Mina said, Kourkoulis had been in contact, a little plot in Kifissia, not bad, half an acre or so, next to the one she'd beaten them down on the year before last, feast of Petros and Pavlos, "splice the two together shipshape-like, make one good 'un, get yourself over here smartish to draw up the contracts," he'd pressed.

Asimina Saltaferou had her people, got her information, did her sums and the sovereigns stacked up. Later, she got Mosca, her big sister would never cooperate, to copy the contracts in fine clear letters, mailed them to that man the same day, you can rot on the high seas, but I'm not wasting my time here, she added a couple of words at the bottom, neither one inclined to waste them.

July '27, the centre of Piraeus up in flames, February '28 fifty shops in Monastiraki reduced to ashes, many went belly-up but not Saltaferaina, though she usually invested in Attica; she'd set her eye on a barber's shop, a tailor's, a little plot, and made a cool-headed assessment, never burdened with memories, teenage reminiscences, parental give and take or undesirable abuttals, all of which stopped her purchasing on her island, though she'd grown up before the last century was out in Asia Minor, Smyrna.

Her daughters were familiar with her devotion to estate agents, Kourmoulis, as if he'd dare do otherwise, kept the bargains for Saltaferaina—the Saltaterou woman—the leftovers for the rest.

So she hadn't set foot in Athens for a full two years, seeing that man off then, she'd stayed on three days at the Ionion to sort the orders out, shoes from Plytas, Arsakion Arcade 5, valuable frames and the like, taxi drivers and bus owners on strike over English Power, national uproar, chaos, and she'd had a hard time getting through everything she had to do, but now the public transport was working to a tee and from the harbor she beat a course for the venereologist, a certain Nikolaides in the center of Piraeus.

"It's like this," she told him, "the father caught syphilis, years ago now, but the damage stayed, lost his sight then his mind, God knows who he thinks he is, but it's the son I'm interested in."

"Neurosyphilis?" the doctor asked.

"How am I supposed to know?"

Saltaferaina laid down the dates, August 15th, 1911, Captain Vatokouzis ashore and, benefactor though he was, having paid for the churchyard flagstones, he didn't show up for the saint's day fair, his sides covered in red spots; "Peach blossom," his wife had whispered in her ear, glum, dragging the child around after her, must have been seven years old. Mersina Vatokouzis, God bless her soul, her daughter she'd had in 1914. Fell to pieces, she did, gave up the ghost just after the forty days were out.

Long ago, when the *Antonios P* sank off the Scilly Isles, dead of winter 1905, they'd blamed Marios, Mina's brother. Three men drowned and the boat, spanking-new, holed and irreparable on the seabed. Mersina Vatokouzis' paternal family, the N. Daniolos & Son Marine Coal Company, kept an office on Syros back then, salvaged the ship for scrap and they got a little back, two and a half thousand sterling. Marios turned to drink. It was Mersina, may she rest in peace, who nagged and worried at her father, got him to take Marios back on, brought him back to life, and he worked like a dog, all the dangerous cargos, ammo-

nia, saltpeter, naphthalene, varnish and tar. In '22, when
Nuredin Pasha reduced Smyrna to ashes, he sailed run after run
with conscripts picked up in Asia Minor, and went to the bottom like a sailor in '23, the English Channel, not a drunkard to
make his child ashamed, him down in Johannesburg now, down
the English diamond mines.

"They can put up with Africa in their thousands, and Africa
can put up with them in their thousands, both are right,"
Saltaferaina thought, waiting in vain for a letter from her
nephew, even one about diamond mining would do.

"What does the patient take for his condition?" Nikolaides
brought her back, "bismuthiol, salvarsan or mercury and
iodide?"

Not a woman on the island didn't know all four, it was their
fate, they'd chew it over round at Mouraina's. He asked about
her son's health, "I couldn't swear to it, Mrs. Farakouki," Mina
had given a false name, "I couldn't swear to it, but there's a
good chance the son was conceived before the father was
infected by the syphilis."

Which means I'll have him for a son-in-law and I'll have to
move quick, Saltaferaina resolved, her eldest very distracted
and otherworldly of late, when he'd been sounding Mina out,
Takis the chief accountant for the Vatokouzis and Hadoulises
had delicately let drop a nicely rounded five-figure number, his
assets, she'd felt her heart miss a beat, her firstborn daughter by
general consent three inches short of a genuine Aphrodite, and
Nikos looked strong, distinguished, the money was tempting,
her daughter expensive to keep and a marriage like that the best
way to repay her debt to Mersina's soul, she'd done a lot for her
family, she owed her a thank-you.

And she sorted out the matter of the Kifissia plot, twenty-five
gold sovereigns, then back to Andros and the contract duly
copied and dispatched to Savvas, the signature dated August 6,
the Metamorphosis of the Savior, she wrote him, noting too her

small contribution to the collection for Italy's earthquake victims, nothing much, last year's quakes in Japan, Yugoslavia, Palestine, India, and Italy again had cleaned her out.

I'll tell him about the match later, when it's all worked out, she decided, and set about her unending chores once more.

The clans gathered every afternoon round Mouraina's, in dribs and drabs till there you had it, the lot of them ensconced in the sitting room gulping down the *kourabiedes* whole without dropping so much as the icing sugar, and Mouraina, tipsy on raki, *masticha*, and liqueurs mouthing all manner of naughtinesses, the more successful earned titters, the cascading hushing and shushing announced the sin to the world at large. The neighborhood kids would crawl up on all fours, the yard wall only this high, eavesdrop and commit the dirty words to memory, that lesson they'd all learned pat in primary school. The schoolmaster, to give Mouraina a piece of his mind, or so he pretended, fishing round till they'd spill the can of beans to him, too, a quiet man Mr. Stratakis, Mosca thought, that his only fault.

"Both from the same hole, one fucked like a Korean typhoon, the other like the sirocco, got it straight from the brides' mouths I did," Mosca heard it with her own ears, hunting down her mum the day before yesterday, Mouraina with such a head of steam worked up, she hadn't time to cut herself off mid flow or patch something together on the spot.

But it was what she saw that left its mark not what she heard, the flushed lady guests not even noticing the girl, as if, this their song, they could hold themselves back, hanging on her every word as the lump of lard crowed "so-and-so couldn't pull it out, because his anchor had fouled in her fur."

When Mosca was eleven, twelve, even thirteen, the curiosity gnawing away at her, she'd grown wise, whenever her ma, not that often, loaded her basket with stuff needing sewing and set off for Mouraina's or wherever else they'd all gather, she of the irrepressible mouth first and foremost, she'd find an excuse to burst in on them and hear what she could hear, she wrote the tastiest morsels down on tiny slips of paper and from then on, whenever she got together with Katina, Kiki, Marie, "his cock quivering like a mainmast," "sixty bollocks makes a crew of thirty," "lardy cunts because they were plump down there," "months and years without a rogering," "Argentina makes the best blankets 'cos it's one big whorehouse and all they ever think about is getting into bed," not forgetting that "too much lemon sours your kisses, your pussy, too, sometimes," were rarely out of their mouths.

Till thirteen, thirteen and a half at most, all that still forbidden treasure, desirably exciting torture, what's that mean, and that, the little girls would wonder, *'tis in the summer love blossoms, yet when it gets wintry, and that's the real mystery, they're all left alone* and the rest.

Mosca strapped for a good way of getting Orsa to notice she was there, three years her elder, nothing could change that, she'd always be three years older and daddy's favorite who'd shut herself in her room for hours on end without being stuck-up, not a sound from in there, or lie faceup on the courtyard wall and stare at the Eye of God, there where two mountains met head on and the clouds were always in a rush.

Orsoula, I hate you, I have to say it, Mosca thought, but never fall for a sailor, apart from your fear of losing him, you'll be hanging off Mouraina's every word, too, and boy will she be well past it by then, thirty-eight years old the she-whale and struggling to come up with anything new, the widows especially wouldn't sit there listening to the same stuff over and over without complaint, they demanded something new. So before they hit the coffee pots, she'd wrack her brains to please the women who, widows or no, slept alone every night.

A few months earlier, Mosca gawping at the man come from Athens to fix the island's bedsprings. Just the one hollow in her parents' double bed, one side only, he'd mumbled something and guffawed and her mother'd sent her packing to the pantry to roast coffee. The end would come and the Saltaferoses wouldn't have worn out a single pair of sheets.

And it was raining, drops like sword thrusts, mud everywhere, the three women stank of musty claustrophobic days, Mosca cursing now and then, her mood only lightening for the hour of English. Milky-white skin, thin as a rake, wavy brown hair, that was David and he had her way ahead of the rest of the class, Tuesday he's given her *The Tower of London*, all 631 pages of it, she'd given it him back Friday, picked to the bone, a feat, she'd wanted to persuade him language wouldn't be a barrier between them, the Brit, disbelieving, asking her this and that, but all the answers at her fingertips. The moment the bell rang, maybe in apology, "stay for a while," he'd said and gave her a postcard just like that, the artist's name went in one of the young girl's ears and come out the other, American, that much she remembered, a Christmas night, the Thames frozen, barges and sailboats pulled up on the banks, her heart racing she confused the details.

Some other girls got stuck there, no escaping fate, their sentence a fate of sorts, squinting hunched up over needlework on endless afternoons, counting and recounting knots and stitches on cold winter evenings, words in the house like drops from a dripper, two in the kitchen and two in the cellar, every day the same. Mosca loathed embroidery, maybe because of the unwritten law obliging them all to embroider that sad square and hang it in the most prominent place in the sitting room, to spy on and threaten them their whole life long, "listen up," it'd say, "there's no escaping fate." If that silly cow Orsa ever shared a secret,

Mosca would let her in on hers, she'd shake her up, "you can escape fate, but with a sailor, no way, just no way," she was terrified of becoming another of Mouraina's regulars.

"Katerina won't say boo, Cavo d'Oro's after you," whenever the sea was rough, some evil little devils would pelt Katerina Basandi with squeezed-out lemons, her husband, a cook, gone down with all hands on the other side of the world twelve years before, the woman couldn't take the sight of the sea's blue since, she'd moved behind a monochrome hill and, with Mosca for company and protection, walked home ten times over in order to steer clear of alleyways with a shard of blue Aegean at their end, sometimes shielding her eyes from any hint of sea with a palm held vertically against her cheek.

She wasn't mad, just unusual.

Mosca didn't want the sea, either, so she was fated to fall for the English teacher and to dream alone, laid out and faded-looking behind the voile of her iron bedstead's mosquito net, of escape from Little England, as Andros had been christened by shipowners with offices and interests in London, and ship's captains with ambitions of establishing themselves in Great, the real, Britain, china teapots, Madeira cake, and couples talking at length in the King's English of matters refined, European, and thoroughly modern.

*M*oney *must be found, without it nothing can be effect-ed,* Demosthenes, he was quicker than Saltaferos, otherwise the captain would have got it in first that morning round ten when the wire came in; the sea's a bitch from her one tip to her toes, Constanza, Cardiff, Diego Suarez, and Maracaibo, whores the lot of them, coast after coast encir-cling the oceans, too many to count, and arch-whore the sea herself, just as she's making your fortune she'll have your pants off before you know it, Savvas seethed with anger and worry.

It is with a grieving heart that I must inform you that the dear-ly-departed, Jason Telemes, who will live forever in our memo-ries, having contracted influenza and St. Anthony's fire, passed away in New York on July 17th, 1929, old Octopus had a pen-pusher for a son, a land lubber, shipping didn't smile upon him, his ships sank, both of them, the *Marousio Bebi* in 1907, purchased for the sum of 11,000 Guineas in 1916, lost off Uruguay in 1917, the *Kymatiani* built 1908, purchased for 27,000 Guineas in 1925, lost en route for the Philippines, spouse taken to her heels, Telemes left without a penny, just debts and promissory notes to his name in that city, the damn city that did him in.

An old friend Jason, seems to be a lot of folk dying of late, thought Saltaferos, torn two ways, he loved the sea but was afraid of where it led, winding up on the beach in a place where his childhood memories, figures, shadows, words, sounds, routes, colors were not, how different the blue of the sea in the

Bay, after the Presentation of the Holy Virgin, November 21st, a dirty grey until the southwesterly whipped up and made them leaden, African waters orange, especially as afternoon turned to evening, and as for the blue of the Coral Sea, something else that, the waters flashing and glowing like Christmas festoons with fairy lights, like the mandarins dew-dropped on the hill-sides walled and stepped, the dawn setting the sky aflame out past Cavo d'Oro, the fruit sparkling like electricity and dazzling sparrows struck dumb at the sight. A small world, but with no end of oddities, its sulfur blue seas calm as thirst-quenching sodas one minute, swelling and raging and drowning the next, like old Octopus, the king of the 32-card pack, Paschalis Telemes, *asi es la vida.*

Saltaferos, fifty now, the courage of ignorance and time no longer on his side, laden with the heavy load of experience and age and a rapidly burgeoning sentimentality, "a touch of sweet-ness," the younger men said, maybe a reaction to his wife, all business, besting various surviving Telemeses, Maridises, Zannises, octopuses, bonitos, crabs, and lobsters right then, weighing them up, making comparisons and wedding plans on the sly, Mina would catch them off guard like a Minister of Finance devaluing the currency, and the captain thousands of miles away expecting to be left bobbing in her wake. He'd never got to the bottom of his wife's soul, they'd let opportuni-ties slip by and now neither one could be bothered, so there was no will but no way either, they just did like so many other cap-tains and their wives on the island, the man looked after the men's work, managing the ship, arranging ports of call, cargo loaded and unloaded, shipboard life, the family income, the woman seeing to women's tasks, managing the home, invest-ments, raising and marrying their children. Just that when it came to the hard stuff, Mina'd put her faith in a leaking life-jacket, her purse; an intelligent woman she knew how risky and futile that was, she should put a little more heart into her strategy, for their daughters' sake at least. Saltaferos's wish as he plowed from one Latin American harbor to another, general cargo, he crossed himself, couldn't hurt, before opening the letters from Andros.

You say I go and stick my nose into the whole neighborhood's business, I say you go and stick your thing into holes in every harbor in the world, she wanted to lay it on the line there and then but saved it, its time would come, nothing goes to waste, Mina reasoned. Mosca had copied down the congratulations from the *Voice of the Aegean*, eighty drachmas it had cost, "Savvas P. Saltaferos, Capt., and family extend their warmest congratulations to Demosthenes G. Glynos, the son of our fellow islander and Senior Pharmacist to the Armed Forces, Georgios K. Glynos, on winning a place at the Naval Academy." Like father like son, losers the pair of them, but how could Saltaferaina know whose help she might need one black day in this small place, so for the sake of the family's interests she kept on the best of terms with everyone and showed the finger to a good half of them behind their backs. She couldn't possibly entrust the running of the household to her absent husband, he had a head for the ocean, on dry land he was all at sea.

"The blue of the Aegean flowed into your eyes, Orsa," he'd write to his firstborn and the other one complained, and if his eldest managed a sheet of note paper all told, the youngest found time to keep him up to date with all the island news, assigning priority to his kin and landlubberly mates.

"Write on cigarette papers," Mina would tell her, "your feelings'll weigh less."

The printer had finished the notices for Sunday's memorial services, "the widow L. Issaris" where L stands for Leonardos and "the widow S. Argyropaidou" where S stands for Sokratis, Stergios's was another widow, time to hit the two coffee shops, they'd agreed to share the grievers, and the square thick with mourning, not a Sunday went by without *kolyva*, boiled wheat to nourish the departed soul, seeds for continuity, raisins and sugar to sweeten the afterlife, it was off with the black and back on with it again, its darkness penetrated their bones, blackened their blood and then off to memorials for friends and strangers, work their fingers to the bone all week long, then the black two-piece and queue for condolences bright and early Sunday morning.

Mina decided to set off for Apatouria with the two of them before daybreak, to mother-in-law's, to arrange for the sale of the figs there and then and to spare the girls the pitch-tar parade, their house just down from the Cathedral and their life one sailor's memorial after another, in the summer especially when the scattered Andrians crowded back to their island, a deluge of them.

Some time before, the Assumption, May 28, watching Orsa. The girl had picked an armful of poppies from the gulley and the straggling dry stone terraces round Three Churches, now hanging from the balcony she was blowing and shaking the petals, which came off in an instant anyhow, she'd filled the alley with a flurry of red which the breeze blew towards the small, white, siesta-slumbering city. Mina on the ground floor, in the vine's shadow, eating cherries and poking her head out to snatch secret glimpses of her, beautiful, distant, the color of honey, a whim of the west wind. He was right, the blue of the sea had flowed into her eyes and let's see if they shed blue tears when she finds out about the groom, no tears, no ifs and buts. Mina wasn't having any of it.

September 5th, around the fifth hour, too, five in the afternoon. The sand, full of the heat of the day, laying down a shimmer like gold dust on top of whatever brown was left, the rocks and earth, the clear water revealing the seabed's secrets, here the color of saffron, there a deep-sea green, with the seaweed wearily turning away from the sun that insisted on pursuing it into the depths. A saint, out of love with Orsa, reclined in the centre of the bay, bone-white Saint Thalassini, blue patron of the sea, the twin of that other perched goat-like on the cliff who'd kept a lookout on those evenings when Spyros Maltambes and her had stolen stooped kisses in her yard.

A swimmer's strokes crack the sea and scatter white slips of saint from a letter shredded by its disappointed recipient, flashed images that filled the afternoon of the 5th of September, 1929, an afternoon Orsa Saltaferou wanted to spend alone, no close friends and so miserable the slightest movement bothered her, even at a distance, like the swimmer, Bozakis's cattle grazing on dried-up sow thistles and dill and the cinnamon calf drowsing in the shadow of the box elder.

Orsa tightened her grip round the three salt-encrusted spoons washed up by yesterday's blown-out *meltemi*, she'd dug them out of the sand and they were green with forgetfulness, "I'll keep them in my bag always," she thought, the afternoon rushed on, her swimsuit just wouldn't dry, the swimmer was out on the shore sprawled on her back, and the whole world in three parallel strips, a white and blue at the top, blue in the middle, and yellow down low, the cherry-red-swimsuited swimmer at its edge. She didn't want to talk to her, not at all, it was better like this, from afar, and if it had been last year or the year before that she might have chosen to store this image of the summer of '29 in her memory, that's how Orsa hoarded the past, the summer of '28, for instance, boiled down to a newly-wed's red hat snatched by the wind on the beach, the summer of '27 was Spyros Maltambes, shirt off, beating and cursing an octopus at the end of the mole, and summer 1926 Nana Bourada-Negropiperi in black, fan black, sitting alone in her shadowy hall with the door open.

Not so many people on the beach now, one here and one there, the market ground to a standstill, the city, ruins of the Frankish castle at its tip, steps and churches galore, marble fonts and mansion houses, Venetian or local coats-of-arms carved on their fronts, loggias, all sturdily rigged to withstand time with carved triangular plaques to remind us of the year of their birth, a city recaptured by the womenfolk as the years went by and the sailors packed their kit, belted up their trunks and left them, and far away Savvas Saltaferos had sworn to come next Easter and stay three months.

It never crossed Orsa's mind to call her mother, mum or ma or mummy, "she's going to Hell, the devil take her," she sometimes wanted to shout, especially when Saltaferaina succumbed to doubt and took a box of Havanas out of the cupboard, to rig her confession, everyone knew Father Philippos's weakness, and the cigars smoothed the way to every sin's absolution and the salving of every pang of guilt. No, there were no flies on old Saltaferaina, the priest tired of hearing the same old stuff, after thirty years, nothing the parish's sailors or wives could do was either original or interesting and he'd half listen before forgiving everyone and everything and heading out into the church-yard, eyes peeled for one of the few remaining males, in search

of a backgammon partner. Coming up emptyhanded was clearly a greater source of dismay than the sins weighing on his
flock's souls.

If mother's got a human bone in her body, she'll soon be
putting her conscience in order with a box of Havanas, the girl
thought.

Spyros uncle, Emilios Balas, had showed up the previous day
for a coffee and to discreetly raise the matter, "I've chosen her
another, a sacred bond, my hands are tied, no can do, tell your
nephew I've given my word, anyhow that Spyros, come on,
seems much too much the charmer to start a family to me." His
uncle, not up to this, swallowed his tongue and any talk of feelings, for her part Saltaferaina skirted the reef and didn't delve
into the matter as she should have and was wont to, supremely
suspicious woman that she was, and Orsa, eavesdropping,
missed not a word. She felt her veins pulse and burst and empty,
saw her blood form a brook, flowing slowly and inexorably, yard
by yard, into the Maltambes circle she adored; Saint Dimitrios,
the bridge, the old graveyard, the rocky cave, surrendering its
redness there until it was no more, as it turned into water, one
with the sea.

Caught off guard, her mother had nonetheless flown into
action, she'd stopped Balas in his tracks quicker than if she'd
pointed a revolver at him, to top it off she'd asked for the droppings from the pigeon loft for her carnations.

"Watch out, or those neighbors of yours will filch it again."

Motionless behind the oak sitting room doors, Orsa held her
breath, heard everything, and could not cry.

"Send the recipe for the *pasteli*, darling, you never know, the
cook might bake us a few," back it came beautifully scribed in
Mosca's hand, so many walnuts, so much honey and sesame, he
translated any which way for Angelita, Angelita Rodriguez San
Pedro, a small woman but a huge source of guilt, location
Argentina, year 1916, accrued by Savvas Saltaferos. He wasn't

no skirt-chaser, just a normal guy whose wife drove him mad with that sour face of hers, "your cholera and my cholera," that's what him and Nicephoros, God rest his soul, had called their wives. Matchmaker, Acheloos, the ship's dog, scared out of his wits by storms, but all hands had fallen for the old yellowbelly with his one good eye and grimy brown coat who'd vomited and broken everything in his path for two long days and nights. The first thing Saltaferos did when they docked in Buenos Aires was take Acheloos for a walk, to bring him to his senses, when the mutt calmed down they went to pay the girls a visit, Angelita newly arrived, "bring the dog in with you, don't want him scaring again and making a mess," she'd nursed him and called the vet; he'd prescribed sedatives.

It was that bloody dog started it all, *como vos querràs, mi amor* and *si mi amor* were bound soon to follow, so the fifth time they hit Argentina she was waiting for him with tomato pilaf and *halvas* and he adopted her son. Father unknown, three years old, she'd called him Odysseus, too, the only Greek name she remembered from the three or four years she'd put up with the classroom, "she'll have me all trussed up in no time, the bitch," Saltaferos thought; that same afternoon he dragged her off to a notary public and made her sign never to reveal herself to his legitimate family, the next morning they finished the job at the registry office and the three of them went for an ice cream.

A quiet morning, September, spring already in the air, Angelita usually on top of the world, sweet talk, tango, kisses, high spirits overcome by her unexpected good fortune, sobbing tears of gratitude.

Savvas kept looking at the little boy, definitely a keeper, he had a dignity in his gaze, he didn't approve of his mother's views on life, quite the little man at three, and with a cloud of brown hair like an angel's halo made of twigs.

Angelita and Odysseus, angels the pair of them, and Saltaferos able to relax in Buenos Aries at least, so he told

Hadoulis father and son, "I've hit fifty, no more China Japan, India Manchuria for me," chaos there what with the revolution, no, Argentina suited him just fine, he knew the seas of the South Atlantic like the back of his hand, the Atlantic Shore, a few years now carrying cargos for himself for Kingstown, Georgetown, Curacao, Paramaribo, Necochea, Valparaiso and back.

The others had no business finding out, sure Nicephoros had been worthy of a secret like that, but he'd gone and kicked the bucket just as he was about to tell and his son remained a secret, fifteen years old now, nearly six foot tall.

And then there were the daughters known to all. He'd got three letters the other day in Lisbon, Orsa, Mosca, Mina, written, you'd think, not by creatures that shared the same house, but by strangers, people from different lands, worshipping different gods, his wife eight and a half lines of expenses and a few half-chewed phrases about some future match, Mosca an eleven-sheet report on goings-on behind others' doors, bypassing the white two-storey house in Riva—their own—completely, and Orsa two spaced-out pages that said a lot in their own way, "be happy, daddy, let me stow away with you, it's like grandma says, in the end Little England's too small for big emotions."

Savvas Saltaferos's face darkened for the hundredth time, his wife had deprived him of their daughters' embraces, when he returned to the island every two or three years, he didn't feel comfortable kissing and hugging the two reserved kids who'd turned into young women in the meantime, age raising yet another barrier between them.

Having play-acted a few times on Andros, he could lay it on nostalgic and regretful while inside he couldn't wait to weigh anchor and set sail again, thirty-six years at sea, no such thing as unfamiliar waters, even afraid of hankering after his bed, his lemon and mandarin grove and little cypress tree, his old mother and a few select folk like Grigoris.

Laid out in the breeze, borne by four sailors, staring at the Eye of God, the sky opaque, the midday moon, "Grigoris flew, daddy, he flew along the main road for the last time, past the woodpile and the night flower's withered branches, yet more victims of the fussy barber, past the twin plane trees in the square, the houses where he spent his evenings between voyages, and came to earth in the church of the Panagia," Orsa had written him. He lay listening to the bell toll from eleven till four in the afternoon, listened, too, to his wife softly weeping, and tried to get used to it.

His soul hurt for Grigoris, and it hurt for Orsa, a girl with a head beset by dark ideas. He stubbed out his cigarette, gathered up the letters and rubbed his temples round and round, his mother suffered from headaches and this was his inheritance, no chance of missing out on that. Coming out of his cabin to go to work, he bumped into the cook bringing him a plate of sausages and couldn't hold it in any longer.

"For fuck's sake, in the end I'll say I miss Andros and just mean I miss Aristos the grocer, let's say, laid-back and close-shaven with a moustache that's a geometry lesson in itself, interpreting dreams as he weighs out butter or dried cod."

"And he makes the spiciest sausages," Christakis added, trembling.

Page 146, Rear Admiral Sir Frederick Bedford RN Retd., on the avoidance of collisions at sea, in his father's book, *Rudiments of the Theory and Practice of Seacraft incldg. all the tables and astronomical charts*, by Pelopidas Tsoukalas, Athens, 1912, old but tried and tested, Spyros Maltambes had it off by heart, and he wasn't the only one, he'd had his nose in stuff like that since he was twelve.

What else was there to do in the middle of the Indian Ocean, where nothing ever happened, just a steamer plowing through an endlessness of white, the monotony had him turning the same things over and over, driving him mad?

October 17th, Surabaya Java, at the quay loading rice, that's when he found out Saltaferaina had turned him down flat, twenty-seven years of age, a captain with tempting offers from shipowners on Andros, Chios, from Inoussa, Kasos, and Kephallonia, she hadn't even asked if there were any feelings between him and her daughter; wouldn't you know it, a woman who bought her olive oil from the top of the hill, her butter halfway up, and her honey at the bottom with no idea how to shop for a son-in-law, God knows what dandified fancy-pants she'd set her sights on, that was her all over: no money, no honey. A body that could keep you up all night gone, I've lost her, Maltambes remembered an hourglass figure, delicate wrists and ankles, firm, well-fleshed limbs. The first time he'd kissed her, Orsa had swooned in his arms in shame, but soon as she came round, after a minute or two of silence, unexpectedly bold she'd answered his first kiss with a thousand of her own, leaving him dumbstruck. As for their last date before he set sail, his uncle's forty birds their witness, perched among the nest holes and fish bones in the dovecote, cooing ragged breaths and words half-unfinished.

A strange girl, submissive one minute, far from it the next, bubbly and gay a third, impenetrable and melancholy a forth, "it's the light," she insisted, "it affects me so, that or dreams."

She hardly ever spoke of her family, "I'll read you a poem," she'd announced out of the blue, and then the torture of having to guess whose it was, she'd muddled him with poets' initials and cities of birth, him losing every time and her loving it, her beloved a bit hopeless when it came to poetry. She'd copied stray verses from here and there into that long, narrow leather-bound notebook of hers, as fat as an ecclesiastical tome, identical to the ones they recorded the wages in on the ships, *papeterie Hautin, fonde en 1856*, she'd learned French from postcards but her accent was good. Maltambes flicked through his own, bound in black leather with *Ostria* inscribed in a brown decorative border, crew's salaries from March 1st, 1928, last year, *Nikolas Zannis, telegraph operator, paid 250 Escudo, Ioannis Polyzos, stoker, owed 37 Pounds, overleaf Athanasios Maistros, ship's engineer, requested 50 Pound advance en route for Calcutta*, and so on, Maltambes had been around the world a dozen times. But last summer he'd been much impressed by the space and hiding places of the little island shielding their romance from view, everyone acquainted and everyone nosey, not a soul got wind of them.

Orsa took a thousand precautions, but then always came wrapped in silks, Spyros knew a thing or two about women's getups, but hers a whole story in themselves, so she'd show up with a little jasmine intertwined with her honey-colored plait, a ribbon the color of the sea and her eyes, he'd fix his gaze on their blue and drink in the cool, eternal shimmer, "that's the ocean I'll sail," he'd declared and pulled her tight against him, on fire, "lucky Maltambes," he'd tell himself, "the girl's a mermaid, your lucky charm," like the one he had tattooed on his left arm, a magnificent head of hair, tail tucked under her, scales finely drawn.

Heavy work aboard ship and the men well used to it, one five, another fifteen, a third twenty-five years at sea, only the first-timers needed to ask what to do. When the weather wasn't playing tricks, everything much of a muchness, very ordinary.

Spyros watched the old hands, each one with his own pace in port and out of it, on the long hauls even the jokers, the troublemakers, all the unmanageable ruffians, had fallen into step with the sea by the third day, it imposed its own rhythm and silences on them all, whatever profession their seaman's papers professed, greaser, deckhand, or cabin boy, like Takis, Mouraina's nephew, the golden boy gone to sea two months past, up for the most hellish voyages, shorn of his appetite for adventure without so much as a typhoon to his name or having had to pray like the clappers, nerves shot to shreds.

There were all sorts going round in Spyros' head. But he was waiting to get his hands on some money, too.

"You saved my ship twice last year, and two fortunes with it," Hadoulis Junior, a special guy, well-bred and well-read with it, just wired him a promise of a share in their new vessel, the *Leonidas II*, on order in the name of their uncle, who'd done great things as a merchant and smuggler and died in his sleep, a ripe old age, having earlier forced the priest to his knees at backgammon.

With a 15% share to his name, Saltaferaina would think him more of a gentleman, and Maltambes, who'd set his sights on her girl, would have her one way or another.

A mule at the window, ten sacks of doused manure round the roots of the damson tree, the chandelier that swung no more, and the electrician finally climbed down off his stepladder, the ground floor speckled with his red and black cables, finely chopped, and bits of copper wire.

Mina Saltaferou cut him down to size, because he'd come to hang the new light fittings after the wedding, but was it Eftychis's fault he'd been feverish with the flu and left his obligations pending?

Saltaferaina had marshaled Orsa's wedding like a military campaign, dividing precise responsibilities between relatives, neighbors, and others so Savvas' absence wouldn't count, so no one had time to catch their breath and weigh up the flaws of this match, to keep her firstborn, too, confused with all the furor, to forget herself and keep her mouth shut.

From afar, Mosca watched them unloading the Viennese chairs off the lighter and onto the backs of the animals down on the quay, four donkeys in no hurry, it took them just short of half an hour to arrive, to negotiate the steps down into the yard, to unload the elegant chairs and a clothes rack, gifts from Hadoulis the shipowner, the guilty parties had all dug deep into their pockets.

She killed time in the pastry shop, beside its mustachioed founder, faded by the summer glare he'd been resting in peace above the *fruit glacé* not giving a damn for a decade now, his only care to smite the sugar-lusting flies with his gaze, as if they'd dare.

Would she wed a confectioner? If it meant not marrying a sailor, she'd have the apprentice lad who baked the almond cookies, hell, she'd even have the little slave who threshed in the summer sun and brought the bitter almonds for the *souma-da*; that is, if she weren't already in love.

David sitting in the pastry shop, he'd finished off a cake, probably chocolate because there was a bit of truffle left on his plate, bent over busily writing cards, Christmas cards, "but they won't arrive till after," she had the urge to scold him, December the 20th already, but disturbed by all the comings and goings, the ordering and purchasing, he'd greeted her somewhat formally and that's how she stood there for an age, a pillar of salt watching the four far-off donkeys bearing the Viennese chairs, tongues lolling from their exertions in the icy wind, until she heard "Miss Saltaferou, the wedding sweets are ready, may it be your turn soon."

Orsa hardly looked real in her ethereal wedding gown, an Athenian house, her hair sprinkled with lemon blossom and a swarm of bridesmaids, captains' and shipowners' daughters, the whole of Andros had given the wedding top billing and sent gifts, they'd packed the house with elaborate baskets of wedding cake, the downstairs house, where the whole family usually lived, not the upstairs, which the Saltaferoses had set aside as dowry for their firstborn daughter, equipped with only the finest, and in the meantime only unlocked for feast days and guests. There was no way Orsa wanted to live upstairs, with the best view in the whole Aegean, Paraporti Bay on the one side and the Eye of God on the other, mumbling some gibberish about wanting the moonflower beside her in the summer, her mother had guilefully got her to fight for the flowers and let her win, and Vatokouzis didn't interfere, Orsa was the greatest stroke of luck in his life, he was not Orsa's, because when Saltaferaina, more resplendent than Athanasios of Syros, Tinos, and Andros, who'd come to bless this union in person, and as the senior prelate to cast out the syphilis more effectively, so when Saltaferaina began to toss "a child's home rests upon the foundations of their parents' blessings" to left and right, Orsa stared at her like a beast for slaughter, but for naught.

The union effected, Monday December 27, 1929. "And thou, oh bride, be thou magnified as Sarah, and glad as Rebecca, and do thou increase like unto Rachel, rejoicing in thine own husband, fulfilling the conditions of the law for it is well pleasing unto God"; Athanasios intoned the words in the centre of the room, beneath the swinging chandelier Eftychios had not had time to take down and Father Philippos, present and sidelined, did too, silently through clenched teeth.

The celebrations lasted until dawn, Mosca watching the somber newlyweds, a waltz and a *ballos*, and thought of her sister without clothes, surrendering herself for the first time to a man in whose blood she did not trust, suspecting all the while she wanted another, someone she had not opened her mouth to proclaim, and most tragically of all this blond, gangling Vatokouzis with the half-closed hazel eyes, seemed neither a bad man nor a fool, Lord God, how the perfumed bed chamber, the starched sheets and satin quilt, the rose petals, shells, and confetti scattered across the bed in which they were to spend their first night together, a night of torment, must have seemed to mock them both.

For gentleman and lady pure torment in the night, God's will performed by flickering candlelight, Katina, Kiki, Marie, Mosca, the four inseparable school friends of old, realized afresh that they were girls and knocked back a raki on the count of three.

David resolved to act, asked Mosca to dance, and she pounced on him, her hopes renewed, clasped herself to his chest, sent the Englishman into a panic, he held her a demure ten inches at bay, the island code's accepted distance. But he must have felt her disappointment, though she sighed to underline it, and her eyes were blacker than black. Four or five times round the room later, his tones even more English than usual, "Show me the steps to the *ballos*, too, after," he said, but there was no after, as though he'd forgotten he disappeared into the corner once more between two giants, Papadopoulos, mathematics and physics he taught, and Madame Hazapi, history, how dainty David was, he didn't even like the wedding feast, sitting nibbling chocolates and cakes, *Kyria* Nana repeatedly proffered him the tray of sweetmeats.

Mina Saltaferou, who had eyes in the back and sides of her head, took note of the waltz but kept her comments for the dawn, when the last guest had left very or a little drunk, searching out their bundles of sugared almonds.

"I paid the musicians, too, a sovereign to the lute and another to the dulcimer, all the fuss and bother over. Let's go and catch a couple of hours sleep ourselves."

The daughter much taller, the tallest in the family, so short stout Mina stood up straight, patted her pitch black curls into place, and fixing not only Mosca with her gaze, but the floor, too—that is, fixing Orsa, who had long since retired downstairs with Nikos—confided the distilled experience of a lifetime, speaking softly, she gently led her younger daughter by the arm to a spot right above the marriage bed, "I've one thing to tell you both, it's a thousand times better that girls don't marry the men they love, it makes the pain bearable when off they go to their fancy women."

Mina Saltaferou, though short and fat, had been considered a catch at twenty with her lily-white skin, crow-black hair, charcoal eyes, plum mouth, she, too, had been someone in her day, and in Smyrna where she'd grown into womanhood, they didn't let their women go to waste. Of course, deep inside, she'd long known the nature of her own marriage, a life spent waiting and a gold medal for fidelity, but her achievement not worth a dime.

"What can I say, my love, for you to forgive me? You didn't want the gifts, you wanted me. The Germans made it clear I had to oversee the repairs myself in Hamburg. On your wedding day, when I'd imagined myself dancing *ballos* after *ballos* until dawn, singing *come Christ and Virgin with your only child to bless this couple in the making*, I'd telegraphed Vangelis and had it all arranged, but ended up drinking myself into a stupor with the men from overseas and singing their songs."

"It was better that way, papa, the island was blanketed in snow and looked aristocratic and refined, like the pictures of icebergs you'd send us from Archangel."

Twenty words if that, Orsa's reply to Savvas Saltaferos. She'd accepted the honeymoon so she wouldn't have to lay eyes on her mother, waving the mute certificates with their seals and stamps and Harley Street signatures, the twenty-year-old bride, too young to suspect Saltaferaina might be scared that in the end, or worse, before the end, she'd see her own life differently and break down into tears.

If only we were all more tender with each other, if only we hugged and kissed more often, weeping and giggling like children in each other's arms, trying to guess whose is the heartbeat, ours or the one we love, Orsa often had such thoughts, since, at the age of twelve, she had resolved to assign importance to love and only love, a decision she made one night when, out of nowhere, she felt a sudden stab of awful solitude; but sweet solitude she would not deny.

Before the wedding, she'd gone to Apatouria, a good hour's walk away, to tell grandma Orsa the truth and to form an alliance. She arrived with rays of winter sun, the village faces east, the two Orsas had just finished their fish soup and were nibbling the flesh from the gills, the usual old folk's food, the older woman put the coffeepot on to boil and the younger stood up to put the dishes in the sink to cool, through the kitchen window she saw the sun already dipped behind the mountain and her mood darkened with it; she liked the way dusk and night fell in westward-looking places, the day dallied, the landscape grew slowly darker, piece by piece, when folk turned on the electric light or lit the wick of their oil lamps, it was as though light and darkness were exchanging a kiss, elsewhere, in places where it all happened of a sudden, she was afraid of losing her mind.

She turned the tureen and the two bowls upside down to drain, looked outside again, an aerial assault, hundreds of starlings plummeting like lead weights, darting like bullets into the two enormous fig trees, their naked branches warped javelins, ashen, beyond, the cypress windbreak, pitch black already, a landscape like an icon to a menacing saint.

"I'm listening," the old lady said. She handed the girl her cup, put a basket of mandarins on the table, and took a deep breath, ready to hear serious tidings, she'd guessed exactly what this visit was in aid of, always loved to go against and undermine her daughter-in-law.

Orsa didn't say a word, she'd swallowed her tongue and felt inert, lifeless.

Her grandma tried to stir her into action with a few choice words, "syphilis," "father-in-law," "fear," "love," and been forced to take another tack.

"How long is it since you cut your hair?" she asked her granddaughter as she donned her coat and knitted hat.

"Since primary school," Orsa replied, kissed her and left.

The few neighbors—blurred figures at their windows—one

woman here, another there, eyes fixed on the deserted lane; they'd got wind of the visit early on and peered out to catch sight of the future Vatokouzaina as she lengthened her stride so night wouldn't catch her out of doors. Two or three hastened to open their windows, part the curtains and shout "all the best for your wedding!"

"Don't touch me tonight," she'd told Nikos Vatokouzis. The wedding guests had bundled them off to bed an hour earlier with the customary ribaldry. Him in no rush, looked around for his cigarettes, "on our second night then, no matter, Orsa," he said, and smoked till morning listening to the lute and the tramp of dancing feet upstairs, what a racket, just a few thin floor boards separating him from them, *monopatosia*, a single-plank partition, congenital flaw of two-storey houses. And the hullabaloo didn't let up in the slightest.

In no time, the bride had learned to distinguish Marie's heels from Nana's, the teacher took little steps, her toes touching the floor first, like the hooves of a young filly, the groom easily picked out Hadoulis' heavy soles when the old man danced his one and only *ballos* of the night, the confident steps of the metropolitan, who left quite early on, and the uncertain footfalls of Father Philippos, who stayed, though being supplanted like that had done for his legs and his spirits, both attuned their ears for a while to a flood of girlish tears, some young girl's *bonboniera* come undone, the sugared almonds had bounced across the floor like pebbles.

They left for Piraeus the following noon aboard the *Afroessa*, stayed four days in the Capital, him running from shipowners and harbormasters to shipping agents and chandlers, attending to the details of the voyage, overseeing the loading.

Hadoulis father and son, Vatokouzis' partners and not just Saltaferou's bosses, sent a snowy mountain of a hundred white roses. Orsa got through it in her room, staring from her hotel window at the comings and goings in the street and harbor below, rain, carts, automobiles, people rushing by, and ship after ship. When night fell, she sat in the darkness and counted the lights outside, so many more than she was used to, yellowish and hazy, as waves of drizzle descended like a dust cloud to envelop the whole of Piraeus.

If things were different, she'd have strolled from shop to shop looking in the windows and going inside, had her nails and hair done, seen people. But things weren't different, this is how it was. Maltambes aboard the *Ostria* beneath the Indian Ocean's summer skies, many an Andrian among the crew and correspondence formal, so and so dead, wed, or bred, so he knew, or would soon enough, that Orsa Saltaferou was now Nikolaos Vatokouzis' bride.

She became his wife in more than name aboard the *Archipelago*, in his cabin, as she sailed though open waters off Sardinia with the wind behind her, the oil lamp flickering as always beside the cot. Nikos Vatokouzis kept his eyes shut, and Orsa, too, only Saint Nikolas's wide open in his icon, nothing ever slipped by him unnoticed.

When the deed was done, Orsa realized the expression "I was now his" wasn't right, it was the first time she'd felt her body hers and hers alone, as much as her thoughts, she turned slightly to one side, inexplicably he undid her endless plait in the depth of the night and brushed her hair, laying it out till it covered the whole bed, as though he'd been looking forward to doing and seeing just that for the longest time. He smoked a cigarette and left, heading for the funnel to check the watch roster.

Orsa's wedding gown, an all-silk, pure white embroidered torrent on the hanger bedside the porthole, did not move for the forty days of the voyage.

A swell, sailing round Finistero lighthouse and Nikos scanning for the rocks off Vigo with his binoculars, many a schooner, tall ship and steamer had docked for the last time there on the seabed, off the coast of Spain.

"Dinner was salty as hell," said Mansolas, the master, Karystinakis's food didn't suit him at all, he'd be sipping water all day long, Nikos and the Radio preferred coffee, the three of them talking, their chat punctuated by the drawn-out groans of the ship's iron plates, smoking and waiting to reach the spot where the *Aegean II* had gone down two years before.

Orsa wasn't going to go against tradition, she wasn't vain that way, the sea held her in its power, totally, sailors' words had always mesmerized her, picked out one by one and never forgotten. So she'd noted down where ships had sunk and wanted to throw *kolyva* into the waters in memory of the drowned. She had four or five bags with her, chanted over by the monks at Ai-Nikolas, as they'd done for many a year.

"Pretty depressing for a honeymoon," Nikos had told her gently, giving her room to turn down the sad duty.

"I'm not superstitious," she told him quietly, without irony, she didn't play it high-and-mighty, either, she was dead straight with him.

A match was made and then a wedding, now these two who'd known each other by sight till then had to spend a lifetime together. Their first time, ice in her and panic in him, the sun was up before they got their act together, Nikos would touch her spine gently, unsure, every so often he'd move away in the berth taking her hand with him, she'd turn onto her other side, him hiding, kissing the air and drinking in his wife's slim wrist like a priceless marble sculpture, her fingers white and abandoned to his breath and lips.

"We're here," the master brought him back to earth, and Stamatis the cabin boy informed Orsa who, ready for some time, came out of her cabin with slickers over her green dress, a kerchief on her hair and a paper bag in her hand.

The sea was rough, arrogant in the manner required by the myth of this place, they crossed themselves, Orsa leant over the rail and scattered the *kolyva* into the foaming waters, "God rest their souls," Nikos said; Sophocles Rodokanakis had gone down with the *Aegean II*, his classmate at Robert's College and the only one of his peers he could call a real friend, they'd rejoiced, embraced, kissed, and wept together.

On the island, sadness for his mother and shame for his father kept him away from others his age, he'd wander Riva and the quay alone, Annezio his nurse called him a spirit of the quay, the summer northerlies—*meltemi*—and southwesters spat spray in his face and he found consolation in the cigarettes never absent from the inside pocket of his duffel coat from eleven on.

At the age of six, six because he'd just started primary school, woken up one night by the clatter of feet on wooden floorboards and staircase, his father on shore leave and must have been a little drunk, "Mersina," he was chasing his mother to get her back in their bed, she, scared and lost, ran out the door in her nightie and set off down the hill for the river. The boy ran to the window and watched the white nightdress disappear into the drizzling darkness, towards the gulley. Annezio hid him in her arms, no need for words, the selfsame thought in their head, him six and her thirty-six, that the poor woman might fall into the river and drown.

He was never desperate for his father to come back home, just to leave it, the expensive toys he brought were left unplayed with, and him every couple of years back with something even more wondrous only to find its predecessors untouched, still wrapped and ribboned.

His son had found a way of punishing him, but it cost him dearly because he was a child, a little boy, and wind-up cyclists, German train sets and bright metal airplanes sorely tempted him from inside their boxes.

He was fourteen when he lost his mother, hypoglycemic shock or some such thing, Doctor Resvanis' answers far from satisfying as he turned his little button eyes to the great Eye of God and the heavens, which, as he saw it, were wholly to blame.

But Nikos had an even heavier punishment in store for his father, then in the North Sea. The captain came back to find his son and sister-in-law in league against him, dead set on young Vatokouzis continuing his education in Constantinople at a reputable establishment, Robert's College, alongside his cousin, though in truth their mutual indifference was unlikely to ever bring them close.

His father's syphilis had served to keep his son from going to sea, ultimately turning him towards mathematics and the University of Athens. He couldn't remember how many doctors he'd visited while a student, how many times he'd taken the Wasserman test. He'd learnt a lot by his second year, not about mathematics but other things. He didn't want to punish anyone anymore.

He resolved to pursue a maritime career, and his decision marked a silent reconciliation with his father, he'd left all the documentation required for the issue of his seaman's papers on the marble-topped table in the hall, the captain had taken a good look at them and probably wanted to take him in his arms, his old man a sailor to the bone, but scared of his son since Nikos was just a little kid.

"My father served on the *Aegean II*, too, two and a half years time-charter in the North China sea," said Orsa, throwing in another bag for the *Asimako*, her uncle Themis gone down with her.

They reached Biscay in the dead of night, the Bay throwing everything it had at them, torrential rain, zero visibility and everyone on lines in case the waves swept them overboard, the sea as bad as it got; Orsa, roped up too, shook out the little bag for the *Konstantinos Voulgaris*, leaving just the *Nautilus*, which had taken all hands to the bottom of the English Channel six years before along with Marios, her mother's other brother, "tell me when we get there," she'd asked the crew; her nice uncle, he'd taught her to tango.

"If the sea had graves, the Biscay cemetery would stretch further than the eye can see," Nikos said; he wanted to touch Orsa, to feel for her soaked to the bone, but since it was her that set the distances from the outset and her mind that was somewhere else, anyway this wasn't the time, he had to keep his mind a hundred percent and then some on the job, at least until the weather let up.

He mustn't force it, on a sailors' isle where so many children had the Olympian forehead or old people's wrinkled skin, the memory of his little sister who hadn't lasted forty days, the superstition and the ignorance had kept him proudly solitary for years, he'd thrown himself into his work, women a source of guilt, and he did not want to lose this creature who had come to him like manna from heaven.

Orsa stared at the sea for hours on end and not because its blue calmed her, she was reading something in its endlessness. Nikos Vatokouzis noticed her eyes moving almost imperceptibly from left to right, constantly toiling away, sometimes all morning long. She was seeing stories, stories written in the blue turned up by the ocean rollers, but by the smaller waves, too; he knew that from experience, they never stopped, washing up stories without end and heroes without pause.

S tray goats were nibbling at the city's gardens, and straying daughters at their mothers' nerves.

"You'd better watch out, you shameless creature," Mina said, throwing the basket of walnuts at her younger daughter's head, who shouted, "no, mum, for goodness sake" as the room filled with walnut shells and nuts; they walked them in and the floorboards stained with their oil.

Saltaferaina had just unearthed the lost hatbox, and wouldn't you know it, among the letters from schoolmates, that fine father of hers, some sheets of paper with songs on them, poems, bits and bobs tied together with colored ribbons, what business had the Englishman's photograph in her house, among her daughter's things?

It was two months since the trip to the monastery, Tirini, a forty-strong mule train to Gerakones, Mina admired the Englishman, how he kissed Hadoulaina, Raisaina, Loukissaina's hand, how he followed the abbot on the tour focused and eager, as though the half-wit's Greek was up to understanding all those dates—when it was built and rebuilt, when the altar screen was made, how the tiles the refugees brought with them from Asia Minor when they fled had at last found peace in the rood screen's royal door.

She couldn't forgive herself for never having been anything but proud about her Mosca's thirst for knowledge, her obsession with the foreign language; she was always trying to get it through to that strange fellow—because a man who goes after a foreign girl is inevitably strange—that different worlds can never meet. Mina Saltaferou was a woman with an inviolable creed and unshakable principles.

Before tearing the photograph to pieces, the silly sop in front of his English house, she'd had a good look, definitely didn't look like a palace. He'd come to eat his fill, a hungry man with a face as pale as canvas and sickly little ribs all shiny under his shirt, she knew the cut of his jib because a month ago, Carnival it was, the Thursday before Lent, that flibbertigibbet daughter of hers had dragged her off to the Club, Hexadaktylos' daughters were playing something monotonous, they had a talent for the piano while her two had tired of it in the third year. Mosca with the foreigner again, talking that English; the Hexadaktylos sisters might have had a bent for the piano, but my girl's got a flair for languages, the thought soothed her conscience.

The mayor made a speech thanking Moraitis for donating a full set of brass for the band, and then it was time for the blue-faced elder Hexadaktylou to play, Mina soon lost patience with the persistent plink-plunk of the piano, deep down she hated that instrument which took up so much room and was as black as pitch, she cast her mind beyond the Club to the events of the past week, a collection for the Athenian Anti-Tuberculosis Society, a five-hundred-drachma hole in her purse, quintuplet lambs born in Messaria, and a bolt from the blue, so sad about Leonis the goatherd struck up at Katakalaioi, went up like a Roman candle he did, but his clothes unsinged, just blown apart at the seams and scattered over the thorn bushes, "a few minutes on the sewing machine and they'd be right as rain," Mouraina's comment, insensitive as ever.

So it was piano, piano without end, and Mosca silently giving it her all right there, leaning a touch towards mister teacher who, woe betide him, Mina was set on condemning the very next morning to the shipowners who'd found him God knows where and brought him here as an act of charity for the sailors' kids, "Send him packing!" And she'd take a few cigars to Father Philippos to forgive her her negligence, though she was thinking of cutting down, cigars were expensive.

Then she'd write to that man in person, "I've got to get her engaged, because she's either hot under the collar or sick of the island and we'll lose her." She'd send him the pictures from London, too, Vatokouzis had smothered their eldest with gold, necklaces, bracelets, earrings, her experienced eye had already drawn up an estimate.

Long ago, long long ago, Savvas had vowed to take her, too, on a three-month voyage to the Baltic and send her home on another Andrian vessel, and Mina had had her sailor's papers issued, but gone and spoilt it all with her big mouth, "other captains' wives," Raisaina, Loukissaina, Hadoulaina, "go away with their husbands for six and nine months at a time," Saltaferaina had been left in port for good.

Tired, she stared out the window and let her mind drift for a while sitting on the ledge, early evening, the days getting longer, the Aegean silent and Tinos opposite.

"I hope that son-in-law sees a way of taking charge of things better," she thought, "the sort of inspiration the swallows have to do the miraculous, inexplicable things they do, like flying all together for hours on end."

Last year had been hard for Mina and this one, too, she felt a weight on her heart, she didn't like hurting her daughters, but life arranged things so love lasted so little and sadness so very long.

The guy fancied himself a prankster, but he was just a lout, Mr. Dinos, the German woman's son, a forty-year-old waxer, worked one day and sat around for five, he'd spent seven months in America gawping at corn fields and cotton plantations, got bored, come back, put a tenant in to work his kitchen garden and talked about his lettuce plantations.

Early afternoon, blustery with fat raindrops, leftovers from the spring storm that had raged all the previous day and night, those that had to inspect damage done to market gardens and boats and get supplies in for the family came out like shell-less snails.

So Katerina Basandi was walking past the *ouzeri*, Mr. Dinos thrust his arm through hers, stuck her down amidst his drinking companions and shoved a chunk of tinned squid into her mouth. The woman was far from happy, he guffawed, proud of himself for having come up with a show for some out-of-sorts actors from "Napoleon Was a Girl," stranded by the bad weather, a dozen men on shore leave and loafers hanging around to see if the cook's widow would swallow.

Mosca was on her way to Thaleia's to pick up the buttons and belt she'd left to be covered for her Easter outfit, saw what she saw, burst into the *ouzeri* and got Katerina to spit it out on the spot, she wanted no truck with fish or seafood and she did right, that was her business, "I wonder who's really lost it," young Saltaferou said straight out, looking the outsize joker straight in the eye, grabbing the woman's arm, pulling her out and setting off for her distant neighborhood at a cracking pace, a half hour's walk, and Katerina, as always, hand held up against her cheek so she wouldn't see the blue, the sight of the sea made her sick and she wasn't the only woman who refused fish and shellfish or to swim, there were others, especially those who'd lost a loved one in waters close by who wouldn't touch fish for fear they'd fed off his flesh. Their calves were frozen by the time they lifted the latch, crazy weather.

"It's been twelve years since I turned them all away," the woman said and lit the paraffin lamp, "still don't have electricity in this neighborhood. When we were little, we'd sit high up on the rocks at night and watch the ships pass by all lit up."

She threw a couple of logs into the stove, unlocked a sailor's leather trunk, motioned to Mosca to rummage around inside and turned her back, standing motionless at the narrow window, looked out at the mountain that brought her night an hour before the rest.

Mosca lifted the lid, Evangelos Basantis written on the inside, sent from Europe before their wedding, stuffed with silk robes, nightdresses and gramophone records, instrumental stuff and foreign songs, *black eyes in the glass, blue eyes at the window*, Katerina's beautiful voice still rang in her ears, five years old at the time, Mosca had first heard it at the engagement party, Katerina and her cook's, she'd thought girls in love got a beautiful singing voice as a gift on the day of their betrothal. The trunk was overflowing with well-pressed densely-embroidered lengths of fabric, tablecloths, pillowcases, curtains; Mosca unfolded them one by one, felt a chill run down her spine and the gorge rise in her throat, well what could she say except let the tears flow like torrents.

Marousio, owned by Iasonas Telemes, sank with all hands off the coast of Uruguay, 22.4.1917, seamen lost, Gerasimos Fakis master, Adamantios Fakis second-in-command, Nikolaos Mandarakas ship's engineer, Nikolos Hazapis assistant engineer, Marios Pertesis radio operator, Leonidas Zannis cabin boy, Evangelos Basantis cook, Asimakis Hiotellis able seaman, Pandelis Vakarellis stoker, Dimitrios Mandarakas greaser, Matthaios Papadakis apprentice seaman.

With cross-stitches and chain-stitches, with black, grey and a thousand shades of accursed blue, Katerina had been bent over her untouched dowry all these years, unpicking ducks, dolphins, stars and embroidering the island's maritime tragedies, one after the other, the struggle with the murderous waves, lifeboats overturned, life jackets floating empty, ships half submerged under mournful, alien skies, here a lighthouse, the lighthouse off Falaina, testified that hidden reefs had trapped the ship, there a cyclone set its seal on disaster, when the causes remained unknown, fate, an evil, black-clad figure stood high on prow or stern protruding just feet above the waters before it, too, sank into the bottomless depths.

Mosca had fifteen or more laid out over chairs, trunk, table, sofa, rugs, tiles, deadly seas in ferment before her eyes, the costly catalog of seamen lost with dates, Charon's heavy hand pushing the island beneath the waves again and again, for it to resurface slowly and weakly, tear-stained and black-dipped.

"Vangelis's godmother sends me the thread, from Kastela," Katerina said who'd quarreled with her in-laws, blood more poisonous than poison as they say, still at the window, outside the darkness had gathered momentum.

Mosca took off her shoes, walked across the embroidery and kissed her on the cheek, still young, Katerina twenty-eight and, as her young friend realized just then, as beautiful as ever, so much beauty in her light brown hair, the thick eyelashes and the moles on her neck.

Mosca's chest was bursting with anger at Andros's fate, Little England, so much for that, which some shipowners called the island and not David, out of solidarity for poor Katerina, out of fear that her father and Vatokouzis would one day be added to her work, "Ah, Orsa," the words slipped out, "so was fate escapable after all?" She often toyed with that fatalistic phrase, on the surface to poke fun, deep down to worry.

The clock past seven, not in the mood to leave, Mosca curled up on the sofa and pulled a half cigarette from the inside pocket of her coat. A Russian started singing on the gramophone, a deep, impressive voice, who knows what he was saying, something sad and nostalgic, as usual, Katerina knew them all by heart by now and sang *secondo*.

"He came ocean rollers, I'd wash the sheets and my nightie every day," the women of Korthi, the simple seamen's wives and daughters, hung out their kitchen linen and aprons and wasted away, Orsa had heard that before, too, Mouraina in full flow, her audience considerable, the cups, saucers, and water glasses rattling inside, I won't look for mum in there, she decided, walked past the two yellow storeys heading for the teacher's green, the city full of two-storey houses, all with a balcony facing out to sea and everyone sitting on the other, the blind one, overlooking neighbors or a wall but sheltered from the north wind. Whether they wanted to or not, the island folk saw the sea every day, and Orsa was convinced that the outstretched horizon, "the horizon without end," as she'd written in the third year at High School, the sea whose waters flow elsewhere, anywhere, taking thoughts, landscapes, voices with them, stopped sailors and islanders from ever feeling trapped.

"The blue flows and us with it."

"You Andrians sail the high seas, yet never leave your island."

Kyria Nana had rested her cigarette on the ashtray and was rubbing lotion on her hands, she had red dappled fingers and palms and didn't know why, perhaps it was her sink's way of telling her to stay away. The unscented coffee served in the salon, identical to every other salon on the island, with its little bookcase, *de rigueur* in any captain's home, half hidden behind the large double door.

May and the perfume of the climbing rose in blooming white floating through the open window. Orsa felt uncomfortable but safe. Madame Nana had once told her the story in so many words, later she'd told it her again with fewer and as the years went by her tale reached its end sooner and sooner, after just seven, six, five phrases.

"And when, my dear, my first love was lost, not in a shipwreck but on dry land, of dysentery somewhere in the Indies, I succumbed to my fellow student's advances for one reason only: he was from Andros, too; and imagine, I'd never once visited the island."

She hadn't the heart to go back home, to Arta on the mainland's western coast, to the unworldly beauty of Mount Tzoumerka, she'd morbidly desired a corner of the dead man's world, so she'd lived a prim, monotonous, vicarious life, fully up-to-date with other folks' loves, others' passions and woes.

"Meaning that in life, what you lose is more important than what you find," Orsa came to a hasty conclusion, there was something eating away at her, an obsession, doubt, something.

"What you find you'll lose again," Nana stressed every word, "what you lose is there forever."

At least that's how she'd seen things during the first years of her marriage to Mikés, but with the passing of time, life treated her to a lesson turned on its head, what you have is worth more, however little it may be, than what you lack.

"They're both equally true, choose the one that suits, sayings, maxims and the like hold backwards, too, always."

Orsa wasn't in the mood for riddles, so they left the past and homespun philosophy behind, the teacher was a dab hand at both, but her former student wasn't nostalgic for the classroom and her modest grades. *Kyria* Nana straightened her pleats and bombarded her with a million questions about London, a place she'd never gotten to visit, because her seasickness was keener than her heart's longing, she'd come to the island fifteen years ago in a storm and not passed Cava d'Oro since.

She didn't ask the usual things, she wanted to know if the English wore coats of fur or cloth, if you noticed the dogs on the streets, if they had rose bushes as impressive as hers, if the girls with the peaches-and-cream complexion went about their business alone or with a chaperone. All the rest, the parks, museums and palaces, she knew already, Madame Nana Bourada-Negropiperi invited all the recently arrived ladies round for tea or coffee and interrogated them with flawless technique, mulish persistence and a poetic disposition.

Orsa handed over her postcards, too, bought in London though not of London, Glasgow's Jamaica Bridge, the Commodore Hotel in New York, Bombay's Hotel Majestic, she already had two of those; the teacher collected postcards of bridges and luxury hotels, fifty-three bridges she had and eighty-two major hotels. And she delivered a photograph of Charles Dickens' house, a special request, her weakness for the author common knowledge, anyhow, David Bradley, the Englishman from the High School, she called David Copperfield and her canary, Oliver, even though Mouraina had told her the bird was either mute or female; the afternoon really was going by more quickly now and Oliver silent and still in his cage, a little yellow statue.

Mikés Negropiperis had died three years before and the time had come to turn the pages of the photo album once again, the dearly departed, a teacher plump and dignified, with a *joie de vivre* in his eyes that twinkled through his spectacles, in the schoolyard surrounded by his students, sometimes in school uniform, sometimes in theatrical costume or sports kit, school years 1917 to 1925 when he succumbed to malaria and everyone had to live without his salty puns. As she thumbed through the photographs, Orsa realized students die as well as teachers, the twins in the typhoid epidemic, Matthios from the coffee shop who'd just melted away, Bakis on his very first voyage. She didn't linger on Maltambes the schoolboy, stopped at fourteen-year-old Vatokouzis, eyes tight shut and towering, just before he went off to that aunt of his in Constantinople, so what was worth more, the man she'd lost or the man she'd found? She took her husband's telegram out of her pocket, read it aloud, and noted the curiosity, interest, and panic, in that order precisely, on her teacher's face.

Kyria Nana spoiled her pleats with a swipe of her hand, glanced sideways at Oliver and waved two or three fingers in his direction, exhaled her cigarette smoke, brought the cup back to her lips, though she'd long since drained it to the dregs.

Old man Vatokouzis had taken the news in silence, too, while Nikos's nurse, who now wiped the old man's ass and kept him clean, faithful to the family from the age of twelve, caressed Orsa's hair, she'd made the sign of the cross over her and not said a word, just went and kneelt before the icon, from her tone of voice and mumblings she was clearly having words with the Virgin.

"Nikos is coming back in ten days so we can travel to Constantinople together."

The telegram was from the Piraeus office, her husband, who didn't disappear off to the other end of the earth, who usually sailed round Europe from the Baltic to the Black Sea "would be taking additional leave to take his spouse to seek the blessing of the Patriarch so the baby would be born strong," Orsa said calmly, took the cups into the kitchen, and bid Oliver good night, too, with a few-fingered wave.

"He's doing it for me, he doesn't think he's sick," she said and left the teacher in the gloaming, leant back in her rocking chair, swathed in pleats, lighting another cigarette.

"I heard you should suck an unripe olive for morning sickness," she advised after a couple of drags and a few minutes silence.

Orsa went outside, picked out a rosebud and headed down the least-frequented streets, unable though to avoid around ten "good evenings" to sailors' wives, sitting still and quite alone at their windows as darkness fell, until they grew accustomed to the chill of the coming night and settled upon two or more companions for the night's *al fresco* soiree.

Years before, her godmother's far-flung neighborhood had just got electricity, ten years old at the time, Orsa had walked up and down in front of the open doors and wondered at the women, one in every hall, still as marble for hours on end in a chair beneath the globe like hares frozen in their beams of light. She walked to the quay, the sea's aura and absence of others brought her peace. She sat on a coiled cable with her back to the city lights looking straight out towards the lighthouse, the Aegean smooth as glass, the moon's sliver semi-luminous mid-sky. The white rosebud smelt of sweat from the palms of her hands, kneaded like a ball of dough all the way down. She threw it into the water. She stroked her breasts, which were no longer girlish, and her belly, which was swelling and straining at the seams, "the last time I wear my coral, it doesn't fit me anymore," she thought and burst into a flood of tears.

The sun broke free of the sea and lurched skywards. All the way to the Eye of God, usually dark blue like a bruise, smeared pomegranate, "and, shipmate, you found the best mountain," Saltaferos told Him, "to enjoy Your works"; things the captain, too, managed again after three years in foreign parts.

A mainland wind filled the elms and walnut trees, the rustled whispers tumbled through the bushes, whipped up the Far Quarter, too, bundling it up in its embrace and setting it down further along; Saltaferos saw things miraculous and inexplicable, in the mood again for romance and poetry.

When it had passed and he grew somber, he admitted to finding the island awash with malaria and typhoid and his family groaning from a hidden itch and an obvious chill, and that in the month of May. His suspicions alerted by things left half unsaid in letters, Mina hadn't set his fears at rest in Piraeus, they'd laid up May 3rd, the families of local men waiting on the dock, the Papagiannises and the Vouyiouklises, Philippakis' Markella and Pitaoulis's wife, Maro, three wives and two daughters from Andros. They stayed at the Hermes for two days and nights, to hand over to Hadoulis father and son, to pick up a pair of glasses for their daughter's wall-eyed father-in-law, to buy something gold for the first grandchild on the way, to take a taxi round their plots.

On the second night, they'd all met up in a choice taverna in Marousi, Argyropaidos had a nose for good food, they'd stuffed themselves on spleen and delicious roast meats rustic style and time to toast pregnant Orsa, Mina an iceberg all night long, never so much as a hint of enthusiasm on that woman's face, *a life without festivity is like a long road without an inn*, unfortunately, Democritus.

"Conger eel and rockling, if you've an appetite for spring fish, honor my table, I'm waiting for Louis to deliver and they'll be cooked by eleven. Take a stroll round your assets and don't be late!"

He'd spent the night at his mother's; the old woman spent March to November in the little house in Apatouria, chatting to family at the Saltaferoses' old place in Plakoura December through February more than sufficed, all she needed the rest of the year was a "good morning" from her neighbor, peace and quiet.

She'd roasted the coffee at dawn, balancing the red enamel cup the captain took with him everywhere on the edge of the wall round the little terrace, her chair right beneath the door frame, sitting half in and half out of her house.

For years now, the city had buried its dead elsewhere, his mother had moved heaven and earth, marshaling anyone with a position however lowly, and heavy guns like the shipowners and the MP for the Cyclades, seeking written permission from the mayor to be laid to rest, when the time came, beside her parents in the old cemetery; her husband lost on the Danube, his paddleboat capsized, his bones bathed in river mud, "my dead man lost and scattered," the old woman used to say, "he's not whole even in my memories." Now, when she sat down to eat, she'd slowly chew the first mouthful, swallow and turn to his faded photograph, "needs salt" she'd say, and forget him again.

Savvas sucked up his coffee a mouthful at a time and his mother's silence brought on, as it was clearly meant to, according to plan, hard thoughts, as though she were telling him, "Mind your corner, take things in hand like a man."

Orsa, who took after her in so much, the day before yesterday, Monday, had rubbed herself against him like a cat, him
going on and on, "Come off it, dad, enough of the big talk and
macho stuff," she'd whispered so the others wouldn't hear,
"when there are important decisions to be made, you're always
on the other side of the globe and don't tell me to 'respect my
elders, Chilon of Sparta'; that sort of thing's for fathers of a different sort."

That same evening son and father-in-law took a stroll
through Plakoura and Nimboriò. Out past the estates, cattle
lowing on both banks of the river, something different from
the sounds of the sea, in the fields the darkness softly shared
their monotone good nights. They walked as far as the quay,
drank raki from the same bottle and talked about ships
launched and events in South America.

A head for figures that Vatokouzis, university-educated too,
had his own opinions on where the pound was going and how
to get a better share in the *Nireus*, which he had with the
Hadoulises. So he'd reeled off some good deals being discussed
by those in the know, the *Kymatiani II*, *Skyros Island*, *Panagitsa
II*, his father-in-law nodding, contacts in the Hamburg shipyards, Savvas agreed again, their MP mediating a bank loan
earned another "bravo!" his intention to acquire another
freighter, in the very near future with a partner or without, no
matter if it was small. His father-in-law's all round blessings and
approval.

A great relief for Saltaferos, Nikos would do anything for
Orsa and *asi es la vida*, he said, a touch galled his little girl had
moved on to another man, that's life for you.

"With the kid on the way, you'll be up to your eyeballs in
obligations."

"Just let it be healthy," Vatokouzis sighed, threw the empty
bottle into the sea and spoke as though he were wagering with
himself, "Constantinople will chase away the shadows, it'll

bring us together forever, that golden, Byzantine city of a hundred palaces and a thousand colors," Nikos had placed his innermost hopes in the city that just a few years since had made him, a schoolboy with a chill heart, love life anew.

Yet all he'd said left Savvas quite convinced his eldest daughter's marriage was not a happy one. As for the younger one, he'd caught her with red-raw eyes, what could he say about the Englishman, it wasn't an easy decision, a week on dry land and the problems had started to get him down, dropping anchor, he'd said "a time to rest, to knock back the wine, to while away the time of day with friends and relatives," but one daughter sniveling every time he clapped eyes on her, the other killing him with what she left unsaid.

As for Mina, after three years away, as always she'd spent the first few days chasing him with that big fat ledger of hers, and as Savvas's eyes grew accustomed to the sight of them again, his nose to the smell of them, as he enjoyed the blackcurrants turning red, the apricots yellow, the newly-planted melon plants in their patch, or as he sat in his vest scanning neighbors' windows from the balcony, his wife kept droning on behind him; family finances, the three thousand seven hundred Drachmas paid back to Singer, the twenty pounds to the shop down on Tzelepi, the wedding linen, plates, electrical items, and general expenses.

"You wrote me all about that," he'd tell her every so often, until he'd had enough, swiveled on the spot, seized her by the shoulders, "go to hell," he said inside and first saw the plait wrapped twice around her head was white as snow.

"I'm going to help the cantor spray his vines," he said at last and left.

"Again?" Mina said under her breath, throwing her account-book into the bureau drawer and shutting it with a bang.

The captain's blood was up, he wanted to go back in and tell her out loud, "go to hell," mostly because he knew how large a part of the blame was his for the fate they'd given their girls, but Father Philippos appeared, the cleric *ex machina*, the solution, keeping watch, he raised his right hand closed in a fist, shaking air dice, boy we've wrecked the guy's throat with those cigars, he chain-smoked the things, lungs shot, Saltaferos hurried on to other, less painful, thoughts.

"I dreamed I beat Jesus at backgammon," he said hoarse but high-spirited, "and the wife put me on a fast."

Maltambes had grave doubts about any household whose members never sent each other to the devil out loud.

Little runt Antonis, Annezio's young orphan, had the *bonboniera* on the blanket, everyone who walked by got treated. As the steamer slid towards night, Spyros slipped a sugared almond into his mouth, rolled it on his tongue, the talk of the Mamaises who'd gone to the wall with last October's crash and the world economy at rock bottom, an avalanche of bankruptcies. A telegraph wired from London that morning, his boss congratulating Spyros on his 15% share in the newly-built *Leonidas II*, 11,500 tons and 388,000 pounds sterling, then a few hours later the wire from Piraeus about the others' disaster, Lloyd's had withdrew the insurance contracts, the European banks applied the penal clauses, and the Mamaises were for the poor-house. Maltambes thought like a shipowner for the first time, even if only a hatchling.

Anybody and everybody was losing their jobs, there'd be many a family putting sons and fathers out in search of a new employer.

Neither his uncle, Emilios Balas, nor Spyros Maltambes had ever served on a Mamais boat, but it sure was strange, as though someone'd voodooed them, it was one disaster after another. There were ships working Chase Bay to Batavia, Split to Danzig, Diego Suarez to Djibouti, the Mamaises sailed their own routes, from Marseilles to the lighthouse on Kilkieran

Point, from Le Havre to the arid Canary Islands, from here and from there straight onto Toronto's treacherous shoals.

Old man Mamais, Nikolos of the Andros Coal Company, had run his barges to the Black Sea, the Mediterranean and England for twenty years without the methane catching once; in 1925, a year many embarked upon new shipowning careers, "& Son", Epameinondas Mamais, a graduate of Hydra and the London School of Engineering, took charge and changed the company name to N. Mamais & Son Transcontinental Shipping, general cargo, three freighters—fine vessels—at its disposal: Maltambes green with envy at their purchases, mad about the *Samothrace*, the *Lesvos*, and their pride and joy, the *Agia Thalassini*.

Four and a half years the Mamaises lasted.

"It was vicious tongues did for them," old Polemis the cook expressed the thoughts of many, "they were asking for it, leaving their females off the leash in Plakoura, one frock in the morning another for evening, perms at Joseph's and high heels ordered by the dozen."

With both his sons out of work now, they'd have to knock on other doors, a hundred men in the same boat, battling the tempest for a wage, who'd get sorted first and where, "I'm real worried," Polemis said, "hey Antonis, chuck us another one of those almonds, my blessings do the trick, too, come on, so may Vatokouzis sail through these dark days unscathed with Savvas' first-born at his side"; his youngest son had been at primary school with her.

Maltambes spat the half-chewed almond onto the deck, he hadn't known whose wedding it was from, "water, captain, get some water down you," they shouted, handing him a glassful and Stathakis administering a fatherly slap on the back, "can't trust them almonds, my boy, deadly they are."

Just as he was beginning to feel himself again, "may it be our turn soon," that was Antonis, the ship's wag, whose beauty gave him courage, seven unwed men aboard the *Ostria*, six of them reckoning on engagements or the whole hog next time they hit Andros.

"Get used to licking almonds and get yourself married the leave after next, you're seventh in line," Antonis wound up the repartee.

Retired a year now, Emilios Balas hadn't notified Spyros of the wedding, he'd found out himself from elsewhere, weeks back.

The night his uncle had come back from Saltaferaina, the wind taken out of his sails, he'd lost it, given him a nasty shove, called him a useless old bastard and the old man had taken it to heart. Not that he'd ever written to him anyway, just short-winded telegrams every 7th of December, "may you live to be a hundred and may God and Saint Spyridon watch out for you always," and again when he heard they'd scraped through some typhoon or such like in the Pacific, the Indian Ocean, the Philippines by the skin of their teeth.

"It's the Mamaises' captains who'll have the toughest time finding a berth, one from Andros, one from Cephallonia and one from Corfu," Maltambes steered the talk back to shipping, that other business over and done with as far as he was concerned, poisoned by Orsa's stale almonds, the Saltaferoses had him running amok inside, he had it in for the father who'd never make a stand one way or the other, he had it in for the mother who didn't see past hard cash, and most of all he had it in for the bride who'd wasted his entire summer with her kisses, setting him alight with poems, pinches and sidelong glances in blue, but her passion doused by the first rains of fall, she'd dived headlong into the Vatokouzises' safe, a chip off Saltaferaina's block that Orsa, "I'll send her a thousand-page accounts ledger for a wedding gift," he thought, "time to kill adding and subtracting, because she won't be lusting after her husband's body, for obvious reasons."

Maltambes hadn't got to know French mademoiselles in

camel coats, English women in tweed two-pieces, Russians in fur caps, he'd made their acquaintance in their underskirts and was grateful for it, they'd never tortured him with aristocratic robes and equivocal verses; in fact if he asked them to, they'd patiently massage the knots out of his back.

Antonis folded the voile from the *bonboniera* into two, into four, into eight, put it in his pocket and, conjuror-like, gulped down the last white almond, having whirled it round and sketched circle after circle in the darkness first. The sky unadorned, where the hell had the stars got to, a flash of anger and Maltambes went to plot their course.

"Lord, when will we make Tocapilla to rest up a little, the damp and the calm have rotted our bones," Bousoulas the first engineer sounded exhausted, but saw Maltambes fit to explode and sat there mute and still, on his black days, everyone knew all he wanted from them was total silence and nothing on the move anywhere.

Spyros pulled out a cigarette and his lighter, sent a searing drag deep down and took the helm, steering straight at the blackness.

As a student at Robert's College and later as a sailor shipping grain and coal from Odessa and Constanza, the sight and soul of Constantinople, Constantine's City or just "the City," were ever-present in Nikos's life.

The sweet light of dawn and dusk flummoxed the Greeks for a time, "but it's a Greek day dawning," they thought, "tonight we'll slumber in Greek sleep," until the mist lifted and they admitted the place was Turkified, but the idea of Constantinople as a many-stanzaed poem was the same, and Nikos wanted to recite it word for word to his wife.

It was on his first voyage, to Carthageni, aboard the *Theotokos*, captain Lionakis, when they heard about the destruction of Smyrna, three times he'd gone on the razzle there with Rodokanakis, the ladies' man, and some fellow students; his boring cousin tagging along, no choice in the matter, not that he ever joined in. Smyrna with its heart on its sleeve, immaculately turned-out family men who loved their work as much as their play, Amoudianos and Samiotis, traders in oil and liqueurs, associates of his father.

His soul in flames, too, at the news of poor, burnt Smyrna, "imagine if they torched Constantinople, too," they'd said with the crew, trouble there too, with fifty dead and the British Mediterranean fleet rushing to defend the Straits.

"May God protect us from the French and British," the atheist master crossed himself, a sworn enemy of Western policy, Western diplomacy, Western food and flesh.

Nikos and Orsa walked round the walls of Haghia Sophia, entrance not permitted, so she bought cards and postcards by the dozen and mailed them daily. She spent more time scrutinizing the postcards than the sites themselves, Nikos knew from their home and London honeymoon that she had her own way of feeling and forming a place she'd visited or was never likely to see, ordering, shifting, even upturning the postcards, mixing gloss and the tidings on the back of a multitude kept in boxes and drawers or dragged around in wallets and handbags.

Le pont d'Anana, she found a series in French, Adana bridge, *l'Hotel Pera*, *le Constantinople Palace*, for *Kyria* Nana she explained.

The patriarch had caught a cold and his fever postponed their appointment by two days. They took the ferry, went to the Proti, the Antigone, the Chalke, the Princes' Isles, photographed and were photographed, wandered the Baloukli and the palace of the Dolma Bahçe by taxi and tram, Orsa sad they were too late for the tulips, real ones she'd never seen.

The same afternoon in their room at the Hotel Royal, Orsa lay staring at the wooden chandelier above tracing delicate circle after delicate circle on her rounded belly, one time she took his hand, traced the veins with her fingertips and laid it there, on her, wordlessly, her eyes moist and glistened in the twilight.

Nikos leant down and kissed her belly over and over, a hundred times, two or three in the air and the fourth on the fabric, pink linen, another two, three in the air then that hesitant contact between her body and his lips, which would have remained sealed and distant with a simple "Nikos, stop."

The next morning, they walked to Phanar a second time, attended mass and took communion in Agios Georgios' and were received by Photios II around eleven, not fully recovered but affable and friendly, "beautiful Hellene" he called Orsa, blessed her and gave her a book, *Hymns of the Byzantine Melodists,* which he seemed to love.

As the patriarch and Orsa embarked on a brief discussion about the donation to the Baloukli hospital, Vatokouzis could hear his chest beating, irregular, the strain was almost painful, perhaps because his wife had relaxed and her beauty was something beyond belief, beyond him. And he wanted the patriarch more distant and imposing, to have something extraordinary about him, something all-powerful and divine, a meeting with a convalescent Photios not enough, what he needed was a tête-à-tête with God himself, Oleg Onegin, he remembered the Tsar's legendary officer, a student still he'd happened upon him one Sunday morning, in a glade on a wooded Princes' Isle, the more than mere mortal living in a wooden hut, making whips for his daily bread.

They'd booked a table for one-thirty, Pandelis' for lunch, Madianos of the Ottoman Bank, Frangopoulos Junior, imports and exports, they'd studied together at Robert's College, with their wives Corinna and Sophia, three couples, his aunt had moved to Egypt *en famille*, his unsociable cousin making a name for himself down there as an engineer.

Only a few mulberries and white-heart cherries had passed Orsa's lips in days, and not just because of her fast. Relieved after their morning visit, she hungrily helped herself to forkful after forkful of Pandelis's *taş kebab*, lamb the only meat she'd eat, tried sweets, all light with rice flour and rose water, and even asked for a recipe, *kazan depi*. She emptied out her bag, couldn't find her notebook among all the souvenirs, postcards, and envelopes, and the three bent, sea-eroded spoons fell at her feet.

"The waves washed them up at Gyalià last year, late summer," she said blushing slightly and kissed them.

Her father, she said to the table, says Cartagena, Odessa, Marseilles, Archangelsk, Biscay, but her father-in-law and husband say Carthageni, Odissos, Massalia, Archangelos, Viskaikos, she loved the Greek versions more, so much maritime tradition, so many seafaring men, "all the world's harbors should really belong to Greece" she stopped, her thoughts shared, leant her head to the left and started to fiddle with the hanging earring that was nipping the skin of shoulder and neck.

Frangopoulos first and then Takis Madianos tipped meaning-laden winks at Vatokouzis, having unconditionally surrendered to Orsa's charms, Constantinople fell and the male diners' hearts with it.

Three days left until the *Oropos*, Hadoulis-owned, general cargo, docked again and they boarded for the return, they spent them visiting everywhere they hadn't had time for, the city's Seven Hills just as they remembered them from classroom visits, strolls in Pera among the charred remains of last January's fire, Tatavla, indifferent to religion everywhere else, in Constantinople Orsa didn't miss a single church, lighting the requisite candles to the Virgin in Galata and the Holy Trinity in Taksim, she even went as far as the Evangelistria in the Yeni Sehir, she liked the churches' cool interiors, too, with their somber wall paintings. She'd choose an icon, pull a chair over and sit facing it, to rest her back most of all, parting her legs and tucking the folds of her skirt down between before her black fan came out to slowly fan her throat and glistening arms.

Vatokouzis could have watched her for hours. The hair in her armpits like ears of corn, her honey-colored bangs broken free of their clips and streaming backwards, the blue of her eyes, sometimes half-open, sometimes closed, as though she were complaining to the saint, "Would you look how my man's tired me out with all this walking!" Yes, Vatokouzis could have watched her for hours. He almost forgot Annezio's request, a lucky charm for her Antonis, at sea with Maltambes aboard the *Ostria*.

"Though he doesn't need it, Spyros is the best captain of us all," Nikos said, "the bosses swear by him, for him there's nothing they wouldn't do."

He'd heard he was to captain their first ocean liner,

Southampton to New York, the *Minerva*, a wonder of ship-building and luxury.

"Antonis would do a thousand times better staying with him on the passenger ship, he'd get to see people," the nurse's only son just twenty, six years under his belt already, tankers and general cargo.

Nikos would have to stay on freighters for the next two or three years, hard-working and with plans of his own, in short he had to be Nikos Vatokouzis, loyal employee to Nikos Vatokouzis employer.

Orsa laughed, "Well," she said, "saints are my specialty, so I'll choose the charm"; and next morning her husband drank slow-boiled Turkish coffee on the quay waiting for the *Oropos* to show, while she, in her white dress and a mole painted on her right temple, like the White Russians flooding the places of entertainment back then, took the boat to Prinkipo by herself and brought back a red bone cross and some little bells from the church of Agios Georgios the Bellmaker, patron saint of boys.

"But you only got one for Antonis," Nikos said and felt a fool, not because he'd given himself away, as some might think, quite the opposite, he wasn't dead set on a son, just clumsy with words and gestures sometimes, Orsa scrambled his wits, she'd almost gotten used to it and would grant him absolution, sometimes moved that her husband muddled things so.

"I'm going to have a daughter," she announced quite certain, licking her finger, and rubbed the mole away.

At dusk, freshly bathed and refreshed, cheeks and shoulders slightly red from the hot June sun, she sat at the prow on a lounger Orginos unfolded for her, a gallant captain of the old school, and bid Constantinople farewell munching on a sesame roll.

Eros esti . . . you, love is . . . me, *ti esti anir eseis*, what a man is me, *gamos esti pistis aionia kai phychon te armonia eseis*, a wedding means faith unto eternity and the harmony of souls, and serve me right.

To hell with foreign languages, to hell with foreign lands, Mosca was wasting her time squinting over all that bloody English, to hell with all those excellents mister squiggly signature had heaped on her.

Full August moon. Fresh risen, madly aflame, too, with all that had happened, sitting on the pebbles, Kiki, Katina, Marie, Mosca watching it rise and whiten, young Saltaferou weeping and heaping abuse on her mother, "the heartless, tight-fisted, pitiful old woman," and her three faithful friends enjoying the unfamiliar sensation, womanly despair over a lost love.

David Bradley had let his house go, packed his trunk, and fled or escaped without leaving a forwarding address, without even a "goodbye, my little Mosca," without even bidding his colleagues or bridge partners from the Club, Maris, Resvanis and Mr. Dinos farewell.

"Sadness is so beautiful sometimes," Marie said, "how it's heightened by strange landscapes, like now."

A red-black blur, the looming ghost-rock, the sea as immovable as dry land, and there, a long freighter with all its lights ablaze, like earrings and necklaces.

They'd come equipped with Papastratos, Gitanes, Santé, Players, Xanthis, cigars, matches and lighters, and smoked them one after another in their camouflaged smoking room behind the rocks. If anyone ever moved that little pile of stones, they'd find a bucketful of filters and butt-ends, two years worth; in town, women and tobacco just didn't mix. What were they to do? That's where they buried their pain when Katina's fiancé called the wedding off, dumped her for a Dutch girl short-ass had, and their sadness as almost all their former schoolmates left on the ships or to study first, shipping & maritime, of course, at the Trident College for the Merchant Marine, Syros, Hydra, England.

"Eighteen's the limit, we're either engaged to the man we love or *lose him forever, 'tis a law broken never, bitter sadness our fate, that to God we berate*, Marie and Mosca especially, though the others too, patched together rhymes to outwit their fears about life, at eighteen no longer a laughing matter.

June, July, August, six engagements and two weddings on graduating from high school, half of them hastily arranged. So every weekend the whole flock of ex-schoolgirls would chew the cud at memorial services, come Saturday evening, fashionably cloched, the four members of the society of kindred spirits would convene at some celebration or other, Kiki, Katina, Marie, Mosca, K.K.M.M., every merger and liquidation signed and sealed, *vide* Katina-Michalis, Aggela-Giannis, Madò-Leonidas and Mosca-David, with deep sensuous drags in the smoking room and twenty more stubs in the illicit ashtray.

Mosca blew the smoke out onto her arms, into her décolleté, "exhale into my hair, all of you, please, I want to stink of cigarettes when I go home," she blurted out angrily.

She'd walked with her elder sister two days before, entering her ninth month she took a long stroll every day as the sun was setting, the bridge to the cave to Agios Dimitrios, the route identical and inviolable, must have been a matter of discipline.

"I overheard her tell our ma London's not the back end of beyond and you don't think twice, do you, about taking your daughters' lives in your hands," Orsa who spoke rarely, and to ma only when absolutely necessary.

The Aegean at its most beautiful, the *meltemi* billowing their wide yellow skirts as they strolled along in step, pockets overflowing with sunflower seeds, little talk and much munching. Mosca told her a little about the Englishman, not much to tell.

"Do you love Nikos?" she asked.

"He's a good husband."

"But do you love him?"

"I'll have an untroubled life with him, Mosca."

"His hands . . . "

It wasn't the first time the sisters had commented on tall clumsy Vatokouzis' amazing hands, long and bony, elbows and wrists a forest of blue veins large and small, hands like a map with rivers and subsidiaries, the Rio de la Plata.

They walked the rest of the way in silence, night was falling and there was no need, they thought apart now, singly, Mosca stealing glances at her sister's swollen belly, and if they'd met their mother then and there, she'd have grabbed hold of her shoulders, "Get lost," she'd tell her, "schooners, wherries, punts, dried-up lardy cunts"; it bothered her a lot that Mina had continued to cross Mouraina's threshold in cold blood; Nicephoros' widow's, too, for weeks now meeting place number two.

A son right off, her mother thought. By the time the midwife arrived from Livadia, Orsa had the job done and not a peep out of her. Annezio, legs crippled by arthritis, fetching and carrying like a girl of fifteen, couldn't miss the birth, couldn't leave the old man at God's mercy, either.

"In the armchair with the blanket over his knees, lost in his sins," she told Orsa. "Didn't ask, it was me told him, a son, eyelids didn't even flicker, but the hand gripping the chair like a pair of pincers relaxed and his fist unlocked, his palm bloody from the strain."

"The husband's away and will always be away, Saltaferos the same, but now we have a man in the house," Mina had got herself a grandson and thanked Her grace with wild-rose-flavored incense from Mount Athos.

The dense aroma broke free in the censer, filled the house, floated through the neighborhood and melted into the sky; it was dusk, the hour when news flits most rapidly through home and café, by dinner everyone knew Orsa had brought a lively, black-wigged son into the world, big-boned and painless, build and coloring Saltaferaina's.

"Name him after the late king," she suggested to her daughter; as heir and as monarch Constantine had honored the island with his visits, and Mina had been feeling sorry for monarchs of late, the one in question had died on Sardinia, and the other one, Queen Olga, in Rome. In reality, she was doing all she could to avoid Giannis, custom would have the child named after its father's ill-fated father.

Orsa looked the baby in the eye, stoppered its mouth with her nipple, her breasts dripping like fountains, mother and nurse spent their time boiling nappies and laundering.

"The more work the merrier," muttered Mina who hadn't stopped for a breath in days, sorting out the baby stuff, making good on vows to numerous saints, seeing to the diet of the difficult new mother, never a good eater, and battling with a mountain of quinces from Apatouria, destined for *retseli*, quince cake, sugared confections, and a big jar for Marika Hadouli, who'd lent a hand with the Englishman.

Two years before, Mina had spread a little gossip about Tassa opposite, who'd brought the monk from Kavkara with an incantation for Paris, her second oldest there for nine years studying law, enraptured, he couldn't find the way back home.

Be afraid, let terror grip, let fear seize hold, take flight, be smitten, get thee gone, thee that from heaven hath fallen, and with thee always the evil spirits of Paris, the spirit of lechery, the spirit of night and of day, of noon and of evening, the spirit of the dead of night, and so on and so forth, Mosca had learnt it by heart and she and her friends had retorted, *Tassa the ass who sucked on grass, exorcising Paris with a poison chalice*! Since the church didn't mind, if Hadoulaina turned a deaf ear, Mina would order a spell for the whole United Kingdom, the act and feel of mocking herself brought relief, especially when she couldn't decide if a situation warranted laughter or tears.

Fortunately, Hadoulaina adored authority and enjoyed confirming it at every opportunity and in every way, they said the anchor embroidered in gold thread on the right lapel of her every coat, the front of her every dress, was there, too, on her knickers, the leak some hard-done-by washerwoman or seamstress's revenge.

An enormous full-figure Jesus loomed floor to ceiling over her drawing room, allowing Hadoulaina to present him as her permanent crutch, witness, colleague, escort, and He stopped her husband thinking himself top dog at home. The old harridan was happy she'd seen to the Englishman and Mina was doubly happy, the devil had packed his bags and she'd got her daughter back to groom, and if possible within the year, for one of the island's five eligible bachelors, Margetis, Rallias, Porphyratos and the two Lavdas, Franka's and Anna's, in order of assets.

Savvas had set sail again in early August, he'd missed the birth, too, she wouldn't have him under her feet though he'd never disagree with her plans and estimations openly or plainly, he just went quiet or grimaced and threw his hands in the air.

Mosca still angry and out of sight round at one friend's or another's, but her mother patient, waiting, anyhow Mina would soon be busy with the pig-sticking, Aposperitis had raised her piglets up in Vourkoti along with his own, those that had escaped the summer blaze that had slid down in a rush and scorched the whole hillside, mostly thyme and oregano, but some olive saplings, pear groves and onion patches, too.

"I see all twenty-nine of them in my dreams, belly up, ready to burst, I wake up and I weep, no more sleep for me that night," he mourned his sows, his lamentations superfluous, since come November the pigs ended up as sausages and tins of lard and took to the oceans, sailors' tasty snacks.

Mina scolded Aposperitis but was grateful to him, as she was to everyone and everything that kept her mind and soul off family matters, which could spiral out of her control now and again.

"October 30th, the feast of Zenovios and Zenovia, spent three gold sovereigns and bought the parents a gift from Issaris' place, Messaria, a russet cow, she'll be needed when the old one's milk runs dry," she wrote to the other.

Saravanos, a pediatrician who came from Athens once a month, had examined the infant that evening, he'd earlier conferred with Resvanis, the family doctor, "the divine beauty of his mother has spelt doom for the infant's every bacteria and

bacilli," the pediatrician noted good-humouredly, simultane-
ously flirting with the daughter and teasing the mother, pale
and wooden with worry.

As he was leaving, his fee paid by Orsa, jasmine and moonflower debris blew through the half-open door, the dried-up
leaves and flowers crept across drawing room tiles like baby
bugs. Mina grabbed the brush and shovel, "let them be, mother, they're so beautiful," her eldest daughter said, lulling the
infant to sleep in her arms, up and down, up and down, and
nudging them with her slipper.

"The Alps?"
"Exclamation mark."
"Patagonia?"
"Three little dots."
"The Sahara?"
"A question mark."
"The Andes?"
"Definitely a semicolon."
"The Niagara Falls?"
"A colon."

Nana Bourada-Negropiperi had come to visit Orsa with a shiny red and yellow balloon for the baby and ideas for new games of question and response, like places and punctuation.

Mina sat with them for a while sewing buttons, she'd finished primary school in Smyrna, back then when her father's boat had carried figs from the estates of Nazli, pears from Parsa, licorice and oak apples from Philadelphia to islands un- and well-harbored, when she'd only known the local geography well, the prefecture of Aidin and its mountains, Sipylos, Tmolos, Mesogis, Latmos, Kadmos, Mimas.

Later, she'd committed the bustling coastal centers of five continents to memory, an ungeographied sailor's wife she would not be.

She served their visitor a liqueur, gathered up her sewing, and withdrew, her heavy steps audible upstairs moving chairs, rearranging, scolding now and then.

"Are they quarrelling?" Nana asked.

"She's alone up there."

In the house, her mother hadn't had much to say to her daughters for a few years now, she talked to her ancient house-bound tomcat, Babis, two stone if he was an ounce, stiff-limbed and permanently asleep, for a few months now she'd been pointing things out to her bankbook, interrogating the side-board, and sending the slotted spoon to the devil.

A hard winter, December '30 and January '31, they rotted in the rain and the old woman's goats drowned up in Apatouria.

People inward-looking and ill-humored, they fell behind with their jobs and come Christmas, day after day of rough seas put paid to the ferry service and little celebrating got done, much unavailable and delays in the sending and receiving of the season's greetings.

"How did you spend winter evenings with Mikés?" Orsa asked.

"We played cards to chivvy time on," the teacher replied and sank deep into a highly personal memory: it was evening and her late husband, content after a double helping of steaming macaroni and several glasses of Syneti wine, had tempted his half-drunk Nana into a farting competition, "that I'll never forgive you," she'd tell him for months afterwards, the memory bringing a smile to her lips every time she remembered, devoured by nostalgia, what wouldn't she have given for another night like the one when, doubled up in fits, they'd farted away like naughty school kids, mid January, windows left ajar fore and aft so as not to stink up the bedroom.

"Penny for your thoughts, they must be happy ones."

"Better not," she replied, she'd never tell a soul. She pitied the young girl who'd be spending most nights of her life alone, thousands of nights, she made a rough multiplication, really, thousands upon thousands of nights. Her and Mikés had been inseparable for sixteen years. "I might be forty something, but you'd better watch out, I have quite a thing for your Nikos. His eyes are so expressive, I'd say they're framed not shrunk by those glasses. And as for his beard," she went on, "what a shame he went and sacrificed it," she'd once seen him standing under a streetlamp in Nimboriò, it was cold and his hair and beard glistening wet, dusted with tiny snowflakes, like a steppe.

Dark Maltambes needed to shave twice a day, Orsa remembered, she scratched her cheek, kissed the baby and thrust the thought as far away as she could, to the far side of the planet, to Canberra, for two years now the capital of Australia.

"Do you think Paris will ever stop being the capital of France?" Nana wondered with charming incredulity.

"And Vienna of Austria?"

"And Rome of Italy?" the teacher continued calling Europe's capitals into question, some changes earned her praise, Venice, for example, for the capital of Italy, or Barcelona of Spain and Petersburg for the transcontinental Soviet state, her postcards encouraged such subversive thoughts, and the more her seasickness kept her anchored and imprisoned on Andros, the more enticing the idea of an eternal geographical fluidity became.

"It's not just impractical, it would confuse the postmen, too," Orsa teased her gently, a little bored.

"Don't you sit there telling me what's right and what's wrong, what's possible and what isn't, I want my little delusions, I need them, all of them, and hope I'll never be deprived of fresh ones," Nana made her wish.

Orsa gently rocked the baby, long since asleep, it was true, the teacher's three-hour visit had left her near drained.

"Do you really think all that up just to while away the evenings?" she asked.

"Twenty-one years old? How much you have ahead of you, my dear," she replied, stubbed out her second cigarette of the evening, stood up, performed a meticulous pleat check and cast round her for umbrella and coat. She stood in the doorway, her gaze scanning Orsa from top to bottom, wanting to confirm her initial impression, and her beautiful former student really was looking tired and somewhat thin.

"Mosca?" she asked.

"In love again."

"Who with?"

"The baby."

At the age of sixty, Annezio learnt off by heart all the most difficult, most sacred pilgrimages in the Holy Land, the Church of the Nativity in Bethlehem and the waters of the Jordan, she memorized the ground God trod, the Holy of Holies, the Dome of the Rock and Al Aksa mosque, and had three good reasons for going to the trouble:

Firstly, she alone could describe as she alone could see, old man Vatokouzis' eyes had blurred over for good.

Secondly, she corrected or amplified his mutterings, improved their meaning, contradicted, deleted some that were completely gaga, filled the frequent silences to conceal his collapse.

And thirdly, although no one asked her to, she wanted to prove that the Vatokouzises' generosity had not gone to waste when they'd sent her to Jerusalem at the sick man's side, first class, too, twenty-one pounds sterling, with second class only eighteen, second economy class twelve and everyone on their own mattress from home, and third class seven with accommodation in monasteries not deluxe hotels.

Athanasios of Syros, Tinos and Andros had invited Mina Saltaferou to join them on the Holy Sepulcher Association trip, too, "next year," she'd answered the metropolitan verbally, and so Mosca's fine hand brought things to pass, she sent two completed application forms and the requisite deposit to the Georgantis Bros United Dairies, Panepistimiou 48, Athens.

Steam ship, Piraeus to Rhodes to Cyprus 532 nautical miles, Limassol to Jaffa 180, 712 in all, the old man worked out, some things some places he'd never forget, he seemed more lit up about the journey than the destination, and Annezio, anyway, elsewhere, in the past, her employer's good old days, before he picked up what he did, back when his speech, starched with a razor-sharp crease, had won him pride of place, sometimes it even set him apart, how could the others follow him, those hoi polloi who stumbled over their words, mumbled through their teeth, or delivered a story's punch line at just the wrong moment, leaving it maimed and useless for the rest of the evening.

Between February and May, the nurse had graduated to every stop on the Easter trip, every ceremony, prayer and hymn, as though she were already back from the longed-for trip, Orsa inhaled and suckled the boy to whom her father-in-law, with flashing eyes, had strictly forbidden his name, Giannis, teasing the curl upon his little head, for him she'd picked out Tchaikovsky's *Sick Doll* on the keys of the out-of-tune piano she hated, and another German one until his ears grew tired of both, "that's it, the piano and our family don't mix, period," the two sisters laughed.

The baby had brought Mosca just a breath away from Orsa's heart, it seemed they'd had to reach twenty and wean themselves off parents to meet like sisters. They took strolls with the pram in the scant rays of winter sun, to unfurl and open up, so they and baby could meet with other folk, to go to Chez Nico's for photograph sessions, Mosca had been photographed with her nephew more often than his mother had.

"He suits me," she shouted; with Kiki and Marie, Katina had left for Athens and nursing school, they'd go steal sweet oranges from Antonia and perfumed apples from the priest, nothing too good for the little fellow, who only had to hear her shouting and joking to break into peals of laughter and demand somersaults and squeezes.

Damp from three months rain, Andros ate its fill of brown-capped porcini, yellow chanterelles and oysters, every hillside ablaze with multicolored mushrooms, tasty and not nourishing in the slightest.

Thomas's Monday, a week and a day after Easter Sunday, Piraeus, evening, Annezio and her father-in-law returned from the Holy Land laden with icons, religious souvenirs and amulets, as though they'd known, you might say, for they found Orsa in Athens, in the Papasarandou clinic with serious anemia, fainted at home she had while rubbing her heels with a pumice stone.

Mina stayed behind with the child, and the two sisters rushed to Athens on Resvanis' orders, never one for medical responsibilities, he dispatched them to Melissia and continued his solitary walks in Riva. Orsa kept the nurse and sent Mosca home, the child would need her high spirits, two days later, sister and wheelchaired father-in-law boarded the *Afroessa* to sail spring seas back to the island.

"They'd gathered from the ends of Arabia, from Syria and Abyssinia for the ceremony of the holy fire, caravans, camels in their thousands and people of every faith, Armenians, Syrians, Copts, even Turks, archbishops and patriarchs in ceremonial robes with the insignia of their office, and our old loon in his captain's uniform. I had to force him to dress up," Annezio stressed, "and I know he liked it plenty, never mind if he spat in my face and called me a whore on Easter Saturday."

Orsa stayed in the clinic right through June, tests for thyroid problems or a peptic ulcer, the lack of iron down to pregnancy luckily, and breast-feeding, so it was injections, vitamins, and a thousand other things until, late August, she moved to Cecile of Kifissia to convalesce, supervised rest with the Hadoulises at her side like family; they sent their own specialists, university professors to a man.

Nikos sent telegrams, meaningful gifts and letters bulging with regret at not being able to jump ship in the North Sea and be close to her, there were loans to be repaid and, though he never said as much, he was probably too embarrassed to ask for further leave, he didn't want to exploit his relationship with Hadoulis Junior, who was gradually taking the company over with seven freighters to play with.

Orsa was sure Dr. Papaeconomou would be sending her back to her little boy any day, but summer passed them by in the hotel with Annezio stuffing her with puddings and bon fillet, describing altogether differently each time the trip to the Dead Sea by car and the ceremony of the Niptiros, the Washing of Christ's Feet, *God's wisdom that leads us through the abyss and holds back the sea* could not make her well, her soul weighed heavy, especially after her Antonakis paid a visit to Cecile's, an afternoon he'd stayed, then off to Andros in a flash, two idle months, then, as expected, Southampton and the *Minerva*, the new ocean liner.

"I don't love Kifissia," Orsa thought, unused to towering trees and so much shadow, honey and cornflowers, complexion and eyes, she was a touch of the Aegean, a little island bathed in Cycladic summer, Sikinos or Sifnos as her father said. One afternoon she walked Melpo Athanasaki to the station, a classmate married in Piraeus, a teenage friendship with nothing left in it, tiresome. The train left, the platform deserted, the hour late. Orsa noticed a white high-heeled shoe lying on the ground, from all the months of illness, Athens, recuperation, Kifissia, it was this image she resolved to file away in her memory.

They packed the next morning, before dawn she made a gift of her perfume to the young chambermaid from Kalamata, then a taxi down to Piraeus, it was September 3rd, Antonakis staying until October 10th and Annezio counting the days.

"Wake me up when Andros comes in sight," she said and closed her eyes.

When they entered home waters, afternoon was well underway and the sky had filled with clouds, "ah, no island summer for me this year and how I missed the little things," mist over the Eye of God, the smell of wicker, vineyards, figs, black-barked brooks, the Virgin's liking for pink lilies; Orsa realized how she needed Andros, an essential condition for being.

The *Afroessa* dropped anchor in the bay beyond little Andros harbor and they disembarked in boats, Annezio supervised the loading of their luggage and parceled-up toys, annoyed with her only son, infatuated, away as always to Aladinou and not there to meet her.

It started to drizzle.

"You've brought the rain," Mina Saltaferou shouted to her daughter, she sat little Savvas, that's what they had called him, down on the quay among the busy travelers dragging trunks, baskets and valises any which way; him standing on his own small two feet, in his sailor suit, he could walk, too, his first steps, "so I missed that too," Orsa thought, she needed a little time to get used to the idea she no longer had an infant but a regular little boy.

The rain grew heavier and spoiled his ringlets.

"Mosca ran home to bring you a raincoat and umbrella, we don't want you sick again, there she is, coming down with her fiancé, they exchanged vows the day before yesterday."

Pleased, taken aback by the surprise and speed of the thing but pleased, five positive thoughts in fewer seconds, that there was no way her little sister would have a man forced on her, that the engagement would save her from that ogre, their mother, that she might forget the Englishman now, that she'd make a good mother, that they'd have the foundations of a firm relationship, and the drizzle turning to rain all the while, setting off the colors of the city, arid from summer, and Orsa home again, relaxed and ready for anything.

She took the child in her arms and turned to see Mosca striding jauntily towards them arm in arm with Spyros.

With Spyros Maltambes.

PART TWO
MONOPATOSIA

Monopatosia. Wrecker of my children's joy, poisoning my life, stealing my sleep those nights, those rare nights he was here and many more besides, the same things spinning round in Orsa's head seven years now, making her unhappy; when the Saltaferoses built the two-storey house in 1917, the date carved high on the façade, they'd gone overboard on doorknobs and window frames and scrimped on the floor, like taut-stretched cheesecloth it dripped upstairs' sounds and lives into the downstairs home, thin cypress boards, plain, joints unstopped with clay, no solid matter to show the homes were two, to demarcate their lives, no buffer zone for safety's sake.

The *Minerva*'s seven came home in June—the ocean liner in a Rotterdam dry dock for minor repairs and maintenance—reckoning they'd stay till early October. Welcome backs and get-togethers for Maltambes upstairs, visitors and comings and goings, "the sweet apricot's still warm, son, the second plate for you, the first for your sister-in-law, in the family way again," Saltaferaina announced, "you didn't tell me," Spyros said and handed out sporting outfits, racquets and nylon toothbrushes to the kids, they couldn't get enough of those in America, but little Savvas in a sulk, he'd wanted Japanese fireworks again, seven years old and fit to explode, he'd driven them crazy.

The rest as per usual, the finest fabrics for wife and mother-in-law, five bridges and three hotels for Madame Nana, he handed Orsa the envelope along with her gift, a little wooden alligator; it seems he'd forgotten how afraid she was of reptiles.

"You always remember us, Spyros," she told him calmly, really she'd lost all interest in gifts, she'd had her fill since childhood, so many women she knew moved by the childlike ritual of unwrapping, wondering about the bottom of the box, was it fragile or not, peeling off the label with the country of origin, slowly undoing the string quite unconcerned by the contents, often the packaging alone enough to guess it was another Argentinean blanket, a dozen or two Polish cut glasses or framed Brazilian butterflies.

In her downstairs home, her sister's above, in all the others excepting none, the corner display unit spanning two walls, a native canoe with dark-skinned paddlers for decoration or the felt lion whose head floats when they open the windows and the breeze leaps in.

"You always remember us," she repeated and went downstairs.

Monopatosia, cursed a thousand times, every sound as clear as crystal, everything heard and overheard Orsa wanted to hear, whenever Mersina or Savvas looked about to scream or fight, "shut it" she'd beat them to it, the children paying for her return to reality from the place where she lost herself between her brother-in-law's voyages, only when he was on the island did she care less for them than she should, a bag of nerves in tatters, her ears cocked for every sound and shuffle from the floor above, and when he set sail again, she'd scoop the children into her arms repentant and craze them with kisses, "that's the last time you upset me, Spyros" she'd swear to herself, but it was enough, full two years later, to see him approaching from afar, womenfolk rushing to windows or doors with that not-so-hidden admiration, for the cannon to fire in her breast, a warm welcome and submission, especially when both storeys grew quiet and the celebrations started up on the bedsprings, gently at first and then not so, Orsa weaker than her desire to trace his cheek with her fingertips and search for what once was in his black eyes.

The guests had left, she heard them pulling in their chairs to eat, Maltambes the same as ever, larger than life, pleased as punch Mosca was frying him meatballs, his favorite, going to the open window every so often, "Andros, I wouldn't change you for the world," he bellowed and roused the neighborhood and lowering his voice, "them that drown don't live to regret it" he said over and over and sighed then started over whistling *mother, ah homeland of mine* again, and, *how fine the moon-flower smells*; moonflower had once been their code, it meant eight o'clock at the watermill.

They'd pass the steps to the sour cherry orchard, head down the deserted lane, fit to faint, Spyros would slip his arm round Orsa's waist to protect her from the perfume and the girl melted like a candle, just like that. When Zanna's sons pried the tree loose and set about it with a couple of mattocks, "because sleep weighed on them too heavy in the hut," always something bothering those too, "look what you've gone and done," Spyros said and they burst into fits of laughter, Lord knows how they'd laughed, "that's my girl," he'd said, "don't take it to heart, we'll fill our garden with moonflowers and sit on our balconies and just breathe in all summer long, we'll stay up breathing all night long."

It was past eleven when they went to bed, Mosca had a time getting the little ones off to sleep, four-year-old Christina still hungry for her father's caresses, wanting to draw them out till midnight, she didn't remember him at all and he seemed new to her, like a toy, but man and wife were impatient, Orsa held her breath like a thief in the night, "Maltambes," she thought, "I stay up all night long and do not breathe, I stay up all night yet do not breathe." She counted the sounds one by one, the shutters opening and closing, Mosca leaning out, as usual, to make

sure Orsa's light was out, then slippers off and head on pillow
first, the creak of the iron bedstead, Spyros wandering from
room to room like he was looking for something, probably taking in places at his leisure and things, the eternal and the new,
"don't be long," her sister's invitation, she never showed much
desire for her husband when he was away, the clink of glasses,
he must have had a glass of water, and him slowly making his
way back to the bedroom, directly above. Orsa rigid, she heard
him take off his shoes one by one, lie down on the left side of
the bed, a deep, manly sigh broke through the thin cypress
floorboards, "you good-for-nothing call-yourself-a-builder, you
murderer," she cursed Halas to hell with all her soul, then
silence, the familiar silent self-consciousness of two bodies long
apart's first touchings, then, a little later, choked fumblings,
heavy breaths, she knew it by heart by now, willingly and not,
she'd lain in wait through it all some nights in '31 when they
married, in '33 and '35 when Spyros had stayed two months or
three at a time on Andros.

Her sister's breasts and thighs she knew from summertime by
the sea, from giving birth and suck, from when she was afire
with fever, careless, always gadding about, and Mosca often
down with a cold, upstairs she'd go to care for her, to change her
sweat-soaked underwear and lay hands on her skin, she'd studied her body's every secret, the wide-spaced breasts, thick nipples chocolate dark, the milky opals of her loins.

Maltambes knew how lucky he was to get his hands on all of
that.

When their breaths fell in with one another's rhythm, she got
up as quietly as she could, a robe thrown round her, slippers in
hand and door closed gently behind, in June's full moonlight
streaming through the open windows she saw a pair of eyes
watching her; her mother's, to whom sleep never came easily.
Listening, too.

Once, a few years back, when Orsa went three days to

Piraeus to see her husband, she'd come back to find her bedroom up and moved to the other end of the house, leaving her suitcase in the hall and her child in her mother's arms, wordlessly and coat still on, she undid the new arrangement there and then; same thing again after a day spent seeking the Virgin's help on Tinos, Mina, who never once let on, had made the bed up with new sheets and hung new curtains, but it didn't work.

"You're used to peace and quiet, you must find our racket so annoying," Mosca had fished around once or twice.

"Mother and Annezio snoring in unison could drown out the sea," her elder sister skirted the hook just fine.

The darkness had a paleness to it, the full moon; Orsa eavesdropped on the neighborhood, silence, only distant Mouraina caught her eye, sitting on her little terrace in the dark puffing away at the heavy stuff, that's how she made it through the summer nights, in her slip, her meaty thighs and flabby ass laid out around her for company, growing old and rusty, cigarette in hand, like the iron railings on her balcony.

What use childish infusions of lime and valerian after years of loneliness, or the Veronal they requested, insomniacs to a woman, from doctor Resvanis; they did the trick, Orsa'd tried those, too, little to write home about.

She darted into an alley away from eagle eyes, unable to take talk, especially talk of men's bodies. Her arms folded over her swelling belly, six months gone, she slowly walked down and round Maltambes' so-familiar route, river to cave to dove cote to Saint Dimitrios to old cemetery on bone-dry hill, by the time I get back, she calculated, they'll be fast asleep, damn them.

She wanted to be a little girl and spend her time hidden alone in the sitting room for hours on end, moving from armchair to armchair, the dark green velvet always cool that way, to take the gold tassels on the heavy curtain in her hand, to caress her throat and cheeks with its fringe, to make it one with hers, and for that to be enough.

When she got back inside, her legs so tired they could barely take her weight, her ankles swollen, her eyelids heavy, her soul empty, round two hours Maltambes' walk, her mother's eyes flickered as she sat up, her blithe snores counterfeit.

Dead quiet up above.

It takes skill to batten down the shutters.

The *meltemi* blowing hard as the curtains billowed white, the windowpanes rattling and Mosca on the run from room to room on the lookout for drafts, securing hinges, beating damage to it.

In the dining room, carefully folded over the backs of chairs, English worsteds, flimsy silks and French velvets, whatever her father had sent her in dribs and drabs over so many years and her husband had made up for since and then some, a little bored with them now she'd had her fill of luxury, no more gripes against her father, and her sister who'd once got the lion's share.

She wasn't overly fond of running to the seamstress in the heat of summer, the sweat dripping off her as she stood motionless for fittings, autumn a more suitable season for sewing and freshening up dresses, for gatherings round her second cousin Archontia Sarri's to decide on fashions, catch up on the news, be the first to taste this year's syruped quince.

Mouraina's reign was at an end.

She'd taken it to heart that her husband, who she'd imagined snared in her knickers till death do us part, would not be coming back, what a waste the full-length offering in wax to the miracle-working icon of the Virgin Theoskepasti, the rakish ship's officer uniformed and at attention, so she'd had them round less and less till one afternoon she begged their pardon and shut her door, her inventiveness in matters of *amour* and *eros* gone for good, the baton passed on without a word to Nicephoros's widow, who'd long since swelled past eighteen stone, a lardy cunt since the day she was born, but less talented than her predecessor.

Last summer had been marvelous, they'd gone to Tinos with Orsa and her four kids, stayed ten days at the Palace Hotel without mother, who always got in the way, they hadn't even asked her, Mina had waited till she'd secretly counted the tickets in the bureau and frostily announced, "I think I'll stay here for the pig sticking and the grape harvest." The cousins very close, Savvas between unnaturally and unpleasantly serious for his seven years, Mersina a tender-hearted scaredy-cat, her two, Christina and Mimis, a real handful, little gypsies on account of their swarthy looks.

She discovered her sister bit by bit, as though she were curled up in a trunk revealing a new inch of herself with every new day. So different from the person she'd thought she was when they were teenagers, Mosca had cut herself free of others' opinions, she had her own, she decided with whom, when, and why to be warm, generous, indifferent, malicious, a bitch even, and no one else.

They buried their calves in the tepid sand, side by side, watching the kids out of the corner of their eye, the impressive swimmers, youths and tomboys diving with flourishes from the high rocks, drawing ever closer to the other's essence without traded confidences or much talk, without even looking each other in the eye. Their men were away and they shared their absence.

"And, of course, there's no escaping Fate," Mosca laughed contentedly, she may have married a sailor, but what a sailor, whichever way you looked at it, there was no one worth a fig beside Spyros Maltambes.

Midsummer '31, the Feast of the Virgin, August 15, Orsa away in Kifissia convalescing, nuts but oozing charm, he hadn't sat his behind down once all night, dancing until dawn, setting hearts aflame and sending the married women off to their beds one by one with a fire in their loins to match that in their bosoms, Mouraina, Tassa, Nicephoros's widow, Hadoulaina, "even if I had a daughter," they'd said for Mina's benefit, "some Spanish tart would get her hooks into him," there wasn't a single woman didn't want him, Mosca wanted him, too.

"Who was it got your daughter sick, *kyria* Mina?" he'd teased Saltaferaina, pulling her up to dance a couple of verses.

"I have another," she'd replied, and that had been that.

Newlywed, Mosca had followed Spyros on a trip to America, New York had seemed a complete and different universe as she walked its streets, her eyes rolling in their Mediterranean sockets at the sight of so many strange things, her husband had taken her everywhere and Mosca had shone in once-off outfits, she wouldn't want to be seen in dresses that sophisticated on Andros, she'd bury them at the bottom of her closet.

Music halls, restaurants, breaking the sacred bread in the Greek community, wedding receptions in deluxe hotels where the height of elegance and style, she wrote Orsa telling her everything, was an enormous flower arrangement in the lobby, one or two hundred lilies, the same ones that sprang up around Andros's pools and streams in spring, the ones they picked for Christ lying in state on Good Friday.

She'd seen Annezio's Antonis, too, he didn't come to Greece anymore, for political reasons, and had left the Loutraki Greek restaurant in Chicago where he'd found work for the International Exhibition of '33; he'd become a hairdresser in the meantime. His salon was in Alton, Chicago, from the island of winds to the windy city, the American women made an Ad of his Ant, turning him into Adonis, the handsome islander in no hurry to set them straight.

He delivered an enormous dog-tooth chest to them in New York for his old mother, he missed her a lot, he broke down just before they left, his beautifully coiffeured locks collapsing, too, as he locked himself in Maltambes' embrace, "Ah, captain!" he sobbed again and again plus some other stuff, about the sea, his childhood love in Aladinou, a summing up of emotions and relationships, a proper dramatic farewell, and that because Spyros had always thought him special too, with his mischievously winning ways and tireless hard work, a sailor, a cook, a hairdresser and political to boot, for goodness sake, the pair of them had ended up in tears.

In the Met, Mosca had sat for ages opposite the painting David Bradley had shown her back then on a postcard, during what she now called that foolish romance, clearly happy with her marriage.

So Whistler was the artist's name, James McNeill Whistler, and apart from the frozen Thames some Christmas centuries past, she found herself irresistibly drawn to nautical scenes, let's say to blue in general, with her reels of cotton Katerina Basandi was a folk version of the same thing, and Mosca remembered her at just the right moment; so this Whistler character painted seas, rivers at dawn and evening harbors, the girl transfixed by Valparaiso at night, but Maltambes, bored by now, not letting the opportunity go to waste, he told her everything about the Chilean city he knew like the back of his hand, how he'd spent his first two years at sea sailing back and forth in that vicinity, how they'd pick up pilots in Necochea for the voyage round the Horn, the terrible cape with the constant threatening roar of the waves.

Mosca had always liked trips and big cities, a metropolis means a lot of stories to find out about, to stick your nose into, to star in, or to just let yourself drift amongst their strangeness, their charm and sadness. After every exclamation of wonder over a skyscraper, a limousine, a bizarre figure, "I wish we lived in New York or London," she'd told Maltambes time and time again, and as though competing deep down for her special place in his eyes, she became more and more demonstrative, gushing, glamorous, she did things not exactly in character.

Anyhow, Spyros had made a down payment on a house in Kastela before the wedding, like he'd wanted to escape the old familiar places, Piraeus was heaving and fascinating and suited him, if he felt like a caged lion now and again, the day could always be whiled away in the ships-chandlers on Lazopoulos Street beside the Post Office, stocking up on British Admiralty charts in Galakatou Street, across the road from Karaiskaki Square, where they dealt in suction pumps, sump-pumps, tow, stokers' shovels and malaria supplies, and next door in the Vichou Street customs office talking shop while the retired Hellenic Navy engineer calibrated pumps, compasses and ship's logs.

So Piraeus was nice, but in the end Mosca hadn't dared shake herself free of her little world. So she had a husband for three months every two or three years, whom she sent long letters like she'd once done to her father, but the instant the ink dried it was back to the same old familiar things, her friends a quorum again with the escapee, Katina, back to nurse her invalid father, asthma, no nursing in Piraeus for her, but despite all their cares the four members of the K.K.M.M. sisterhood retained a touch of their crazy sixteen-year-old selves, all married except Katerina, they'd invested a lot of effort in their new, elegant signatures, their husbands' names now, puffing away, stubbing out their butts in the ashtrays of a smoke-filled drawing room, though they did keep the shutters half propped open, reading serialized novels and especially after Sunday memorials, dreaming up escapes from things worrying, galling, and banal, ever more childishly since they knew full well things like that never happen.

Some folk sit at the window and wait to watch their life pass by—"look, an adventure, a way out of this, strolling along like nothing were amiss, meets us, greets us, and walks on by, leaving us with naught but a sigh"—Marie rhymed married, too, hinting at things the others, more fortunate with their husbands, avoided taking further, anyhow, since she was a kid, they could never have said Marie was crazy about men; Marie was crazy about strappy dresses.

They were spared Mouraina's lexicon, but their bodies had ways of confessing, sometimes, thanks to private matters suddenly on everyone's lips or because of the weather, they had a tendency towards debauchery of the provincial, adolescent kind, sitting on the sand skirts rucked up thighs touching, or getting Katina to unbutton her bodice with the same old time-worn gambits and take out her breasts, twelve pounds the brace at least, delicate green veins marbling the expanse of pink.

That's the sort of thing girls do and novels call them carefree, Mosca thought and couldn't excuse some authors their flippancy, they should dig deeper.

Quite a few of the girls at school had wanted to leave, they didn't, to study, they didn't, falling for one man and marrying another, many pushed into it, like her sister, the old story now thankfully forgotten, anyhow there was nothing Vatokouzis would not do for Orsa, in fact he'd hit on exactly what she wanted, sending her hugely expensive lavishly illustrated volumes, biographies and photographs of wintry mountains from around the world: Orsa adored the snow and spent winters ensconced in her paper refuge, a little nightstand in her bedroom.

But it was high summer now, the breeze plucked at the delicate curtains that danced in and out of the windows, the tomcat transfixed by the sight and Mosca folded up the lengths of cloth and put them in the closet, she'd wanted to cook a perfect roast, Spyros's special request, but there really wasn't time now.

A *ves marinas e algas*, seabirds and seaweed, Savvas Saltaferos had hit sixty-three, the age at which those who've steered clear of the dogfish crossed themselves and tried out every way of taking their leave.

On his last South Atlantic voyage, Buenos Aries to Rosario, beef, just a few days at sea, he'd taken his son with him, a kind of son, anyway, Odysseus, a nineteen-year-old sapling, twice his mother's height, *cabello largo i rizado*, long dark hair, the men on the freighter and folk in the harbors too shy to even look at him, a beautiful boy.

His old man set to retire, they wouldn't be seeing each other again, the young man prepared for this emotional journey, "where'd you find a passenger like that," they all asked, he kept up the chit-chat and songs full of passion one after the other, *asi es la vida*, that's life, a voyage across the ocean waves, *las olas del oceano*, dark and white-capped, often thick with the seaweed that thrived off these shores and stuck to the hull, the deck, the portholes.

The young man loved the sight of cities from a distance, leaving them behind as he slowly drew away in a boat or a plane. When Boeing, the American, had launched his 714 a few months earlier, the airplane with the bar, "one day," he'd said, "I'll go round the world with a drink in my hand, by air." An apprentice mechanic for the time being, working and setting money aside.

October 1938, a chapter closed in Saltaferos's life. He wanted to go back. His maritime career spanning half a century, from a night in 1888, the eve of celebrations, long before the sun rose to rouse the city, the smell of anise off the Easter bread making him hungry, when a thirteen-year-old apprentice dropping firewood and oven clothes for the baker. His mother had backed down, too, leaving their home unswept on the day of his departure, standing on end, the slice of moon promised fair weather, she didn't want to bring bad luck down on the voyage. His old lady, a lifetime pitted against the River, she wrote it with a capital R and meant the Danube, lots of Andros folk in the Danubian principalities back then, trade and give and take; widowed by the River at thirty, she didn't want to see her little orphans sailors.

Return just weeks away, Savvas recapped and calculated. To please him, Angelita, his little angel, had come to love all things Greek, her flat a state within a state in the Argentinean capital, three rooms filled with Greek bric-a-brac, souvenir dolls of Greek kilted soldiers, tins of sugared sweets and boxes of Turkish delight empty and orderly on the shelves, yellowed copies of the *Voice of the Aegean*, Matsangos cigarette boxes, bottles of *masticha* and ouzo and chocolate almond wrappings; Ita, Angelita-Ita, threw nothing Greek away, "never *mi amor*," and it wasn't so much the things themselves, the junk itself, as her feelings for her Greek captain and benefactor that papered the walls and the furniture.

Savvas was in no doubt when they parted for good, his faithful Argentinean mistress would not be going back to her old haunts and habits, she'd never forget the steps of the *ballos*, and as long as she lived her special food would be meat balls *avgolemono, con huevo y limón*. His conscience was clear, he'd given and taken of everything, caresses, care, money, a good chat, gave a few slaps, got some wicked scratches.

No one knew the truth aboard the *Marousio Bebi*, word went round, a favor to the Hadoulises, he couldn't touch the boy, not even to pat him on the back, a lad he'd known since he was snot-nosed and three years old, they'd grown accustomed to each other, Ita's big and little man, how many times they'd sat on the balcony drinking lemonade in the tepid rays of the setting sun, and her living the illusion of the perfect family, preparing dinner in the kitchen, something very Greek but usually a little watery, she never could get the hang of the sauces.

When Savvas held the woman tight in his arms for the last time, in her fifties now, Saturday October 7, 1938, he caressed her hair, he'd always had a weakness for a woman's hair. Thin from the dying and the peroxide, *cabello largo i rizardo* no longer, and what, fuck my funnel, was going to flow down onto her shoulders as she arched her sensuous way through the tango, the captain thought, and was brought up short, Angelita almost had a bald patch.

Braids, plaits, buns, perms, ringlets, waves and ponytails, no finer adornment, he'd often pad out the hairstyles of the women in magazines with his pen, so he turned his eyes away from the scalp of the woman with the tired dull locks, kissed her on the cheek, slapped her familiarly on the behind, thrust his keys into her pocket, and closed the door behind him. No looking back to catch a final glimpse, he didn't want to have to remember that, too. Suitcase picked up the previous night, finances and such taken care of gentleman-like, Angelita looked safe and sated, tranquil. So all this was coming to an end, his favorite harbors, too, destined soon to be out of his life, because he'd fallen for America, even the North with its names stolen from the cities of Europe.

Coal-black, Odysseus' eyes looked at Savvas without asking for a thing, without pressure, thank God without gratitude even, just a very simple love. He'd wish him bon voyage, *buen viaje*, and he wouldn't mean *hasta pronto*, till we meet again.

Anyhow, war was in the air.

The Germans had been arming regiments, ordering submarines and planes for two, three years now, Britain had tripled its air force and announced a partial mobilization along with France just two weeks before.

The oceans were set to turn deadly, an ebb without a flow would wash Savvas onto his rock once and for all, a crab with a broken pincer, to contemplate his sons-in-law, Vatokouzis, made of shipowning stuff, his seamanship would go to waste, and Maltambes the sea dog, nothing he wasn't capable of on the high seas.

The aristocratic passengers aboard the *Normandy,* the *Queen Elizabeth II*, the *Queen Mary* and the other floating palaces were not all enjoying the luxuries of the transatlantic crossing undisturbed, the prospect of war frightened and disturbed, conversation in the first-class lounges revolving around the latest news, the British and French had launched ocean-going vessels with an average speed of thirty knots, the Third Reich submarines—only the very young in the mood for dancing and flirting, only the very old still faithful to the time-honored agenda for long voyages—what are the Japanese really like, the kingdom of the Pharaohs, and mouth-to-mouth resuscitation.

Maltambes sick of being dressed to the nines all day every day, trouser crease, savoir vivre, wanton rich dames draped in furs and ennui who put their husbands to bed then off for a last drink with the captain, bombarding him with hints that were anything but hints, where's the excitement in that, seven long years at this game he lusted for other seas, other cargos, for danger and the unexpected, so while the *Minerva* was in Rotterdam for the necessaries, he'd arrange with the bosses to move to the *Leonidas II*, look after his share better, with war coming there'd be lots of folk in deep water.

In the meantime, Tinos came to him on the breeze which had strengthened and begun to eddy, enveloping him in the distinct aromas of the Cyclades, one by one.

The city, a long strip between two bays, whitewashed for August 15th, the Feast of the Virgin, gleaming like a flawless ocean liner tied up at the quay as they rounded Pitsiklas point.

Before setting sail for tempests new, Maltambes banked on resting, eating, drinking, dancing, making the priest's day, a backgammon board in hand, he'd taken to wandering the two-stories casting imploring glances to left and right, and he wanted to feel dry land, soil, stones, bugs, grass, cobbles under his feet; he'd had it up to here with decking.

Even if it was a memorial service yesterday, the chief of the Lighthouse Service, forty days now, Maltambes had danced till he'd dropped, the band struck up in brass, meetings and greetings, little surprises, and in the café, round the trestle tables of solace, those with a gift for a tale, for the others, touched up the dead man's greatest hours with hook, line and sinker, and word by word turned the conversation from moray eels and sea bream to ships flying the Panamanian flag, old passenger liners being converted into freighters, the war drifting inexorably closer, set to wreck the floating fortunes of the brine with mine and torpedo.

Uncle Emilios, on the beach now, didn't shirk his duty, anyhow he'd always nurtured particular respect for the lighthouse men, their diligence, how they took the loneliness, his wanderings over hillside gully and crag for mushrooms, snails, wild greens, and even more for his personal relationship with the island's secret nature, bolstered his conviction that the lighthouses guided, too, the planets of dry land, the lovers of deserted, barren, windswept spaces hours and days from the abodes of men.

Spyros slipped a tidy sum into his pocket, "don't refuse, uncle, please, for the soul of my mother, I'll pick you up tomorrow, we can all eat together, Mosca's slaughtering a rooster."

But the rooster escaped his fate.

His sister-in-law went into labor, Mosca parceled out children, nieces and nephews round the neighborhood and shot downstairs, and Spyros forgot his uncle and ran to fetch the midwife.

Vatokouzis plowing his way through the Baltic in the *Archipelago* and Saltaferos aboard the *Marousio Bebi*, waiting for the South Atlantic to sign and seal his retirement.

Maltambes alone in the upstairs house, leaning out the window, smoking. Orsa in pain, her cries strangled, trying not to shriek, maybe she was thinking of the little ones waiting, seized by fear and curiosity in equal measures, counting every sound.

He was surprised to see Mersina surface in his embrace, standing up between his elbows resting on the window frame, she'd crept in, barefoot, crossed the room bent low. He stroked her hair. The little girl leant her head to one side, till it was resting against his left am, lying in wait for her mother's cries.

"Uncle, show me your tattoo," she said conspiratorially. And she waited for him to roll up his shirtsleeve, she stared at the mermaid paid for with his first month's wage packet, her nose almost touching his arm.

Mersina, at six, quite convinced the oceans were teeming with mermaids; stroking his arm, a gesture she'd inherited from her mother, "I'll tell you a true story," she announced, eyelids flickering and clinging on tighter whenever a louder cry got out of Orsa, trying to chatter away her fears.

"Many years ago, my mum says a hundred or two hundred, a boat they called the *Palatinos* was on its way to America packed with poor Dutchmen. But everyone fell out with everyone else on the way. The captain and a lot of other men were killed. And then the *Palatinos* couldn't find America harbor on its own," the little girl ended her story.

The tale of the *Palatinos* she told every December, on that very night, the night the great sailing ship was due to arrive in America, folk seeing the ship, mutinying, in flames from the shore, before, buffeted by the sea, it was lost to the winter's night once more.

Maltambes had told Orsa the story twelve years before one peaceful summer evening, a secret tryst at Gyalià, in the cave, a crab stowed away in one white court shoe; when her feet were half-dry and fumbling round to slip it on, he'd nipped her big toe with his pincer, how scared she'd been until she saw it wasn't some viper curled up in there.

The baby crying downstairs, plangent and agitated, jolted them back to reality, "a girl," Mosca shouted up to him, her head stuck out the window, the tension flowed out of the little girl and a few tears ran down her cheek, in fact, slipping free of his embrace to run downstairs, she scolded her uncle, "you cry, too, uncle, mum says it does you good."

Maltambes was alone again. From the window, he watched relieved neighbors arrive with bouquets of flowers, red Virgin lilies and baskets of fresh-cut grapes or damsons.

Though it was her third birth, Orsa's belly ached all day, the sun long since set, and him, forgotten, not a bite to eat, and two whole packets smoked.

He went to the washstand and splashed water on his face, rinsed out his mouth, washed his hands and took a clean shirt out of the wardrobe.

Halfway down the kitchen stairs he met Mosca coming up like a whirlwind, "I left you eggplants on the table, covered, hope you took care of yourself," she said and pecked him on the ear, "the baby's beautiful," she shouted flushed and breathless disappearing through the door.

Before entering his sister-in-law's house, Maltambes reached out and broke off a sprig of moonflower, he sort of knew he shouldn't, but the devil made him do it.

His mother-in-law, here there and everywhere, counting out the midwife's money, some neighbors were lending a hand gathering up bloodied cloths and basins, Mersina curled up under the table, fiddling with the tassels on the tablecloth and talking to the tomcat, "send the kids over to me, I've stuffed tomatoes for them" Mouraina, wedged into a little armchair, offering over and over.

Maltambes sought permission from the women with his eyes, got it, and entered the bedroom without a sound; Orsa tranquil now, the infant, so tiny, resting by her side, her bun undone, soundless waves of honey-colored hair undulating across the crisp white sheets at the slightest movement.

"May she live long and well," he said, drawing close and bringing the moonflower up close for her to smell.

"Thank you, Spyros," she said, tired, without raising her eyes to look at him.

Maltambes waited, and waited, the baby sound asleep, the first newborn he'd seen up close, the color of wax in the half-light, its three hours of life gave it the look of a souvenir from a land of unprecedented secrets; the silence weighed down unbearably until Saltaferaina saw red and thrust her head through the door, her gaze smoldering.

He left. It was night.

He patted his pocket for packet and lighter, heard Annezio on her way, talking to herself, she must just have put the old loon to bed, not in the mood for greetings, questions, answers, he lingered a moment in a well-shadowed corner.

Walking slowly, he made his way down towards the shore, the route, hour, empty streets, quiet, and aura of night bringing back memories, torturing him, and him with his hands in his pockets, sinking his shoes deep into the sand, into the water even, his moccasins wet and heavy, his turn-ups damp, the fine sand gritty in his socks.

He was in a piteous state. On top of everything, he had to put a cable together for Vatokouzis. "Dear Orsa has borne a daughter. Mother and child in the best of health. Heartfelt congratulations . . . Your beloved wife Orsa has brought a beautiful little girl into the world. May she live long and well . . . Beautiful little Orsa's had a third child, her eyes bluer than ever, her hair uncut since she was ten flowing softly across the double bed in the light of late afternoon . . ."

No one in the family, none of the assorted near-relatives roundabout, had ever been red. Annezio wouldn't hear a word about communism, until Saltaferos sent the radio that changed all their lives, she'd thought the Horned One was roaming wild, mainly in Antonis's Chicago hair salon.

Alton Chicago they'd said, Bog-town Chicago she'd heard, with age the murmur of the sea had settled for good in her ears, "fancy going and settling in a swamp again, the malaria will steal him from me," she muttered angrily, tired of illnesses. Neurosyphilis had rotted her old boss away, suit flapping, blind, nailless, witless, his punishment well beyond the bounds of justice, too cruel.

Saltaferaina consoled her, Mosca's father-in-law would soon be on his way to heaven and there was a extra bed for her round Orsa's, her eldest ate little, blow away in a breeze she would, couldn't manage with three kids, the crux of the thing she wanted an ally with brains in the household with her two daughters in the enemy camp since they were little.

That's what she reeled off to her husband, some of it straight up some of it not, Savvas Saltaferos had gotten his retirement, she'd gone to Piraeus, January 1939, to meet him, relieved the sea hadn't taken him in the end but vaguely fearful about life together, Savvas sixty-three and her fifty-three, they'd have to train themselves in cohabitation, in putting up with the other, the love driven off by rivalry and not having agreed on a single blessed thing in three decades of marriage, but they hadn't separated, thankfully the captain always set sail and was gone.

In Piraeus they stayed at the Capital, Saltaferos had brought trunkloads of gear back with him, the usual Argentinean blankets, dowries for Mersina, Christina, and his newborn granddaughter, he had loose ends to tie up at the Mariner's Retirement Fund, career at an end, he wanted to bid farewell to all the bosses whose employ he'd passed through, to kiss the hands of mothers, wives, sisters, to give gifts of coral bracelets.

Three years before, sailing from South America to South Africa, Giorgakis Liakouras, his chief stoker, burnt to hell by a ruptured steam duct, Saltaferos husband and wife had traveled out to Megara to visit his young widow and son, six years old.

There in that little house, with the pair of unpruned roses and the claustrophobic lemon-painted rooms, the captain's wife felt heartache, real heartache. The sea-going souvenirs scattered any which way on the sideboard, the girl morose, she served up dreadful coffee in cups and saucers Savvas, too, had sent his daughters, asking nothing, answers spare. The child was away, she didn't say where. They left in the rain, not asked to stay until it passed, soaked by the time they reached the bus. Saltaferaina had her umbrella with her, like she did on every winter's day, but how could the two of them come together beneath it?

Winter, too, the last time she'd gone to Piraeus, in '36, three years before when the warships had sailed into harbor with the mortal remains of a king, Constantine, and two queens, Sophia and Olga. They'd been put on display, for pilgrimages and Saltaferaina did her duty; despite the ruined knees on which her heavy body barely balanced, she'd discharged all her obligations, deposit down on a promising little property, orders placed for Christmas, distant relations visited, going everywhere in her good black outfit with that self-same umbrella, it hadn't stopped drizzling for a moment then, either.

The yardstick for every city, the mythical Smyrna of her childhood, beat all comers hands down, but she enjoyed herself, alone, being her own master pinching pennies, in Athens and Piraeus, haggling, squeezing the notary's every last drop. She went to the market and noted down the price of fish, to compare them with the island, recorded the prices of clothes and shoes, haberdashery, dairy products, sweets and liqueurs, the subway, electrified now, taxi fares, anyhow, when she got back all they ever asked about were Athens prices, certain *kyria* Mina would find time for everything in just a few days and then make comparisons and predictions.

On the boat back she sat looking at her napping husband, he'd always had a handsome hull on him, but his nose now twice the size, blue-veined and pore-pitted, hairs protruding from nose and ears, blue eyes shuttered from view by eyelids firmly closed.

"May God save us," she sighed, more out of habit; she was tired of calling upon God, she was tired of sighing.

The Hadoulises held Maltambes up, something to do with the freighters, Vatokouzis returned to enjoy his third child, with Savvas retired all three couples complete and together in the house for the first time in eleven years.

"Fancy that," again and again she said it, to herself each time, haughtily turning to face Cavo d'Oro, her way of not accepting that her husband might fake sleep to avoid her; like Savvas's hair, the waves whitened a touch, lucky she'd never suffered from seasickness, just the fear of earthquakes that froze her in her tracks, a few weeks earlier, in Chile, twenty cities razed to the ground, neighbors with husbands, sons, sons-in-law loading copper in Valparaiso all at sea till word came through their menfolk were safe, a few, Franga, Zanna, Pepi, no time for dawdling, quickly reoccupying Nicephoros' widow's sofas for more of the usual. That, too, a way of keeping the twin chills of loneliness and death at bay.

Her daughters, thirty and twenty-seven years old, never set foot in Mouraina's or her successor's, either. The youngest hardly greeted either in the street, the elder's thoughts elsewhere.

Saltaferaina didn't like old man Hadoulis's stately gesture, leaving Maltambes an extra three months so all the family could finally, for once, be present and accounted for. She went and told him.

"There's a war on the way, Mrs. Mina."

"Not just one," she cut him off mid-stride.

That same evening, down on the quay, the sailors sank into their loved ones' embraces, the threat of war made people cling more tenderly or desperately to one another, in no rush to disentangle.

It was windy and cold. Savvas Saltaferos, upright hale and hearty, kissed and caressed away, shook hands, grew misty-eyed, lost himself among the crowd of grandchildren, daughters, his old mother, remaining relatives and acquaintances all around him, when he reckoned he'd done his duty to them all, he took Orsa's arm and pressed ahead, the signal to go back home.

His eldest leaned her head on her father's shoulder like she'd never leaned on her mother's, not even when she had exams to take, when she was feverish, when she was giving birth.

Saltaferaina fixed her gaze on her own shoulder, wondered how available it was to her girls, and couldn't take her eyes off Orsa's long honey-colored braid as the north wind plucked at it like a ship's cable all the way home.

At the youngest Vatokouzis' christening feast, in the spacious drawing room with the two-seater sofas up against the walls like pews, the valuable frames enclosing their photographs of mainly men mostly missing in shipwrecks past, with the display cabinets reconciling souvenirs from countries at war, delicate Orsa took her husband's breath away.

They'd gathered after church, Nana Bourada-Negropiperi, the godmother, who'd stuck an Artemisia on the baby beside Asimina, she'd call her Arta and call to mind the city of her birth, relatives, neighbors, shipboard friends, high spirits through till the dawn. Orsa downing her wine in one, her cheeks on fire, her father for a partner but the other men, too, in turn, maybe all of them, pouring her soul into the dance; Vatokouzis watched her body, sweet from three births, her breasts and hips quivering, there was something extraordinary about her, such slender wrists and ankles, so impossibly slender, the girl not of Savvas and Mina's making, she was angels' work, his sister-in-law Mosca a classic beauty, Orsa something unexpected, no description of features and coloring adequate for those that hadn't yet seen her to form her image in their heads.

Sipping his drink he stole glances at her as though she weren't his own, but some other man's who could take him to task for it.

Resvanis was scolding the godmother beside him, "excuse me for the indiscretion, but you drink, I've been told, seven or eight coffees a day," he'd heard about the cigarettes, too, but that he couldn't handle so kept it under wraps, "excess, my dear Mrs. Negropiperi, will undo us in the end." The teacher evaded the rest, with goddaughter in arms she sought Balas's company and expertise, Oliver, Orpheas, Ovid had all croaked, the strange Indonesian cage vacant.

Vatokouzis had heard her many a time, tweet-tweeting to the baby in that deep voice of hers, shaking her head from side to side like birds do drinking and foresaw her disappointment when the little one first spoke and didn't warble.

Doctor to all five children in the house, Saravanos had come from Athens, he didn't drink, he didn't dance, and Mosca kept his boredom at bay by dedicating five minutes in the half hour to him, Mr. Dinos the master of inanity, "what do you say, Nikos, to a fat-ass competition" he'd whispered in his host's ear whenever the dancing brought them close, and his mother-in-law had cornered the confectioner, grilling him on Pitrofos syrup, Theophanes raised in Asia Minor, too, from the valley of Bournova and the fine city of the same name.

The children were clapping their hands, his son Savvas wearing a grown-up tie that spoiled his whole outfit, Orsa dominating the packed room with her purple dress and high spirits; as for his *batzanakis* Maltambes, a superb dancer and his trunk packed ready to sail for the Indian Ocean in ten days or so, shoving sovereigns into Vangelis' pocket as the lute player sang *my beloved bird, I got the note you sent me, I thrust it in my breast and told my heart to hush*, "just once, let our day break to a *ballos*," he shouted, "and not the murmur of the sea."

The infant's other grandfather absent. The end near. Nikos spoke to him of the mining of the seas, hoping for a spark in those dead eyes, war doesn't happen every day, and his old man aboard the *Irene* when it was torpedoed in May '17, fortunately without loss of life, off cape Spartivento, Sardinia. Alone, ruined, playing with his dressing gown's silken belt, towering skin and bone, crooked in the armchair he'd pissed on a thousand times but would not leave day or night though it stank to high heaven, head resting on its right arm. The two men with nothing to say for many a year now, though, after the relapse, the old man less and less in touch with reality anyhow, ordering Annezio and her alone to jettison the anchor attached to a buoy, to pour oil on the sea, to send up flares, to shut the ventilators, to batten down the shutters because a typhoon was descending on the dining room with dizzying speed. This back when the disease was in remission, before, the situation desperate now, he saw how bad he was and sank, heavy, to the lowest depths of silence, guilt, and sadness. His arrogance no more.

Monday afternoon, after the English lesson Mosca gave his children, Nikos took them by the hand and they headed up to his father's house together. He'd point and they'd see who could shout out the English word first, quay, lighthouse, mule, baby, gate, step, hall, old woman, carpet, grandfather. This gangling grandfather frightened the children with his captain's hat stuck to his knees and who Annezio, with furious gestures—I'll have your hides if you do—forbade kissing, a grandfather his grandchildren never once kissed.

Vatokouzis climbed the wooden ladder from the kitchen up into the attic and brought dozens of dusty boxes down two by two, colors stale, filthy with mouse droppings, fancy bows moldering and cobwebby. He dusted them off roughly on the balcony, tore open the paper and the ribbons, and brought the packages into his father's room, where Savvas and Mersina had turned their back on him, uncomfortable, and were looking out onto the empty street.

In a few minutes, a heap of unworn outfits, the captain never could remember what size his son was, give or take a couple, and all the most sought-after toys in London, Odessa, and Constantinople's most exclusive shops thirty years before, everything from ice skates and kaleidoscopes to train sets and battalions of lead soldiers, untouched and unplayed with, laid out on the carpet. The children couldn't believe their eyes, they'd had no idea what was stored up in the attic, but still up to questions. The sudden burst of color left the old man cold, he couldn't see it, didn't register his son's final gesture of forgiveness, and words were of no use now, I left it too late, Nikos thought sadly, but Annezio, who did supremely well without them, made it clear for the hundredth time that the old man had lost it completely, then pointing up at the wedding wreathes in the cabinet, she clarified that God had had good reason for imposing the harsh punishment. Only thus could she feel at liberty to love and care for an employer who was paying for his sins with interest on top.

She found her voice again, "since you've been up there, you'll have seen the roof needs a serious seeing-to, the wind shifted a couple of tiles, too, and the rain's come through in the hall," she said.

Nikos hugged her to show he didn't hold her responsible for the wear, tear and repairs, then, from his jacket's inside pocket, he took out a folded envelope and pressed it in her hands, dark, worn and patched like her long-sleeved housecoat.

Her Antonakis, a Communist, the little bugger, a twenty-nine-year-old little bugger, couldn't come to Greece, they'd been locking them up in Nafplio's mediaeval dungeon since '33, trying, exiling, executing, and before war broke out, the nurse to those in their first and second childhoods as she poked fun at herself, had got a special visa to travel to America at just off seventy.

She scrutinized the papers and the ticket with interest, "you're not a son to be joining up and writing home," her mother had told her back then before not sending her to school, she'd never learned to read and write, but Vatokouzis had arranged to send her with an Andrian crew, they'd look out for her.

"Hey, Nikos, my boy," she said deep in thought, "I want to take that red-assed bum in my arms, but you'll soon be weighing anchor, I have to stay at the old bastard's side now the end is near, I have to be there to close his eyes."

Hail's a disaster for farmers and a gift for lovers of strange sounds, little balls of ice the size of apricot pits or cherry stones tumbling onto the window panes, the polished cobblestones, the tin roofs of the hen houses, the heavy hail storm, "a commotion from God," grandma Orsa said, enraptured though with nature's explosion, standing hands clasped behind her back just listening, an unbelievable sight, the old woman not busy about her household tasks.

The soup ready, February fish left over from old Vatokouzis' funeral, he'd popped his clogs at the eleventh hour so his son could be there for the funeral and Annezio not miss her ticket to America.

The two eldest were at school, the two Asiminas had stayed home, the baby Asimina in the end, Nana's favored Arta fallen into disfavor, poverty-stricken Epirus didn't inspire the prosperous captain's family, as for the two Orsas, they were bent over their plates, the elder silent because the other was grown, it was up to her now to start the conversation. Their relationship rooted deep, words not necessary.

Having lost her silent godmother to a fever that wouldn't break in Kato Ipsilou, whenever Orsa Vatokouzis was on the verge of cracking she walked out even further, to her grandmother, to Apatouria, so they couldn't easily come and fetch her back, of course she'd regret it and not open up her heart, not wanting to break the old woman's, but what point confidences when she'd call her husband kindhearted and a caring father on these visits that were always just days before Maltambes put to sea.

"I came because I had this inexplicable urge to talk about fish, I woke up and said to myself, I want to talk fish with my old gran," she was exhausted from the funeral, the crowds, the omnipresent black; these things she could not take.

Even as a child, though the eldest, she hadn't gone, it was Mosca from six or seven on who accompanied her mother to the homes of grieving relatives, to decorate the tray of *kolyva*. Mina Saltaferou had a talent for the rites of death, much sought after, she'd drag the little one along too, an hour and a half's walk, sometimes two, on a summer night, to last minute boil the wheat so the *kolyva* didn't sour.

The old woman sucked on her little fish, sick of the endless bones, she'd laid them round her plate, turning to the photograph of her dead husband, she pronged the wrasse, waved it in his direction, meaning, fine tidbit this. Fortunately, the funeral feast quite flawless, Annezio in charge, she'd put all the small and damaged fish to one side, gotten out the best crystal and porcelain and buried her old pisspants with homemade mayonnaise and chicken broth very successfully finished with egg and lemon.

"So wrasse, acara, and red perch are fine-looking fish and make a good soup, they're fished till March, taste like cardboard afterwards."

The old woman went on with her spring fish, the conger eel round cut for boiling, sliced thin for frying, she forced the conversation on as far as May sardines and roe-filled picarels, and as she approached the Assumption and high summer sea beds clear and uncluttered, when sea urchins were bounteous, "good with lemon and better with vinegar," as she pointed out to her granddaughter, listening with totally feigned interest, "it's better," she thought, "right now" and told her to continue with September's baked dolphinfish, but no, she had no business keeping it all inside, she pushed her plate away and, the tone of her voice still hovering, uncertain, put an abrupt full stop in place of the comma.

Orsa brushed the crumbs off her black dress, looked her grandmother in the eye and demanded, "don't ever breathe a word of this, the war's coming to cover it all up."

Warmer now, a rainbow bridge connecting Andros to Tinos.

So the two were to be linked by a secret that wrung her aged heart, but thrust her, too, at eighty, into the centre of a human story, her brief, to be a source of comfort, prudence, and clear thinking.

She swallowed her many questions forever, facts unaffected, anyway, by details, laid her hand on her head and stroked the much-loved hair, "the war's coming to cover it all up," she repeated, "or it'll cover it from here to here," she thought to herself; that was most likely of all!

Maltambes felt ashamed when he entered his uncle's house and saw how shabby it all was. The six identical chairs, once the height of elegance, seemingly gone for years without a coat of varnish, their delicate legs come loose, they rocked back and forth. The blanket thin and bare, bald as a sheet without its chestnut wool. Arrayed on the little kitchen's sink, an orange, a lemon, a mandarin, an apple, and an egg. And the coffee had just run out, a shame.

Impulsive and spoilt by his solitary uncle, the only relative that was there during his adolescence, he'd send a hefty check whenever his conscious and compassion pricked, then he'd forget about him for a long while or punish him, as though that harmless unassuming man could ever be to blame for anything, he just didn't shine.

They shared the herbal tea, pouring it into two cups, men's conversation of the minute: the coming war; and a couple of hours went by with the old man marshalling the news about the new destroyers, the *King George I* and the *Queen Olga*, ordered from English shipyards and the Third Reich launching the *Bismarck*. And Pope Pius XI had died, the old man had seen him from afar, in Rome, Saint Peter's Square, the world abuzz with the Germans' gall at sending a delegation to the cardinals demanding a fascist pope.

"What's on your mind?" he asked his nephew, asking not about the pope but his own plans, the war inexorably approaching with a cowlick and an itsy-bitsy square moustache, and the veteran collier swore that when it was over, sailors, as many as survived, wouldn't recognize the harbors anymore. His time was up, he wouldn't be finding out firsthand about the butchery and the destruction, what bothered him most was that the docks and quays, the customs houses, shipyards, fuel tanks, and from close range sailors' homes and bed and board hotels would be first in the firing line.

"It'll change the map of the world's harbors."

So what did Spyros have in mind? A nice account with an English bank and impatient for Hadoulis junior's advice as to the agenda. His father-in-law, "invest in freighters," he'd told him but took it straight back, his mother-in-law, who deep down couldn't stand the sea, "turn it into land," she'd insist, handing him notices of plots for sale and purchase, grocers' and butchers' shops, too; himself, what he wanted was to risk another year or two in far-off waters, to round up the balance and with the war at an end, no way it could drag on for more than two, three years, sell his share in the *Leonidas II* before it came due for the scrap yard, and buy a freighter all his own.

You could find 4,500 registered tonnage give or take a hundred for seventy thousand pounds, 7,500 to 8,000 tons of cargo and not that old, ten years at most; twenty to twenty-five thousand more would get you a new one. Vatokouzis had already pulled it off, two freighters in partnership. Replete after the serious conversation, which meant a temporary break from being sidelined and ignored, the old man catnapped, but Maltambes was in no hurry to leave.

His uncle was his mother's brother, not his father's, and for that reason alone, Spyros thought of him as a sort of auntie, which is why he'd missed and lacked the company of men all these years; but Emilios Balas was far too undemanding and dignified to clamor for Spyros's attention.

He left a little money under the ashtray and without the guilt brought on by wife and children, let himself think of Orsa, furtively as with every forbidden act. As though the clouds of drunkenness had just cleared, he wondered how everything had gotten so tangled up, if Nikos, who overdid it in the saintliness department, knew anything, if Orsa had ever spoken to Mosca or Mosca found out from somewhere else, what was his father-in-law's role in these family dealings Saltaferaina managed like loan repayments and financial transactions, why the Orsa who'd shuddered and shaken in his arms hadn't dared stand up to her mother and, more than anything else, how he'd behaved so shoddily to both the one sister and the other out of stubbornness and wounded pride.

In the end, Maltambes, a demon when it came to dealing with combustible cargoes in the hold, running before the wind and sailing into it, taking the sea's every whim and challenge in his stride, like all purebred seamen, botched things up—feelings, friendships, family matters and inheritances—the moment he stepped out of his element, suspecting Hadoulis junior of doing him out of something somewhere.

He lit another cigarette, covered the old man with his jacket, finally admitted that Orsa had been avoiding his gaze all these years and that he'd been deliberately provocative and indifferent towards her with his spiteful little barbs, his choice of souvenirs, or certain words dropped into conversation as if by chance, moonflower, for instance.

Staring at some olive pits in the ashtray, the remnants of his uncle's snack, it crossed his mind for the first time, perhaps he was fated to be lost at sea in the war, meaning he urgently had to get her on her own and look Orsa in the eye, Orsa who'd kept a ring that belonged to his mother, maybe because she'd mislaid it as it no longer meant anything to her, maybe because the exact opposite was true, maybe it meant a lot . . . "Where did we leave off, my girl? Let's get this thing over with," he'd tell her, "because there are five kids in the picture now."

Savvas eight going on nine, not proud deep down of his

father's decision to restrict himself slowly but surely, year by year, to the Aegean, it was his daring uncle he admired who tamed typhoons and cyclones, who'd drunk every drink and smoked every smoke. Every tale of perilous voyages, ghosts of the sea, dogfish with rotten flesh spilling out he'd once told Orsa between caresses and lovemaking, Savvas knew them all.

Maltambes stood up without a sound, his eye wandering from photograph to photograph, mostly coal ships and postal vessels, olives from Volos to Braila and the River, Sarakatsani homespun to Cyprus, coal from Odessa to Trieste, his uncle had used up his solitary life muttering to himself, "halo round the sun, before the wind ye'll run, a circle round the moon means the start of winter gloom," "damn the sea and bugger the brine," he grumbled through his teeth, the only thing he wanted, madly, was to take Orsa in his arms, to hide the head that burned and buzzed in her hair, to drag his palms crosswise, magician-like, and for the mistake to have never been.

He closed the front door behind him; the woodworm fit the tenant like a glove.

The north wind did him good, enough of this nonsense, he told himself, deciding to go round the Hadoulises' office to sort out a few looses ends, but they'd have been expecting him for dinner long ago, he'd already overdone it.

The table was set, his children, used to eating whatever and whenever they liked, tired of waiting and torturing the cat, Mosca had taken off her apron, wearing something fresh from the seamstress in red, sitting on the edge of the table painting her nails to match.

"Meatballs again." Maltambes glumly took his seat.

Vatokouzis and Annezio sailed for Piraeus aboard the *Iris*. The old nurse had gone up to Vourkoti with Spyrokotsos and his mules and picked out a young maid for Orsa, an honest hardworking lass of fourteen who let the oil burn black in the pan and mixed the good side up with the back when ironing the embroidery, but with a nice voice, a healthy appetite, a talent for fish sauce, and a love for the open air, "so our delicate madame doesn't get all melancholic," Annezio thought, "no matter if the flour's all maggoty when I get back," in five months, midsummer she reckoned. Two sailors' trunks belonging to that fine husband of hers who'd lain low in Eastern ports and hadn't so much as asked for a photograph of their son, she'd decided then and there to remember neither eyebrows nor the line of his nose, not his private bits neither, and every other body part singly, itemized, so he wouldn't come to mind as a whole, dead now, years ago, the two empty trunks all she had to show for the marriage, so she'd packed them full to bursting with embroidered curtains, lace covers and double sheets, hers untouched, for his bride to find, even if she was American.

Nikos was never bored with Annezio, it wasn't only things past that linked them together, it was her determination not to give up a single one of life's rights to the young, even if she was pushing seventy. She had an opinion on everything and the guts for a fight, she knew her love's worth, because it was special, for the chosen few, and welled from deep down in her heart, she didn't hide her dislike for Saltaferaina, "old clencher" she called her, a closed book, not once had she seen her off-guard, unscheming, that Savvas did right calling her his cholera under his breath, and she had no qualms confessing her disgust for venereal disease, but not only hadn't abandoned that boss of hers, a real mess who'd earned God's punishment, or so she'd say, again and again for all to hear, she'd licked his wounds till the very end like a faithful hound. Nikos and that inexplicable Orsa who'd come in the half-light and put a Turkish delight in her mouth and two drops of French perfume behind her creased old ears, who sometimes hid in her embrace, whose tears dampened her robe, and the kids, three of them at that, were a world whose care filled her days and nights.

Her bulging calves bore witness to the miles she'd walked, she knew every inch of the island, where the toadstools grew for the poison, poppy-greens for pies, where the capers dangled, a bouquet of stems with flowers and fruit, which path led to which distant chapel, which platan had the densest shade up at Dipotamata, which rock at Vori the rockfish pass by, and against which dry stone walls to lean at Fello to wipe the sweat from your brow and surrender, motionless, to the sunset entire, from beginning to end.

"Nature always rewards the patient," Annezio used to say, there's no one color for dusk and that was that, and she was right. And she agreed totally with Orsa, when she confessed to her so serious, "I've thought so much about the sand, sand's often in my thoughts."

Nikos enjoyed his old nurse's calm, the transatlantic voyage and foreign parts held no fear for her, "I've been to the Holy Land, too," she'd remind everyone, *flanked by angels sent from God, grimly demanding my turpid soul*, she'd repeat to audiences willing and unwilling, and to check the efficacy of her memory would reel off details for the thousandth time of the liturgies of the Niptiros and the Resurrection, the priestly magnificence in damask and cloth of gold.

Chicago would not don her Orthodox best, but Annezio was ready and willing for strange lands, Mother Nature may have assumed a truly artistic and luxurious mantle on Andros, but other places would be just fine, too.

Vatokouzis looked after her like a son, from the heart, not that he hid his devotion to this fascinating woman, he walked her aboard the *Patris II*, spoke to all the right people, "Don't beg him to come back, because you'll lose your Antonis," he whispered softly in her ear; the hunt was on for Leftists, he'd heard a lot firsthand.

"Just take the one bottle," Katerina Basandi, the poor woman with the blue and the rest of it, sending two bottles of rosewater for Antonis, a drop to sweeten his water when summer came.

In his brown flannel suit and matching overcoat, Vatokouzis stayed on the quay and waved his handkerchief until the distance had shrunk the figures on liner and Tzelepis quay alike, the departing and the staying put just dots, twilight fell and Nikos walked to the dock where the *Penelope* was moored, successor to the *Archipelago*.

He boarded the freighter to make some final arrangements, they were setting sail for Braila and Odessa at six in the morning, he'd come to love those melancholy cities, brazen and fallen they'd never aspired to greatness, not like those American ones that barely went back fifty years but had already ousted the Promised Land in poor men's dreams.

Hands in pockets, the mate for company, Vatokouzis did the rounds of the ship's corridors again and again, committing steps, twists, turns, motors, doors, the positions, mugs and names of the crew to memory, hearing out the tale of the terrible chef again, the crew close to fainting from hunger, SOSs to wives and mothers, "Send Over Sausages," he dismissed the mate and made himself comfortable on deck, wrapped in his overcoat, watched the city lights of Piraeus.

First time in years he'd been in the house the same time as Maltambes. And he'd realized the high-ceilinged, two-storey mansion with its double doors, porcelain door knobs, plaster-molded ceilings, delicately-carved furniture and abundant silver had one incurable flaw: its meager single ceiling boards, its *monopatosia*, especially at first, when Maltambes seemingly couldn't get enough of Mosca's abundance, a storm of nightly groans and creaks descending on them from above, proof and display of riotous lovemaking Vatokouzis hated but did not suspect.

"Have upstairs fallen out?" he'd asked Orsa on their last night, a lull in upstairs' bedspring barrage, ten days or so.

"She hasn't said," his wife was slow in replying.

A thousand thoughts through Nikos's head in a few moments' silence, in the end both men headed for the sea and the cities of the world, the women nailed to the spot, "which is why I love Orsa and my daughters," he thought.

He'd miss sonatinas by Clementi and Couleau from Mersina's little fingers, not a hint of talent the poor thing, she scrunched the keys like she did the cat's tummy, but what matter.

"Our house we can't change. The bedroom, at least?"

Nikos had parted his wife's hair, whispered his suggestion in her ear.

"Oh, come on," her hurried reply, "only you notice things like that, I'm fast asleep in an instant. Anyway, like all of you, Spyros is away, he's almost always away."

They made quiet love, Orsa breast-feeding still and no fear of a fourth, Nikos's touch imperceptible, like a thief's, details other men would never know, her oval belly button, the little moles on her stomach, the Plough, Orsa Minor to a tee, the fluff on her coccyx, the bushy honey-colored fur on her pubis, always moist as though washed by the spray of a secret, gentle wave, barely touching them, one after the other, not taking liberties, "like he's afraid of an electric shock," Orsa thought, tired.

Piraeus was bathed in light, Vatokouzis knew where every building was with his eyes closed, lit a cigarette and when the first drag had brought relief, stood up to get the blood flowing through his frozen legs.

Halas and his apprentices would be starting work on his father's house in the spring, he'd gone and arranged it half an hour before setting sail again, new tiles, saddle roof, the plumbing, modernize the bathroom, coats of paint, a broad arched window where Orsa could sit in her rocking chair gazing at the Aegean and agree with Nana that a landscape really is more beautiful with a bird flitting thought the clouds or a mule panting in a country lane.

Annezio wouldn't be put out, the house had a lot of bed-chambers and alcoves, they'd keep the maid on, too, the in-laws wouldn't be squashed into a couple of rooms anymore, with kitchen and bathroom right next door, Mina could reoccupy downstairs in its entirety.

"It's just that it's high up and blustery, Nikos, and the wind whistles by as though it were weathering a sea in the Bay of Biscay," Orsa would say from time to time, still in two minds about the move.

Mosca hit the shops in search of a blue-green shirt. She'd packed Spyros's trunk with all the usual: sets of underwear, sweets and such like, and some things more unusual, an exercise book in which she'd copied down the words of the songs her husband sang and danced on saints' days and nights out, something of his grandfather's, a tortoise-shell shoehorn with which to slip his feet into the two new pairs of shoes she'd had him made, locks from her and their children's heads tied together with a red velvet bow from last year's evening gown.

She kept a tight hold of her umbrella, rain, wind too, blowing one way one moment and another the next, high heels, calves already half wet, not much life in the shops yet, the hour not yet nine and a lot of folk crammed into church with the school kids for the Three Hierarchs, patron saints of education.

She'd be accompanying her husband to Piraeus the following morning, and as she walked along bent over and shivering, her thoughts ice, all Spyros and his temper, how he'd been talking half and smoking double for days now. The shirt folded, she paid, did an about-turn on the way out and quickened her step, she hadn't visited Katerina since her name day, November 25th.

Like every year, after the liturgy she'd walk as far as the outlying house, the celebrant unable to worship at the little chapel of Saint Aikaterini which, the whole city to choose from, Her grace had perched at the top of a sheer cliff, another female saint had beaten Her to its foot, and the waves, Saint Thalassini.

"Why not invite her to the dinner party tonight," Mosca thought, angry with herself for not thinking of it earlier.

She found her under the awning in her yard sharing cheese scrapings between three very white, very lean cats, a *pas de trois* of Russian ballerinas. The water on for the coffee, liqueurs, and the ashtray out in a flash, "if I won't be in the way, I'll come with you now and help with the cooking," Katerina suggested and Mosca breathed a sigh of relief, Annezio's years of experience were at sea, New World-bound, the little maid was looking after Orsa's youngest, and her sister going that afternoon to fetch their old gran, who was getting older at a rate of knots and wouldn't deign to conceal her weakness for Savvas's firstborn daughter, the whispering and private glances keeping the two Orsas in complete solidarity.

As she waited for the coffee to boil, Katerina put the foreign songs she sang along to on the gramophone, the Italian-Russian-German sounding much the same, but beautifully, each with the feeling it deserved, the fresh fresh, the passionate passionate, and the sad just that way, exactly.

Cigarette . . . she didn't ask, just offered Mosca the packet, glanced at the untouched liqueur, used to silence, that's how the widow would ask and answer, by pointing and looking.

"My stomach's upset, might be another child."

Katerina, who only smoked for Mosca, stubbed hers out on the spot and put the ashtray out on the windowsill, so it wouldn't smell.

She opened the wardrobe, took out one of the dresses her friend had given her over the years, and slid the pick-up arm carefully back in its place. Quite still, she watched the record slow and stop, hunted down her comb and kitchen apron, grabbed a brown silk dress on its hanger, and pointed at the door.

They ran into Maltambes outside Joseph's barbershop. Freshly trimmed, fresh-shaven and never less than a sailor to the marrow, he greeted Katerina with respect, for him she was a colleague's widow, and though that might not sound like much it meant a lot to Spyros. He touched her cheek and a lock of her hair, "you'll give me the *kolyva* and the names of the ships on a slip of paper, the names and places I remember by heart, too," he told her.

It was windy still, but the rain had stopped, the sidewalks dried quickly, the clouds in a rush to overtake one another, the two women still short of a few things for dinner, cinnamon cloves and extra honey for the dessert the most important, "Spyros, hello," they said, "I might be a little late," Maltambes' reply, some little things still to do and a goodbye here and there, trivial last-minute stuff.

Palm upright against her cheek to evade the sea's blue, though grey due to the weather, feeling safer with Mrs. Mosca Maltambes close by, Katerina negotiated the lanes and steps behind her friend, keen to keep her mind busy with the pork crackling and the leek and celery roast, grateful to Mosca for remembering her for the farewell dinner, but all at sixes and sevens at the thought of spending so many hours in the company of shipowners, and on the eve of war at that.

The radio bewitched her, a brown box that made the household stop in its tracks in the hall, pause in the living room and turn to face the well-varnished little set that had the power to change moods and dictate the topics of the day. They forgot to light the oil lamps, they were sautéing the meat and cutting the potatoes thin for the *fourtalia*, listening to the voice of an invisible other in the twilit kitchen describing the arrival of the newly-purchased *King George I* at the naval docks, the destroyer the work of English shipyards; Mosca cheered, never one to repress her feelings, that bloody David occupied her thoughts for a minute or two, skinny and a fussy eater, he'd be called up just the same, but that children's stuff over and done with now, her excellent English all he'd left to remember him by.

Downstairs, Mina Saltaferaina was baking *baklava*, Eleni the little maid was playing with the little ones, some still-unbroken Christmas toys, Savvas and her eldest grandchild had popped round the priest's house to witness the crowning of this year's backgammon champion, though his wife was in a fury already, slap and rattle, dice and counters ringing in her head twenty years now, she hadn't even made them coffee the last five, which turned the priest into the devil himself, lurching into the inner room, a clout to show her who's boss and back to the championship fit to explode, an approving glance earned from the competitors.

Anyhow, eightish, round the walnut dinner table on the first floor of the mansion, Helmis-made on the island with all three extensions so there'd be ample room, they'd taken their places, the priest, without his wife because she cramped his style, Savvas, Mina, Emilios Balas, Hadoulis Junior, fresh arrived on the island, Mosca's inseparable Marie, Katina, Kiki with her husband Bousoulas, who along with Zanakis and Maistros served in Spyros's crew, and Archontia Sarri, seamstress and second cousin with a love for striking prints and dressed, as always, like an armchair for her Zannis to curl up in, their love undiminished since time immemorial, her first and last, absent tonight in the Red Sea, a steward on the Marides fleet.

The two Orsas arrived at the last minute, "I'm tired of counting time and making mistakes with the arithmetic," the old woman announced and took her seat, welcomes and comments she answered with a glance, that she intended to sit silent for the rest of the evening obvious to all. Young Orsa hurried downstairs to check on the children, they'd be slow getting off to sleep with all the commotion upstairs, fed the baby, changed, choosing her dark green, dribbled a little perfume at the pertinent points as duty called.

"So," she offered and looked around for last-minute jobs needing doing, a decanter of wine to bring to table, a saltcellar.

"Now that you've deigned to put in an appearance, Madame, we'll see what to put you up to," said Mosca, the chef, pointing to Katerina and signing the artworks of the night's dinner.

"A dinner in honor of an absent friend," Hadoulis Junior, elegant and urbane, public relations his thing, his visits to the island spent running from dinner party to dinner party till past midnight wishing Godspeed to the men in his family's employ, some he admired sincerely, others he accepted out of duty.

The radio, volume turned down low, offered snatches of information through the open kitchen door to those not taking part in the conversation or letting their minds wander a moment, so recent and so invaluable an acquisition; "shush!" Saltaferaina hushed them, her vision, hearing, and touch let nothing slip by the newsreader announcing a first, the government's intention to introduce ten days of reduced prices in the shops next March; so they were nibbling at their starters, the sausages were sizzling in the kitchen and Mina Saltaferaina steering the conversation towards matters economic, a sphere in which her knowledge extended well beyond household needs, Hadoulis's compliment, charming and at ease with everyone; he felt at home at the Saltaferoses, a powerful friendship struck up out of the blue with Nikos Vatokouzis, five years ago one humid evening drinking beer and trading secrets in a central Piraeus tavern.

They entered at the same time. The tray with the *fourtalia* through the kitchen door and Maltambes through the front. Orsa, the priest, who didn't eat well at home, and most present turned towards the *fourtalia*, Mosca, who'd just laid down the platter, and her mother to Spyros, grandma Orsa to no one. Katerina was still in the kitchen, apron off and washing her hands, she'd opened the window to let out the steam and frying pan smells.

"Where've you been a-wandering? You left the office hours before me. Where've you been supping?" the shipowner asked, handing Spyros a raki.

"Walking up and down the quay, ten times maybe," for days now his departure had seemed a mountain to him, so he downed the raki in one, took off his jacket, threw it on a sofa and took the empty chair at the head of the table.

He knocked back a second raki, and with an "ah!" as the alcohol seared his throat, raised his eyes to his wife with a look that shook her, a look of farewell if ever there was one; Mosca was taken aback, lay down her fork and sought succor in her sister's eyes but found her ally's cast down and half closed and silent, receiving repeated communion with the ruby wine from Syneti.

"The damn war," Mosca thought, "that's it," seemed her husband was afraid he wouldn't be coming back to them.

Hadoulis, office-trained, broke the silence, the first subject that came to mind the bloody war, Estonia, Lithuania, Denmark signing non-aggression pacts with the Germans, Norway, Sweden, Finland refusing to do so, he said, "so that's the news from the oceans for you, and all of it bad, mean, and topsy-turvy."

"Will the Indian be better, worse, or the same as the Atlantic?" Mosca wondered.

"Keep posted for the latest developments," Hadoulis said, "we'll have to wait and see."

Then a flurry of toasts, beautifully cooked dishes, and self-conscious jokes. The priest, though he'd performed miserably in the championship earlier on, was in fine form, Mosca's girl-friends not far behind, *To the Indian Ocean and that dervish Maltambes, may your company be of the best*, and something for the crew, *To Messrs. Maistro, Bousoulas and Zanaki, come home safe to your Penelope and Ithaki*, clinking glasses with the priest and improvising toasts they were soon blind drunk, uncle savoring every mouthful and acknowledging with succinct, precise phrases the sailors' debt to prime minister Metaxas for the introduction of special improved meals, grandma caressing a piece of crust and nibbling on the crumbs, Orsa sitting quietly as though her mind was high among the mountain peaks once more, Mina Saltaferaina shooting inquiring glances at highly specific targets, and Maltambes, though he'd thrown his right arm round Mosca's shoulders had it resting mostly on the chair back and his back turned to her as he added and subtracted profit and loss with his three men and Hadoulis, exchanging questions without answers.

The serving dishes gleaming, father Philippos had mopped up the sauces with a hunk of bread, the wine brought the drowsiness and touch of resignation they all needed, but the war had something to do with it and so did Spyros's high-strung mood; the liveliness and brio of their conversation gradually gave way to emotion and sadness.

"How will I ever have time to embroider the men lost to the war," Katerina wondered to herself; she hadn't uttered a word at table except for "Cheers!" and "Bon voyage," so she was taken all the more aback when, unplanned, her voice, of its own accord, quietly at first then with more confidence, struck up a beloved Russian song hidden in gray winter skies.

A hush descended, they all turned towards her and settled down to listen, and under the table Mosca sought out the woman's hands, palms clasped and pressed against her knees, stroking them soothingly to the rhythm of the song, the fingers pierced by crooked needles and swollen with chilblains, *ogtavarila rosha zalataya beriozavem, veselim yazikom*, of course none of them understood the words, but if a Russian had come through the door, he'd have taken them all for compatriots, so absorbed were they in the song's meaning, even the priest granted dispensation for the melody's perilous nationality, *i dzouravli pechalno proletaya, oudz nie dzaleyut bolshe ni a kom.*

M osca's third was a girl.
She was born the day the Reich leased Trieste harbor from Italy for a decade, July 13, 1939. They heard the news on the radio, always on, which broadcast the government's decree a few days later that all radios should be declared to the Press and Tourism ministry. Her pregnancy had rushed by amidst worries and developments, the Italians invading Albania in April, the English beginning to mobilize, conscription, and the Soviet commander-in-chief, Voroshilov, called to London to set out a joint military strategy, something that had made a great impression on Annezio most of all, less of a handful after her return from America, where she'd quenched her thirst for her only son's caresses.

"The Romanian officers wear corsets, that's why they look so erect and broad-chested," Nana said; she was sat way back in her rocking chair with her godchild asleep in her arms, ten months old and plump, only the teacher's right hand not at rest, raising the cigarette to her lips and occasionally tapping ash into the ashtray.

Orsa had brought the radio with her, she'd tell Nana about her sister and other family news, the appliance could fill them in on international affairs.

"Mosca's still without milk and the child looks hungry, her nipples are bleeding, chewed."

Laid out on the table, postcard albums, monuments of Venice, antiquities and tropical landscapes from Egypt, lots of singles; Orsa had patiently weeded through her husband's treasures, almost moldering in the attic, and Nana quite satisfied, her collector's passion only now beginning to wane.

Evanthia Chiou honeymooned at the Calvi Hotel, Corsica, Nena Bei at the Grand Hotel Miramare in Genoa, Maria Dardanou at Nice's Ritz Hotel, Maria Kanaki there, too, Lena Vardakosta at the Grand Hotel du Pavillon in Paris; untraveled Nana, who'd now acquired rheumatism, constipation, and insomnia to keep her sea-sickness company, kept a list of the photographs of hotels where her students, beloved and otherwise, had been fortunate to sleep beside their captain, mate, or engineer on honeymoon.

It was a long list, because Nana had been adding to it for twenty-five years, and Little England's young, thank goodness, traveled far and wide. Orsa felt lucky, so very lucky, that Nana babbled on ceaselessly in that deep, almost manly voice, and didn't ask questions; between cigarettes she'd gently rub the young woman's back, fidget, stretch, fidget some more and attend to the pleats of her navy blue skirt, she desperately needed to talk, not to listen, the sound of her own voice brought relief as it poured out slowly onto the linen tablecloth and furniture covers, laying down a resonant decorative epithets here, an equivocal adverb there; separate high schools for boys and girls, fewer visitors to her silent salon, three years now.

Orsa had been using Nana for a decade, but she'd come to think of her as a person who must have had a lot on her mind, for a while now she'd been examining her face from scratch, the double grooves in her cheeks and the crow's feet at the corner of her eyes, details of the house, too, a faded photograph of the childless Athenian uncle who'd put his studious provincial niece from Arta through college, three or four pairs of heels and sandals sticking out from under the royal blue divan cover, her dearly beloved husband's hats, winter and summer, carefully dusted on the clothes rack.

"It was your mother pruned it this year, the climbing rose is like an Alpine avalanche, the sun goes down, the heat softens and its perfume drifts in to us through the French windows, more and more intense."

"Nana, do you like white?"

"It's too bright in the summer, too sad in the winter."

Orsa, too, with thirty cards at least from Norway, Canada, Tierra del Fuego, a random amalgam of wintry mountain scenes; yes, white exudes much sadness.

Nana had long since exhausted the chapter marked "Roses" in her thoughts, rightly comparing May buds to little girls, pink rosewater roses to fiancées, wild roses to elegant ladies promenading down an Athens boulevard.

Twilight already, the child licking an apricot, soft women's voices singing on the radio, and in the yellow house on Andros, Orsa and Nana began once more to talk of places many thousands of miles away. Because they lived on Andros but their stories unraveled to spread across the globe, truth be told few took place on their little island and most elsewhere, in the harbors of other lands, other continents, or on the high seas. On the radio, too, their ears tuned not to events in Thessaloniki or Corfu, their interest drawn to matters international, they could imagine that way. Nota, the confectioner's wife, never had to imagine, "it's six in the morning, Theophanes will be baking the *pain d'espagne*," she'd think, "it's five in the afternoon, he'll have gone out to get some eggs from Stavroula, butter and flour from Batidis." Her and Anna, the hotelier's wife, and Joseph's Katie always knew exactly where their nearest and dearest were.

"A sailor? He might be five thousand miles away or more from where his wife thinks he is."

"You must mean your brother-in-law, my dear," Nana remarked.

Orsa didn't reply. Yes, her husband wintered nearby, in the

Black Sea, and she'd twice nipped away when his boat moored in Piraeus to unload scrap iron and take on timber.

She got up, rubbed her back a little, her kidneys, "I left the nappies and a knitted top on the hall table," she said and went to the mirror to fix her hair a little; the baby would stay with her godmother and Orsa could represent the family at the elder Hexadaktylou's piano recital at the Club, Hexadaktylou junior had given up music, well-married in Athens to an importer of sanitary ware.

When their maid delivered the invitation, Saltaferaina had slammed the door behind the unfortunate woman, all that plink-plunking, where's the sense in it, she took umbrage at Mersina's piano lessons, too, "you go, I've got a headache," she'd commanded all and sundry, Mosca couldn't go, forty days still to pass since the birth, Annezio would stay in mourning for her old employer until she joined him in death, the little maid not invited anyway, she was minding the kids, a little girl had died from an adder bite and Orsa hadn't let her kids so much as look at the orchard or fields for ten days now; so it fell to her to undergo a tedious evening, and she was already on edge, her appetite shot to pieces, her powers waning.

"What about Mersina?"

"Archontia can take her in a new skirt."

"Upholstered in some splashy print, as usual."

"If she has time for hers, too, it still needed sewing and hemming this morning, magnolias and dark green shiny leaves."

"What does that Zannis see in her to kiss?"

"There must be something."

"But her lips are so thin. Just a line . . . "

Nana, babe in arms and straightening her pleats, that obsession of hers with pleats large small and French, came up to Orsa and brushed a few stray hairs off her white blouse, "she'll be playing some compositions of her own this time, says so on the invitation."

"Then that's us done for," Orsa replied, though she didn't mean it; the elder Hexadaktylou wore elegantly serious two-pieces, usually in some shade of brown, and walked at night alone from the Archway to the Castle and back, understanding of those bored silly by her musical accomplishments, she didn't keep a register at her recitals.

So Orsa planted a kiss on her child's forehead, a gentle nip, almost a caress, on Nana's ear, took necklace, earrings and bracelet out of her bag, hurriedly put them on and glanced at her watch.

"Off you go, dear, and move up here, we'll be closer," the teacher said, she'd loved her former student ever since she'd penned the most beautiful and irrelevant compositions in class, and she loved round little Arta and not Asimina, she still laid claim to the name though with less fight in her now, she was lonely and needed them both.

"Oh, please, no talk of moves," Orsa whispered, on tenter-hooks for months, unable to make a decision and Vatokouzis pressuring her in his own way, even addressing his last few letters to that empty house, with Annezio and her mother at each other's throats, the bickering was driving her away from the white two-storeys, straight to familiar, secluded spots, to Saint Dimitrios's churchyard, the little bridge with the dense cool shade, or the rocky cave, evening, so as not to run into late-come swimmers.

Once, when she changed course to avoid a bothersome neighbor, up into Loukissas's densely-planted vegetable garden, she'd discovered the most beautiful pool she'd ever seen in her life, with goldfish, water lilies and the aged giant aloe all round, five yards long, two wide and two high, a Roman scene in the cool of spring, meeting place for beekeepers, blackbirds, butterflies, and entirely at odds with everything around it, an African oasis for those two or three day stretches of July doldrums when the *meltemi*-spoilt islanders succumbed to headaches and dizziness, she was sorry she and Spyros hadn't included it among their special meeting places, the Maltambes circle would have come to an end at the pool's stone wall, beneath the shade of the lotus tree, beside the bulk of the well-head and the enormous aloe, an ash-green sculpture unbending in the wind, unchanged by time.

"I've been looking forward to being neighbors for years now, your mother's been round to Halas a dozen times to complain about the *monopatosia* and after advice, 'it's a real shame about the elegant mansion with the beautiful staircases and the wrought-iron railings,' the builder told me, 'there isn't anything can be done,' those stampeding kids will have her out, I hoped, wild things those little ones of Mosca's."

"You didn't tell me about the cards Lily sent you from the Baltic," Orsa changing the subject on the way out.

"At last I've seen what those lights, the red and green ones, look like that keep the traffic in order in Copenhagen . . . "

Nana sat in her cane armchair on her little balcony with the child in her arms, no light, it attracted the mosquitoes, anyhow, the rose so white the dark of night never really set; Orsa rushed down the three little steps, turned the corner, took an old gold ring with a tiny green stone out of her purse, slipped it on her finger, and joined her fellow citizens, music lovers and other-wise, hurrying towards the Club, because Hexadaktylou senior was an unlucky woman as well as a pianist, her fiancé, mate on the *Stenies*, one of many lost in the shipwreck of 1927, leaving the girl alone in a sea of *Morceaux Lyriques* by Grieg.

S unday, September 3rd, Britain and France declared war on Germany and five days later, on the 8th of the month, Greece stopped all men between twenty and fifty leaving the country.

It was Friday, the *Penelope* had just anchored off Kountourioti quay and Nikos Vatokouzis, thirty-six, was caught in the trap.

A few days later, he was flat on his back on a beach, half lulled to sleep by the mild rays of the afternoon sun; September light was always strange, yellowish, lemony, not a month to wear its heart on its sleeve like April, not grueling like its summer cousins or foul-tempered like some mid-winter Februaries. No, September was an enigmatic month, the dry stone walls on the hills roundabout draped in aged gold, the sea pale and motionless, the family picnic underway with Mersina yelling she was going to be sick as they stuffed bread spread with butter and raspberry jam into her mouth, the little one, who'd reacquired her Arta, passing Asimina on to Mosca's newborn and was now banging the boiled eggs on the pebbles, and Savvas on his rock, Snowy, baiting hooks to get down to some fishing when they'd all cleared off.. Orsa had lost sight of him moments before, forced to search amongst the swimmers and on shore among the shorter and slighter. When she finally made him out gliding through the sea like a dolphin and coming ashore, she realized, astounded, that Savvas was a little boy no longer, only from a distance could she see how much her son had grown. And he was angry, despite his mother's and grandmother's objections, his father had promised to take him on his next voyage, Piraeus-Constantinople-Odessa, the dream put paid to, of course it wasn't Vatokouzis' fault, but in the child's boyish head all grown-ups without exception, prime ministers generals parents, shared in the blame for the turn events had taken, he had his own sailor's trunk, oilskins, jacket, binoculars, and guiltlessly prayed for some disaster or other to befall them on the way so he could prove not only that he wasn't seasick, but that he knew how to save the ship all by himself, of course, on the island, he'd wander round the men playing backgammon and cards in the coffee houses and, just like that and to no one in particular, come out with "the British Admiralty anchor's hard to lash in place," he'd win a warm glance, sometimes an annoyed look, but go on just the same, "line apparatus can catapult a rope three hundred yards to the shore or to another ship for rescuing survivors." He'd go up to his aunt's and unearth these amazing, ancient books, Spyros's they were, in English, Spanish, Greek, try to decode symbols and scribbles among the notes, with Mosca's forbearance lay the Hellenic Navy Hydrographic Service volumes on the floor, over forty, fifty in all, and leave nothing undigested, *Lighthouses and Naval Signals*, *Table of Nautical Miles between Harbors*, *Instructions Concerning Meteorological Observations*, *Naval Charts of Greek Harbors*.

"Want to go to the Club tonight?"

Vatokouzis was proposing a manly outing to his son, Savvas nodded a serious OK and, relieved, allowed himself to lick off the jam and throw the bread in pieces to the grey mullet impatiently circling his rock.

"He'll be short and fat like his grandmother," Vatokouzis thought looking at the boy, no longer long and skinny like a rake, owing ever more to Mina Saltaferaina's build as he grew up, but with a head like an antique Greek statue, curly black hair and long shadowy eyelashes half hooding his frank gaze, at nine years of age usually disappointed. Old man Saltaferos was out of there at dawn, not even a coffee with his wife, the poor kid bored hemmed in by so many women, godmother, mother, aunt, sisters, female cousins first and second, Annezio, Eleni, and a swarm of lady visitors nattering away without pause in the kitchens, the pantries, in the courtyards and in the drawing rooms, a real loner the boy, Vatokouzis was worried about his son, he'd snoop on him with tact, watching him finger his tools, opening and closing pincers or pruner, just like that, purposelessly, gouging a mark into eucalyptus trunks all alone and muttering to himself, scanning the horizon for hours on end, unmoving and immovable.

He had still to come to terms with the boy following the path that led to a lifetime at sea, he wanted to see Savvas on the ships and he didn't want to, German U-boats had sunk a British troop carrier, the *Athenia*, the other day, an uncomfortable silence blanketing all at the news, young Vatokouzis examining his upper lip, begging the Virgin to sprout him a nice moustache double quick, to unleash himself on the oceans in search of revenge.

It was twilight, cooling, night's haze descending, Orsa propped on her elbows with her calves in the water, some distance from her husband, a coolness between them for days now over the damned move, "they'll be lighting the lamps in town," she shouted to him, the watchword for reconciliation and departure, the straight beach and oil-calm sea darkening perceptibly and sending the Vatokouzis family away at top speed, the few other groups, teetering from pebble to pebble, already far away.

Father and son, serious in their suits, entered the Andros Club round half past eight, Danioloses, Maridises, Mamaises, Hadoulises, Mandarakases, skippers and ship owners, sailors, landlubberly nabobs, talking politics and panic-stricken, the ignorant and irrelevant sticking close by, Mr. Dinos and his cronies, sprawled on the leather sofas, hastening to add their tuppence worth, to share their wisdom, see if they could make sense of it together.

The entrepreneurial drive and strict discipline of the island's navigators was going to waste, the state hadn't taken protective measures, lots of Greek shipowners resorting to flags of convenience in recent years, Liberia, Panama, Honduras, in 1939, last year's census, 192 steamers still on the Andros shipping list and many a man whose eyes were open sneaking glances at New York and London, their little island no longer big enough, their homeland a corner grocer's of a state passing laws made to clip its people's wings, seemed that way at least.

Behold the war that would wipe out crews, boats and bank accounts, wouldn't compensate for mourning with the much-bandied profits of war, like the first time round, when some folk started out with rowboats and ended up as shipowners.

Nikos Vatokouzis listened and took note, "Savvas, what was Mandarakas so angry about?" he asked the boy who could be relied upon to catch what his father missed, when the storm was past and Vatokouzis had decisions to make, why not England, an excellent education for the kids, more and varied business opportunities, too.

"You've got a half share in two freighters, let them escape unscathed and we'll see, when the time comes, if we're still in one piece, will there be anything to keep us on the island," he pondered.

His parents' graves with carnations and fuchsias, queen's earrings they call them, flowers crimson, black-currant, bright red and pink fearlessly caressing the funereal marble, fortunate they didn't look as desperate and repulsive as the way those laid out within had departed this life, Vatokouzis had come with his wife, Annezio and Mersina, Orsa wanting to water the plants, to light the incense on her godmother's headstone, like every time, the cat had accompanied them to the grave, not the old one, Babis, he'd eaten himself to death, Haralambis the acrobat, who jumped from gravestone to gravestone and had a whale of a time chewing on the leaves, only Christ's thorn escaped and some immortals that lived up to their name. Annezio had foresight, and their two photographs, portraits, were positioned diagonally opposite one another, it was just that the deceased weren't looking at each other, so the quarrelling wouldn't continue into the afterlife, too, she'd craned her ear at first for hollow curses and seemed relieved: "death's been good for the two of them," she ruled and made the sign of the cross.

Mersina copied her. Vatokouzis, panama in hand and tie loose, looked from his daughter in her little white dress nodding in the wind, to his mother in the frame, he remembered her in the white nightdress, a knife slash rending the night in two as she escaped, his pants-down father's delirious advances. His daughter the spitting image of his mother, just a few dozen sizes smaller for now. Brown eyes, chestnut hair, tears like pearls, nostrils moist, nibbled nails on chilly hands she'd cross over her bird's breast a hundred times a day and sigh, in a world of her own, just like the poor dead woman had done, oblivious or broken hearted, one or the other.

Autumn arrived bitterer than ever.

Saltaferaina commanded it to sweeten, lining up bowls of must-jelly, jams, and quince preserve with silent hysteria, but autumn did not obey the woman who'd abandoned men and women in favor of dishes and desserts.

Amidst the crowds in the two-storey house with its housework and endless comings and goings, "where the hell are you, Orsa, in that head of yours?" Vatokouzis wondered, threatened, his wife never pulled her hand away from his, never took offence when he slipped his arm gently around her waist or encircled wrists and ankles, never slipped away from him those nights he guiltily removed her garter belt and underwear piece by piece, just stayed cold, unresponsive, some mornings she'd wake with the reddest eyes.

Saint Dimitrios' day, October 26, up to Mosca's to wish her son all the best, and in front of family and assembled others, "this move must be sorted before winter sets in," his mother-in-law, emphatic, "Go to hell!" said breathless Orsa, on her feet and heading for the door before the others realized what, her skirt caught on an upholsterer's tack and tore.

Vatokouzis found his wife in floods of tears, in the yard downstairs, beside the moonflowers whose yellow dispelled the darkness. He leaned on the wall and smoked a cigarette, another, then a third and fourth.

"We've another five Dimitrises to see tonight," he reminded her.

"Go yourself," she begged him and touched his cheek, she was in a state and her husband didn't insist, he opened the barred wooden gate, closing it silently behind him as he left.

Saltaferaina keeping watch from the first-floor window lit-up above, a bad fright that, but why was she really up there; Vatokouzis walking up the lane confused and disappointed, gone eight already and the streets full and a lot of folk, women mostly, their finery glittering and tinkling, rushing from one Dimitris or Dimitra to another.

It was to sailors' homes that Nikos was heading, he'd leave his greaser till last, Dimitris him and Dimitra his wife, they were set to make a night of it, October 14, the *Royal Oak*, a British destroyer, torpedoed with a crew of twelve hundred, the loss had shaken seafaring men to the marrow, a night on the booze, by God, a serious session was what Vatokouzis yearned for, and leaning into the gusty sou'-westerly in his good suit, alone, dragging his gaze from the lonesome rock mid coast to the lighthouse at the harbor entrance and back again, Tourlos-Tourlitis and Tourlitis-Tourlos, he felt his eyes grow moist behind his glasses and cut into him like lashes.

October 30, 1939, the *Thrasyvoulos* torpedoed a hundred and sixty miles west of the Irish coast, the first Andrian ship, twenty-two sailors lost.

Like a black wave, the black news stained the island black.

Family names and homes scattered round the villages and Chora, the capital: Voyatzides, Tsiknas, Ballas, Goulandris, Kampanis, Manoussos, Adamopoulos, Sotiros, Ginis, Krousis, Rombos, Peppas, Parliaros, Printezis, Sapountzakis, Stylianos, Philippidis, Foundos, Loukrezis, Lavdas, and Malatandes, Saltaferos the steward, too, a nephew of the family, Little England curled up on itself, it could not take so much lamenting and tramping down its narrow streets at once, so many people surging as one from house to house, those that hadn't lost family or friends indistinguishable from those that had, they too had loved ones on the oceans, from October 30th fear took root in their souls.

"Wasting my life away playing backgammon, I'll go mad," Savvas Saltaferos muttered to himself; the priest's wife's beloved only godson gone down with the *Thrasyvoulos*, she didn't cook any more; Father Philippos, robe unironed and stained, his strength overtaxed with all the funerals and memorial services, back shot, had taken refuge, hunched and scared, behind the backgammon board and five simple words: draughts, dice, sixes, rolls, gammons. He wasn't moving an inch.

When he lost, "vanity of vanities, all is vanity," which fitted his defeat but his take on life, too, like a glove, *vanidad de vanidades, todo vanidad*, Saltaferos translated at once, now, his naval career at an end and a war gathering momentum again, spreading death and destruction, the melancholy dictum slipped out often, his grandchildren had seized upon it, a fine tongue twister, and would shriek it at the top of their lungs, challenge or watchword in all manner of games and escapades.

His daughters glued to the BBC, Mosca, always one for duty, would write out a summary of the news and the women of the neighborhood, busy with their chores but never failing to pop into the courtyard and knock on the glass, "what's happening," they'd ask and continue down the hill to the market and the grocer's.

Daily gatherings at the printer's, the harbormaster's, the Club, the town hall, homes, not that anything came of them, just people in need of company, even Emilios Ballas, Spyros Maltambes' uncle, worried, about his nephew's fate, wheezing his way from place to place, ubiquitous, dragging behind him his guardianship, of which he was not forgetful, his sadness, and an umbrella with half its spokes poking out.

The coffee steamed in the red enamel mug, old Saltaferos, who refused to drink from any other, took it with him to the meetings, to the *ouzeri*, and to the funerals, "truth be told, how many men did I lose as a captain?" he wondered to himself, not that he didn't remember the number, rather because it was something he'd never forget, boring its way into his thoughts every now and then: Biscay '18, the waves had severed the rope tying Maris to his post, a lighthouse boat had brought the body back the following morning, swollen like a drum, then a fiendish storm in '26, the Atlantic Shore had plucked Karystinos, Polemis, Rallis from him off the bridge, his friend Nicephoros, Dokos lost to a bad chill in '29, in '36, Giorgakis, the young stoker from Megara, gone up in smoke, six men lost on a voyage lasting forty-three years, thirty-seven as captain of eight ships, the *Danube*, the *Panagitsa*, the *Aegean II*, the

Mariogoula Hadouli, the *Hydroussa*, the *Poseidon*, the *Theomitor*, the *Marousio Bebi*, some already scrap iron, the others an added worry in these troubled times.

Annezio had let him into a secret the other day, his "unbearable and tightfisted wife"—Annezio made no bones about describing her so—had thrust a purse in her hand, out on the bay it was, so no one would see, stuffed with twenty sovereigns, for deposit with the Monastery of Agios Savvas, near Jerusalem, "for the good health and longevity of her husband," all this back when she and her employer had taken their trip to the Holy Sepulcher, "now don't go telling everyone" she'd enjoined her; the wasteful donation didn't sit with her reputation.

"And that, Mr. Savvas, is how she secured your salvation from the sharks"; with an eye on long-term investments and profits, Mina Saltaferaina had bribed Agios Savvas and God once and for all.

The old captain consciously avoided any involvement in his daughters' family affairs, but some things his mother left half unsaid, some falsely imperious looks from Orsa, a slipper that came out of nowhere straight at Mina's head, Vatokouzis who sometimes seemed more a guest in his own home than its master, all these had chilled his soul, but unschooled in shore-board relationships he'd withdrawn, a mere spectator to things implied but deadly.

"Vanity of vanities, all is vanity," Father Philippos, a wreck by now, borrowed from Romanus the Melodist the maxim had become his refrain for all idle chatter.

They were sitting in the Club, men's conversation hubbubbing all around, Saltaferos slurping scalding sips from his red mug and nodding agreement.

"I mean what they call condoms," the priest clarified and cleared his throat, the revolutionary invention now in mass production had brought relief overt or covert to millions of sailor's families on every continent, "but then what, the war! Spared syphilis only to be blown up by a mine," that the fatalistic cleric, who'd buried many a victim of the disease in his long career and heard confessions that had made his stomach churn, what he really needed, at any cost, was a Havana cigar, to envelop himself in plumes of aromatic smoke and cut himself off for a time from the baser aspects of earthly existence.

Sicker by the day of the priest and the nagging, angry with his family, too, the captain, that eternal departer and worshipper of the waters, would reminisce about the shades of blue that set their seal on seascapes, seek out the company of sailors, sometimes, when he saw, let's say, the surreal spray-whipped southern Australian coast in his sleep, haul his grandson and namesake to lighthouses and cliffs' sheer drops, the only voluntary concession to his normal self his adoration for women's hair, whenever Orsa went to the hairdresser's, he'd go with her for fear she'd have it cut, in fact he'd told Joseph "if my blue-eyed girl ever comes without me, throw her out, tell her your stomach hurts, I'll make up your loss."

And as he lay at night on the left-hand strip of mattress, in which he had yet to leave his hollow, his eyes were slow to close, he'd listen to his cholera gently snoring, listen to the splash of waves at Riva, remember and repeat like a prayer, "I commanded my ships with few words, missing the murmur of the sea I caught myself filling the silences with blather about blue, ruining my mind with nostalgia."

"Any news from Spyros?"

"No."

"Poor girl."

Grandma Orsa, slow to speak, smoothing down the tassels on her shawl with an old woman's fingers.

"Mosca?" Saltaferaina asked breathless, betraying herself without meaning to, but it was too late to take the question mark back.

Her mother-in-law brought the exchange to a close with a sigh.

A Spyros sirocco, a searing incendiary Maltambes gusting over desert wastes, playing with fire again before weighing anchor, but the presence of the unsuspecting nurse inspecting the dead folk in their frames one by one, as though saying "nice to see you, too" to each in turn, stopped them setting to one another with tongues or worse.

It was two in the afternoon, the three of them silently sipping their coffee, Saltaferaina had gone up to Apatouria with Annezio, to her mother-in-law's, between Christmas and New Year, she'd brought her two sets of underclothes, a nightdress, a comb, hairpins and a basket with sausages, hard round cheeses, sweets and angel's hair, vermicelli for the soup, much heavier now at eighty-two, she rarely left her corner, didn't hide her unwillingness to have much to do with the two-storey riffraff, and couldn't stand her great-grandchildren for an instant.

Marriage had failed to smile on all three, they stared out the window, the light quit the gorge before anywhere else on the island, and perhaps their brief exchange, too, had brought down the heavy shadow that was working against the point of their visit.

Saltaferaina thrust her hands into her bosom, nails digging into her breasts, she'd lost control of life, everything was topsy-turvy, and she who considered it the ultimate in security to deposit money in the bank separately for each grandchild and learn the interest off by heart, now with nothing but bad news which she turned into paid-for commiserations in the *Voice of the Aegean*, in some cases even drafting and redrafting the notices in her head well in advance of the event, convinced of so-and-so's death, such and such disaster, "the newspaper doesn't inform," Saltaferaina thought, "it recaps and reminds," as she unerringly ticked off her dead one by one.

Accursed 1939, in with the earthquakes that shook Chile to bits and out with earthquakes in Turkey, eleven thousand people buried in the rubble and she mourned them, *thou makest the whole world tremble as a leaf upon a tree*, she prayed and shot the Eye of God a sideways glance, she'd stop kneading the dough or darning just like that, hearing hollow creakings from the depths of the earth she'd issue warnings twice or thrice a day, "earthquake!" and her heart would stop.

The earth quaked before the Germans, Mina Saltaferaina quaked before something else, the prospect of fate's backhander knocking both stories clean off their foundations, as the seemingly endless hollow rumble of pained love rose up from the bowels of their property. The radio, permanently tuned to the BBC, was transmitting an unbearable tension to the house, she may not have understood English, but whenever the broadcaster mentioned Hitler or the Gestapo, her eldest daughter, who usually sat with her back to her, would wheel round and grant her a look weighted down by unhappiness.

"Ateni's at the mercy of the weather, Vori's sheltered," said Annezio, not a word from the others. She tried to steer the conversation to great-grandchildren. "That Saravanos really cares about our nippers," she said; truth be told, whenever the pediatrician came to Andros, he'd just take a short stroll round to confirm with his own eyes that the children were brimming over with good health and that Mosca's son's fingers and toes hadn't bruised again, meaning no worries of white finger for Mimis. Mr. Saravanos used many an unusual word, but what was the point, in the little house in Apatouria, Savvas's wife and mother refused the disorderly retreat to matters medical but painless, and went on facing off and torturing each other with silence.

Annezio went out, wrapped her coat around herself, and sat down on the yard wall to listen to the ravine.

Five o'clock already, today over with and quickly too, "how much are lemons fetching?" the old woman had asked her daughter-in-law, starting the conversation she'd so quickly and irrevocably brought to an end with that "ah."

The *Panachrantos* was declared missing on January 15, 1940. It had left the Downs the previous day with a crew of twenty-six on board, made contact later with the Land's End station, and then nothing, gone without a trace, probably torpedoed and sunk with cargo and crew, meaning Katsikis, Bafaloukos, Mileos, Karamalengos, Falangas, Makris, Karras, Knakotos, Sifnakis, Tziotis, Tourlos, Petrakis, Fifis, Raisis, a second Mileos, Mihas, Protopsaltis, another Petrakis, Foleros, Veinoglou, and Piangos the cabin-boy.

A child in primary school still, Maltambes had spent summer and winter alike on Chora's breakwater, admiring the freighters moored or departing, heaving up with the anchor apeak and putting to sea with three whistles sounded in a row. During the first Balkan War, the freighter on which his father was serving had been requisitioned as a troop transport and off the Strymon delta he was no more, he'd lost him, dead of the cholera that was mowing folk down back then, and the nine-year-old an orphan, suddenly ward to uncle Emilios, who didn't have much when it came to fighting but lots when it came to love.

Spyros Maltambes, trace his line straight back to Poseidon he could, the Paraporti boatyard mascot since he was knee-high to a pelican, master of the arts of captainship and naval history, with a thousand dates, feats and heroic names at his fingertips, salty as a salt cod, took every lost ship badly, every lost sailor worse, and news like the fate of the *Panachrantos* personally, how much more so when he'd served with three of those lost for many a moon, best man to the sailor from Piraeus, and then that unforgettable all-night session the three of them had thrown themselves into in a Marseilles brothel, the whores had made merry and let their hair down, sent a case of sparkling aromatic wine to the ship the next afternoon they had, with a book of nude photographs and red satin charms pinned to a pad for good luck. Those days were gone.

Apart from the calamity of the *Panachrantos*, on February 4, in the Atlantic, a German U-boat torpedoed two Greek freighters without warning, the *Stathatos*, twelve dead, and the *Keramies*, four more, the British decided to arm their merchant ships and the following week, February 15, Hitler's response: from that day on he'd consider them vessels of war. The *Queen Elizabeth* had just made it into New York's dock 90 when the cancellation of all its routes was announced.

"What the hell am I doing in the Indian Ocean," Maltambes raging, frothed at the mouth, the Japanese blockading the river in Canton since last July to stop the British trading, and him awaiting the bill of purchase for the long-awaited ship, his Anglo-Cycladic Company underway, that was the name he'd come up with, times looking far from good for freight, not in the Pacific, not in the Indian, not anywhere, the Anglo-French had even mined Norwegian waters to stop them selling metal to the Germans.

And no news from the island, after all he'd left a wife and three kids up there, *instead of dolls and games and toys, take me with you on a voyage, daddy you're the best, you know it, and quite handsome, when you show it*, Christina was following in the poetic footsteps of the K.K.M.M. club for ladies, at seven he was her male role model and he liked it, but the news that Vatokouzis was stranded in Greece and that Orsa, spending every day with her husband, might forget about him again drove him into a frenzy, Orsa with the blue eyes and the vibrant flesh, whose ears never stopped changing color and temperature, amber and frozen one minute, pink and steaming the next, then all over again, but maybe it was better he hadn't been caught by the exit ban too, because how could a love concealed not break out powerful and destructive like the war itself. The hostilities were just beginning, and Maltambes getting a hint of what he reckoned would happen when they ended, because if he got through the carnage alive, as a war veteran, as a man, he wouldn't let this mess go on any longer.

The carmine sunsets meant nothing to him, he'd had it up to here with the chain of coral islands, too, and gone to a brothel in Bombay to vainly thrash around on damp sheets for an hour, with prohibition in force for years now in the Indies, he couldn't even knock back some beers, to clear his head, he was close to cracking.

So when the cable came the next morning, tender accepted for *Little England*—Mosca had insisted on the name for his Anglo-Cycladic flagship—a shipowner now, he treated the crew to soft drinks and three hours off and sat in the lounge in his underpants to smoke and drink endless coffees, to dream of his very own ship as a white steed with rounded haunches and the smoke from its stack streaming the length and breadth of the globe. *Little England*, 4,978 registered tonnage, 7,500 cargo tonnage, spanking new, 92,000 Pounds Sterling worth.

It was humid, the sort of underhand humidity that makes a man's skin stick and drip dirt and his mind obsess pointlessly.

Maltambes looked at things this way, looked at them that way, he loved his children, Orsa, the ancient yet youthful power of the Aegean, the Greeks' maritime heritage, and the freedom of the oceans, just like he'd learned at school and from life, seven Maltambes gone down with their ships plus his father dead in the Balkan war, so when he heard that total on the BBC, fourteen Greek ships lost in a single month, June 1940, and twenty-one sailors drowned, he knew he was fated too to join the war and didn't feel in the slightest like running or cursing his fate, no shortage of soul, his pluck known to all, and Spyros, with one poisonous exception, tending since childhood to blaze out and rocket well past mediocrity.

Under British orders, requisitioned vessels from every allied nation were forming convoys to ship supplies from America to Europe.

Even if he could Maltambes would never hoist a neutral flag and never skulk on the sidelines, a shipowner now, he sent the appropriate cable and committed himself and his one and only ship to the fight that very same day, leaving everyone speechless with his high spirits; they should have known, because he was Maltambes and he was in his element.

First up second cousin Archontia Sarri, who decisively hung her wedding band, followed by Mosca with the *Little England*, delicately-wrought in silver, six inches long, a fine offering, Orsa, third in line, hesitant, in two minds, the fingers of her left hand encircling his oval cameo, an old Viennese heirloom her grandmother had hung around her neck for this very purpose, the fingers of her right hand clutching at the blue-green linen of her handbag, searching out the jewels of her most precious memory within, the three brine-encrusted spoons. In the end, she unclasped the cameo from her neck; the Virgin collected valuable trove and Orsa too ashamed to explain.

Thousands of pilgrims from every part of Greece flooding to Tinos for two weeks now, since the start of little Lent, the forty-day fast before August 15th and the feast of the Assumption, and the Megalochari, Tinos's Virgin Full of Grace, had been accepting entreaties, complaints, requests for forgiveness and repeated beseeching for the usual, illnesses of the body and mind, emigration, matters financial, unrequited loves, conception; in 1940, no prayer complete without something, a postscript, concerning the war, until the war wasn't someone else's problem any more, meaning at eight-thirty or thereabouts on the morning the *Elly*, a destroyer anchored in the Bay and not the harbor in honor of Greek Orthodoxy's greatest feast, Lieutenant Commander Hadzopoulos in command and a crew of two hundred and thirty-two, took two torpedoes and was under Tinian waters in less than an hour, the miraculous icon paraded through the streets as planned.

The enemy's choice of time and place numbed the people, adults and children alike in their Sunday best, with the official expression faces take on at crucial moments when they hope something will happen at last and for life to right itself.

The two sisters and Archontia Sarri, the seamstress, conjured up worst-case scenarios; for sailors and their kin, war always starts earlier and ends later.

The procession of the icon was something else, the crowd trampled Orsa's straw bonnet, unable to keep on following in the sun Orsa made for the Tinos Palace, familiar surroundings, her stomach in a knot and with a deeply desperate urge to take her sister in her arms and weep until her eyes had shed their myriad teardrops.

"Come with me to Tinos to make an offering for the *Little England*," Mosca had begged, who often took the micky, depending on the situation, there's no escaping fate or we can escape our fate, but now it couldn't hurt, she wanted to take every possible measure to protect her family and fortune. Just three letters from Spyros, short, from a different Spyros, she said bitterly, but while she read bits out to her friends, to Orsa she just showed the pictures on the postcards. On the trip back from Tinos, exhausted Archontia slept leant against a fat and obliging Gypsy woman, and Mosca took some letters out of her bag, she wanted to share the few spaced-out lines with her sister after all, ten or so all told, odd indeed for a man as die straight as Spyros.

"Don't," Orsa interrupted, "don't read them to me," and because the whole family thought her vulnerable, someone with whom misunderstandings could easily arise, Mosca gathered them up and turned her attention to the horizon.

She'd tried other times, years ago, to read her verses and paragraphs she'd written before mailing them or careless bits from Spyros's letters, Sourabaya written Sorebaya two lines further down, Sorabaya four lines on, with a double rr on the following page.

They returned to Piraeus in convoy watched over by two destroyers, the *Olga* and the *Georgios*, under the command of vice-admiral of the fleet Kavvadias, they were scared women and didn't feel safe, like all the travelers who'd watched on as the flag-strewn warship disappeared so unexpectedly into the baby blue innocence of the Aegean.

Orsa thrust her hand into her bag, she felt so guilty and unjust, even thought to hurl the spoons into the sea, as though the act could reshuffle the pairs by magic, or at least let them chart their course through life stripped of passion.

She reached out towards Mosca, to touch her baby sister's flesh, she felt for her, it ate away at her that Nikos wasn't a normal Greek husband who'd make the move without awaiting approval, who wouldn't stand for too much, thinking nonsense like that to keep the old sadness at bay and from gnawing at her heart.

Three hundred Greek sailors rescued from ships attacked by German U-boats arrived in Piraeus from Lisbon on August 21. The news announced on Greek radio.

Maltambes wasn't among the three hundred, he wasn't expected to be, the BBC, too, had nothing positive to report, the house breathing heavily, silence, spirits low, nerves in shreds, tears, the children dulled now the adults had no time to spare them, and one afternoon Orsa got up from the table just like that, they were eating all together in the courtyard's cool beneath the vine, abandoned her fried zucchini flowers, "I'm going to Nana's," she said, just that, and was gone.

She found the teacher on her cool north-facing balcony folding up her ironing, invited round the headmaster's that afternoon, she'd just pressed her pleats and lapels, "I'll wear the light grey silk again," she said and hung the hanger in the hall.

Her back a fraction bent, "occupational hazard," she said, she'd lost weight but her walk had always been deliberately girlish, she liked being called the little schoolgirl, some playful souls happy to oblige.

"Portugal-Kythera," she said returning with ashtray and cigarette and sprawling on the chaise longue with evident pleasure.

"Sicily-Karpathos," Orsa replied, they hadn't played this game for a long while, which place goes with which, Nana Bourada-Negropiperi, unmatched in this department, always coming up with a thousand new ways of keeping her mind occupied, she'd been nowhere and yet drawn up a globe in her own unique way that brooked no objections.

"Epirus-Ireland."

"Meteora-Karpathia."

"Canada-Aitoloakarnania, but why . . . "

Nana didn't have answers for everything, not that she tried to, Orsa escaped from her problems, found temporary refuge in the questions answers and geography of dispositions, mediating, too, though to no effect, to have Nana reach a decision on something that had been torturing her for years now, to have her choose:

"Paris or London?"

Two hundred Nazi aircraft had bombed the French capital in June, a few days before a whole lot more, eight hundred, had crossed the Channel sky and dropped bombs in their thousands on Britain.

Ever undecided, Nana knew both metropolises from her reading and her postcards and didn't have the heart to prefer one above the other.

T he natural order of things in the two-storeys, as in most houses in Greece's coastal cities and villages, fish on Monday, so off Mosca set for Plakoura bright and early with Lenio for company, fishing out weevers, rockfish and scad, "soup or bogues for frying?" she asked herself and bypassed the bogues her mother so liked; the Aegean breeze lifted the weight in her head, of late she'd come to know insomnia's exhaustion for the first time, "the time's come to get myself off to old Resvanis, too, for the usual," she thought, defeated.

Mosca, quick-witted even sleepless, paid for the best fish, sent Lenio to the grocers for the rest, and set off home, mustn't forget to send a pot of soup round to Emilios, too; Spyros's uncle, always discreet, too shy to come calling, didn't want them thinking he was after handouts and hand-me-downs, actually, he'd send a bag of candies now and again in the summer with common acquaintances passing by, for the children, in winter the mushrooms he picked out in the fields.

George II's proclamation, signed off in the palace of Athens, left Saltaferaina in no doubt that war had been declared, she'd sat down to dunk in her coffee and heard it on the radio: "at 9.30 this morning, bombers attacked Tatoi, Piraeus, Patras, our armed forces are defending our sovereign territory," up on the borders that, anyhow, every church on the island had been ringing the bad news for a fair old time now, Saltaferaina's expert ear could make out the ding and the dong of distant villages, distant islands, the cities of the upside and downside of Greece, of a Greece turned upside down.

"As we speak," she said and pursed her lips, she was alone, the other women all upped and gone, Orsa had abandoned her brush and shovel, she'd been sweeping up the dried jasmine flowers in the yard and leaves shed by vine and moonflower, Mosca's fish half-gutted and semi-scaled, that shameless chancer Haralambis had made a right mess of them, Lenio absent without leave again and they ought to clip her ear, Annezio round at Archontia's from early on for a fitting, a black dress, why she needed a fitting anybody's guess, thirty years now with the same pattern hanging off her bony frame.

The square thick with people, kids in their school smocks, women in their kitchen aprons, captain's ladies and nannies, grizzled old men tired out, close it was, hunched over their walking sticks, folk bearing the mark of syphilis, and boys and young men, too, of course, rushing to enlist, set to take the boat to Syros, many of them coming down on foot from Vrachnou, Pitrofo, Strapourgies, Stenies, Apikia, and Vourkoti still further up, in groups, singing, whistling, in insanely high spirits the women didn't share one bit.

Father Philippos, always one for an ambush, had sprung one on the quay, pulling box after box of cigars from under his robes and offering them to the soon-to-be draftees, he forgot to bless them Christian-wise but remembered every name, tens and hundreds of them, ruffling the boys' hair, winking at them, even kissing their hands.

Nik in action, immortalizing boyhood friends, families, couples, Nikolaos and Orsalia Vatokouzis, Athanasios and Katie Boulakas, Zannis and Archontia Sarris, Georgios and Maro Zannis, fully aware the photographs he took that day, Monday October 28 1940, would be the stuff of history, the most-kissed under pillows, in bedside table drawers, framed not on sideboard shelves but beside saints up on the family iconostasis.

The elderly high-school teachers besuited, seeing off their younger colleagues, Madame Nana unsure what to clutch, beloved former students lest she lose them or her pleats lest they fall out, the few white roses left, half plucked by the breeze, she'd shared out among the first young men to appear before her, truth be told, they'd helped themselves, to give to the girls. The girls . . . how they whirled like tops that day in a daze, blushing at five minute intervals, dazzling they were, appearing on street corners like sprites, like ladybirds, four or five together working up a head of steam at a moment's notice, airborne plaits crossing the square to come to rest on the stone wall opposite, and others like lonesome statues remaining motionless on balconies, their eyelashes alone aflutter at Manoussos's every clumsy cymbal clash as the Brass Band marched for victory. Even Hexadaktylos forgave them their wrong notes, present and charming with it; for the first time Mosca noticed how her hair had grayed, roughly unpinning a lock of her own on the spot and bringing it before her nose to inspect the state of her own.

All gone, Vatokouzis too. The ship on its way and Nikos watching Andros shrink into the distance and feeling Orsa's honey-eyed head leant on his shoulder, as though he'd taken it with him.

In a few days, the town emptier and life different. Folk headed for the fields with a saint's icon in their pocket and headed back late huddling round radios on fire with the news they had to broadcast. Interest no longer focused on just Liverpool, Antwerp, Baltimore, Panama, Cristobal, Batavia, Chitagong and Santa Fe, for the words Pogradets, Korytsa, Premeti, Delvino, Argyrokastro, and Kleisoura had entered their lives, internationally insignificant names of Albania's nationally significant Greek towns, captured one after another by the Greek army, instigating a fiasco of operatic proportions among the Italians, the guilty parties, according to the report at long last published, for the sinking of the *Elli*.

"What's Albania like?" Mosca wondered, they'd never got a postcard from there; Nana Bourada-Negropiperi declared herself inexcusable for having let an entire country slip by her collection, not one of her girls had honeymooned there, Greek ships just sailed past on their way to Trieste, Dubrovnik, Venice.

Mosca, sometimes Orsa too, crossed the threshold into the widow Nicephoros's home, of their own free will now, her still called the widows, wives, and fiancées crusty fannies, though with no hint of sexual seasoning, like a pet name with a pinch of pity, "you poor things" she seemed to say, Mosca with the news from every front, the women sitting dazed to hear the Americans had taken Danish Greenland and were building military installations and air bases, those with no English at all couldn't get by now without Mosca and sent their kids to her for lessons, sometimes it was "Bless you, David," when things looked black or the kids unlikable, it was "If I could get my hands on you, you bloody Englishman."

The wet winter of '40-'41, an eight-day downpour demolished dry stone walls, pens and sheepfolds, swept away flocks and henhouses. Saltaferaina calculating the losses from drowned livestock, multiplying and adding the fortunes of others, a real shock and right they were to be shocked, her so nearly carried away by the torrent in the ravine trying to save Haralambis the cat, at least silly little Mersina had loved her for the attempt.

Vasilakis the gravedigger mourned the wreck of the ocean liner *Edison*, a lifetime joking about his ineptness with money, "I lend to the dead," he'd say, and since he hadn't succeeded in becoming some important shipowner, he'd called his donkey the *Edison*, laden with lemons, drowned in Nimboriò's swollen stream.

Something funny happens in war, the hours packed with earth-shattering events, but in the small places reached only by their echo, it's as though there's something wrong with time, maybe because the usual things, letters, bank transfers, court cases and all the other bureaucratic stuff come to a halt, and with everything frozen or in slow motion, just when you think it's January and will be forever, it's April they tell you, think how time loses its flow and its significance, for it was late April when the Germans took spring-decked Athens and the Stukas blotted out ten Greek destroyers and torpedo boats in just five days, the *Psara, Hydra, Thyella, Doris, Kydoniai, Aigli, Kios, Kysikos, Pergamos,* and *Arethousa,* something Mosca didn't even want to think about, once a joker, opinionated and unflagging, now a little yellow, a tad high-strung, barely half her former self.

In the meantime, the war getting less and less impersonal, two schoolmates, nurses in Athens, drowned when the floating hospital *Attiki* was sunk by German bombers, wounded men, nurses, doctors, not one survived, some local boys, limbs lost to frostbite or shells, farmed out among this hospital or that, hecatomb after hecatomb in the game of wave-tossed hide and seek, the British retaliating for the sinking of the *Hood*, thirteen hundred dead, chased the *Bismarck* one thousand seven hundred and fifty miles into the Atlantic and sank her, another thousand dead, "what's going on with the numbers," Mosca angry and sleepless, "they're gaining on us and we're losing count"; she was afraid of Spyros becoming a number, two hundred and twenty-one or six hundred and fifty-seven.

After Crete's crazed resistance, the island submitted after cutting the elite German 7th paratroop regiment to pieces, the invaders, on May 31, imposed a curfew on the streets of Greece, from ten in the evening until morning which left Mosca suffocating, she asked her sister to take her on that long walk she'd take some afternoons for relief: Agios Dimitrios, the reed thicket, the old cemetery on the hill with the carved sailing ships on the marble tombstones, the bridge, the rock cave, and thus, without knowing it, the two of them walking along arm in arm munching sunflower seeds, Mosca, too, did the Maltambes circle.

French broads have wobbly bums, English beams are broad and white, Spanish asses are weighty masses, the frauleins' Krupp-made butts roll like armored trucks, Russian girls have ham-like haunches, Italians artsy asses, the Chinese none at all, a black girl's behind you could stand your beer on, and Argentinean arses steam.

Old Saltaferos, stuck in the hospital with an attack of angina, instructing his grandson, the youngster in seventh heaven to have grandpa all to himself, his heart trouble and frequent spells in bed ushered in a golden age in their relationship, it happens, people become more useful, priceless, when the everyday slides beyond their reach.

It was an unexpected, let's say fortunate, accident that freed Savvas Vatokouzis once and for all, at the age of eleven, from the influence of the two-storeys' throng of females, the coal-dark lad, barely an adolescent, saw the day in and out at his grandfather's pillow and had learned so much—naval, technical, geographical and manly—he couldn't imagine ever having other questions in his life. The enforced rest made the undisciplined patient think up all manner of original curses, on purpose, to provoke, "bugger Columbus blue with a barnacle," "fart and the Führer will shit on his head," "Deutschland dick-droop," "U-boat buggery," "we went up to Albania to take a piss."

Something positive at last, thought Nikos Vatokouzis, watching father-in-law and son having a whale of a time the last few months, hissing secrets into each other's ear, ever since his return from the minesweeper they'd stuck him on when he enlisted, something had been fencing him in on Andros, he felt more like a neighbor than the man of the house, so when, after a cigar in his home's half-lit study, Hadoulis Junior suggested they cut out, he sensed the absurdity of his relief but could take no more, their secret admiration for Spyros's exploits belittling, and his dark mother-in-law would be the end of him; was she lurking behind half-closed doors and heavy curtains of late, or didn't she want them tripping over her? So many difficult women in one place was more than any man used to absence could stand.

He walked up to his father's renovated, empty house and hid a crate of multicolored silk quilts in the attic, he'd had them in the Hadoulises' warehouse for ages, when they moved in he'd wanted to make up the beds with the brand new bedding he'd bought in Western shops in Constantinople pointed out to him by his schoolmate Madianos, the move never happened and Nikos called off the surprise, disappointedly dredging up the attic's childhood use, a dark hole for swallowing up unused gifts and rendering them useless.

He entrusted his fortune's fate to Hadoulis Senior, begged Mosca to give their children intensive English lessons, if circumstances allowed, he'd have the family out and in England or America in no time, America seemed easier than moving two streets further up the hill, he had bold friends who'd made their pile before hitting forty and escaped the little island's irritations once and for all, he gave the dizzy maid strict instructions not to leave all the heavy jobs for Annezio, paced the quay for hours on end in the dark and the damp, alone with a thousand thoughts for company he'd sometimes chase away and sometimes call back to sort and order, and when, come midnight, he lay down in his wife's arms, he attempted a general going over of good caresses for old time's sake, tending to her hair with that spotted American brush her brother-in-law had sent her, gently kissing her familiar constellation and kissing it again, rubbing her delicate wrists on and on, till he'd near worn them down to half, they made love, glasses still on, forgetful of himself in the darkness, wetted unbeknownst to Orsa by ever-weeping eyes, "but I adore you," he'd whispered, "take care of yourself," her answer, "please take extra care of yourself," because long before dawn Nikos set off for the Middle East.

His ship's name covered, darkness, general torpor and Spyros's head, not the best time for it, there, meaning elsewhere, lining them up one by one, dresses, his mother's dresses.

"Come on, let's pick some out," his old man had shouted up to him one night, the three months mourning passed, the kid eleven, "come on, son, let's get a woman's chore out of the way," and he opened wide the wardrobe doors.

The wicks in two of the fitting's five lamps burnt out, long ago, "I'll change them first thing in the morning" Spyros swore to himself felling useless, but his father not in the mood for chiding, "let's keep one of those sails to remember her by, share out the rest in her memory," he said, he wanted to send them to Arni, to some wacky aunts who were on the best of terms with the man Above, they'd cross themselves, "God have mercy on her soul," and mean it.

"What I don't want is to ever see them again," captain Mimis had made himself clear, he'd studied to be a ship's engineer in England, the old-time shipowners hadn't skinned their flints, they had vision, during the steam decades they'd showered serious money on men with brains, making gentleman of them at the finest schools and engaged them for life.

He pulled a rose dress off its hanger, little greenish leaves scattered over it here and there, if you'd asked Spyros then, a boy, he didn't notice such things, didn't know what rose-colored was, years later he'd salvaged it from the ocean floor of his memory and remembered every detail.

On shore leave his father, come saints' days and bank holidays, early bathed and shaved, ready in his English suit with the sun still to set waiting for mother, God bless her soul, to get herself ready, but, God bless her, there she'd be, hanger and the dress held straight out in front of her, like a bayonet, back in then out, round the rooms she'd go, to wear it to wear it not? She never did.

"Keep the plum, son, from Liverpool, for our engagement," then he'd picked out her black two-piece, brought it to his nose, "don't think we should give this away, she's wearing it in so many photographs, lets keep it close by," the caramel silk for the christenings to one side, too, the flowery one, "no, not the flowery one," in that they'd danced an unforgettable awful waltz at the New Year's Eve ball, 1903.

An hour later, surrounded by dresses, Captain Mimis weeping messily, sobbing like a woman, "It's my fault," he kept saying, "seamen leave widows behind them, that's the rule, my boy," but his wife had rode roughshod over the law and slipped through his hands first, at exactly thirty-two. Theirs was a posthumous love, alive he'd crammed her full of dresses but sought the arms of strangers more than hers, and the poor woman knew it. With Christina Maltambes gone after eating poisonous mushrooms, Spyros would often spy his father, coffee and cigarette in hand, sitting in front of the open wardrobe, suddenly reach out and rustle the fabrics, as though his dead wife were sending him some whisper or gesturing to him with glove-clad hand hidden behind the clothes, perhaps that's what imprinted his mother best on her son's mind, and left him with an appreciation for the range of colors, texture, and qualities of fine fabrics.

"Crimson doesn't suit you," he'd told Orsa in 1929, and she'd promised to purge her wardrobe of the hue that very night.

"And blue?" she'd asked, unresistingly surrendering herself with sweet trepidation, the sweetest, to his approval.

"Your color, your very own, is cypress green," he'd suggested, she'd chosen it often ever since.

Archontia Sarri, who'd relinquished colors any which way, "black flatters me," said one, "yellow doesn't do me justice" another, and the customer is always right, she'd been glad to bestow cypress exclusivity upon Orsa.

Later, whenever Spyros had leave on Andros, there she'd be in her green, and then that booming voice of his, "like a red rag to a bull," what a racket he made, and twist it round right away, to his wife Mosca, who lived in scarlet, cherry, plum, plum velvet, the cloth of empresses, his father with a weakness for it, too.

Maltambes father and son knew about fine clothes, they had luxury in their blood.

Captain Mimis's fateful voyage, eleven months after the sorting of the wardrobe, into the Balkan conflict, the century's first total war, but enough with family, "enemy in sight," the convoy commodore gave the alarm signal, German U-boats had just torpedoed a French steamer, then they got another three, one Norwegian and two Dutch, hitting a couple of tankers, too, the Atlantic caught fire, it flared up like a torch.

Convoy disbanded, best of luck, Morse code received, the next secret rendezvous with it and it was every merchantman for himself, the others with anti-aircraft guns on their bridges and forecastle bulkheads, gunners on all-night watch on the prow, Maltambes aboard the unarmed *Little England*, with cotton and sulfur loaded in New Orleans before joining up with the rest of the convoy in Halifax. Five Greek ships among seventy-three all told, Belgian, Panamanian, Brazilian, grain ships, Argentinean freezer ships, troop carriers, ass-heavy ships from the English coast, whalers that had skewered their peacetime prey in mute Southern seas; Maltambes swept away by the injustice of war.

Seventeen ships lost in the first night's attack, ten on the second, fourteen on the third and the transatlantic escort belly up, that gone too.

"Form convoy, hoist number signal," the commodore issuing the command yet again. When the radio operator finally saw the Irish lighthouse on the shore, thirty-one badly beaten ships were left of seventy-three.

Maltambes counting planks not men, survivors hard to pick up, loitering officially forbidden, the English broke the rule, the unfeeling Americans never, the canvas bags tied to them with their sailor's papers, diploma, a letter or two, all to identify their corpse, Spyros remembered a sweet frightened boy from Chios, Giannakis, who wouldn't put his beloved's photo in the bag, didn't want it getting wet. Him they'd handed over to doctors, in Canada.

The evening after the convoy's arrival, a pub in Garston, the world and her aunt all scared and pissed, gulping down beers two at a time, Bousoulas, Kiki's husband, almost burst.

"Those Chios types, thick they are when it comes to spherical trigonometry," Maltambes yelled; that Batis, the most awkward examiner for the captains' exams, how stupid he'd made them feel, barely time to get his head round the heavenly sphere, a month cramming in Piraeus, Horse's place, and straight to sea. The family home gobbled up by his father's debts and Emilios Balas, the uncle, had already given his soul to Spyros, just as Spyros was to do for young Savvas Vatokouzis, who'd taken the sea and its wiles to heart at the age of eleven, if you can say such a thing. He sat drinking, relaxing, ashamed that amidst all the confusion, him a captain of forty-one, he'd climbed into the three-doored wardrobe that hadn't fit in his parents' bedroom, they'd calculated walls and window frames wrongly and had it in the living room. How could this long stroll down memory lane not end with Orsa? He remembered their assignations and how carefully she'd dressed for them, one afternoon they'd got up off the damp sorrel and sat for a while in the shadow of the lemon trees, half an hour at most, then she'd straightened and pulled at the tucks in her white skirt, to hide the green stains that broadcast their secret to the world.

Around him, the others downing their beers or laid out drunk on the pub benches, buying rounds, pulling out photographs of their children, nostrils twitching, aroused, every time a woman walked by to meet her friends at a table in the snug, sucking up the details of the three hundred and sixty Japanese warplanes that had attacked and destroyed the American naval base at Pearl Harbor and brought the Americans into the war; Maltambes had sailed those waters a thousand times, knew the lay of the land, the look and the hearts of the people on the war's every front, he could take war and that was that, he sank back into the past, passionate Orsa twelve years before round noon, them lying together, a stolen half hour at most, on the sorrel, in the shadow of the lemon trees, then the poor girl trying to rub the green stains off her white skirt.

The price of things her joy and her undoing, a source of wealth and pain, and more specifically the price of onions and lemons, because the mine-strewn Aegean, financial ebbs and flows and the notary's loss, mourning his son, second lieutenant Agisilaos Kourmoulis, dead in Albania, disinclined Saltaferaina from looking to Attica for investments, the occasional Andrian mountainside all she'd haggle over now, disregarding wild dogs and wolves.

What else could she do? Saltaferos either sick or convalescing, she didn't want him home, and he'd turned his grandson into a carbon copy, neither daughter paid her much attention, "too late," she'd tell herself maliciously from time to time, but no longer meant it, and Maltambes' poor old uncle almost engulfing the two-storeys in flames. End of December, they'd thrown a party for all the men in the family, Vatokouzis December 6, Saint Nicholas's day, Agios Savvas, husband and grandson, on December 10, and December 12, Maltambes, Agios Spyridon, the usual band came round, four birds for the price of one, the same things over and over; Balas ate and drank too much, cornered her in the hall and gave her an earful for refusing the match for her firstborn, snorting she pushed him out into the yard, snow in the offing, and plunged his head into the water trough to sober him up, "get out and don't come back again, you dirty old man, want to blow my family sky high, do you?" to make sure, she half-carried him a couple of hundred yards down the road, the old man as light as a feather and weeping, how had he gone and let the drink get to him, he muttered, he'd only ever moistened his lips with wine since then, and that only so he wouldn't say anything he shouldn't and hurt the two, as it turned out, very fine and Christian, as he called them, families, discretely praying to God to intercede for a happy end.

Time did nothing to erase or soften the matter at hand, and Saltaferaina, too tired to conceal something so onerous, took it out on the Americans, cursing them for taking blacks into the navy for the first time, the Germans for going up the Danube, the Italian soldiers who'd cut down the sycamores in Apikia, her mother-in-law who with just one phrase, "Mina, you've done for your girls," had plunged a knife in her heart, Halas the builder antichrist and the impish hosts of joiners and cabinet-makers she sneaked into the house for the *monopatosia*, because that's what was to blame, the single-weight partition, those bare cypress boards, so many messed-up marriages made it, so many unmatched couples took the plunge, but they didn't have upstairs' moans and groans, grapplings and bedtime feats dripping through their ceiling, that she knew for sure, because she listened too.

That Spyros, his nice suits wasted on him, forever unbuttoned or wrong-buttoned, hair uncombed and half-shaven, no socks or no shoes and his belt unbuckled and dangling, shameless on leave that Spyros, an indiscreetly smoldering fire.

The only elated, blessed moments in the house the news from the Russian front, especially when the others were away and Saltaferaina and Annezio, anti-Communist out of seemliness and a Christian upbringing, had Mersina laboriously translate for them; the old nurse celebrated the Germans routed at Moscow and their losses in the Crimea, a million and a half dead Gerries, no need now to bite her tongue and take it to heart that her little Antonis, the hairdresser from Chicago, had turned out red.

And that was something. Because everything else was doom

and gloom, fighting, occupation, torpedoed ships, mourning, shortages, hunger. And the war winters pitiless, on the pure white island with snow down to the sea, a rare sight that, black-clad folk digging and brushing it away for a radish or two, the grandeur and the sovereigns forgotten, the beluga caviar finished, and the mountains soon licked clean of greens.

P ansies at the root of a bright yellow acacia.
"Lemongrass and rosemary."
"Decorative fern and queen begonia in the conservatory."
"A loquat tree and beside it, a pink wild rose climbing a herringbone-plastered wall."
"Pansies and moss."
"Olive and oleander."
"Lilies and ferns on the river bank."

Nana Bourada-Negropiperi had taught all her girls to ceaselessly search for plant duos, jasmine and morning glory, she brought the game to an end and joked about Klairi Delavogia, a neighbor who'd planted morning glory but never enjoyed its impressive blue flowers because she'd lie in till noon, they close round eleven, before the sun reaches its zenith.

The K.K.M.M. quartet, Orsa, Hexadaktylou, and Nana had visited Katerina Basandi, Thursday, October 1st, 1942, her fortieth birthday; Mosca always felt for Katerinio. The other day, some local kids had walked as far as Ammolochos and Varidi in the north to exchange linen for food, Katerina had given them some lace covers and asked for a hen or at least a little flour and eggs, she got yellow lentils, but no matter, there she was, not put on a spread for years, determined to now with the island hungry and at war, not that it wasn't a grand idea, because, alone, the women relaxed, their tongues loosened, they confessed their fear, admitted the chill in their hearts and the white hair denser on their heads with each passing day.

"Nana, why do you sometimes want people to call you Bourada, sometimes Negropiperi, and other times Bourada-Negropiperi?" Kiki asked, who'd wanted to get to the bottom of that for years now, chatting away all familiar and sharing cigarettes with her former teacher, she'd plucked up the courage to ask.

"I've used Negropiperi since I lost Mikés, when he was alive he'd grumble about me flying my standard in his parts, among his relatives, it's a pity I wasn't mature enough to allow him that joy in time, my priorities were elsewhere, it was only once he'd died that I made up my mind I was his wife." Nana granted herself a rare luxury, a deep sigh, she'd always steered every detail of her conversations to avoid being taken by surprise, but Kiki, somewhat forward since she was a girl, rode roughshod over poise, distance, and pleats.

And the hours went by demanding secrets shared, it was one of those exceptionally bright, autumn days when nature changes color before our eyes and we all share a need to unburden ourselves.

Hexadaktylou, who only ever answered to her surname, Vasso forgotten to all, in a few dozen words, and under no pressure from anyone, said she loved another but would never marry, Little England had anointed her life pianist at ceremonies in memory of the drowned, and she'd come to agree, someone needed to shoulder the role in small places. Her forehead, cheeks, and fingers were flecked with the familiar purple, the veins branching beneath transparent skin, on very cold days Hexadaktylou turned blue, there was something unusual about this woman that made the other islanders respect her, but hit back too, a little.

Kiki clarified right from the start that Bousoulas was the man of her life, her fatty and her scruff-bum, the pair of them a tight-knit duo, when he was on leave, the others saw neither hide nor hair of her, Katina mocked her fate, given there was no escaping that bastard providence, been through two engagements she had, and both fiancés married Dutch girls in the end, Marie confessed her whole body ached from lack of love, her belly and breasts swelled at night, her nipples itched, the sleeping pills did nothing any more, if she'd lived in a city, she'd have taken a lover, she declared, just like that, "caresses and kisses, kisses and caresses, night and day, day and night" Kiki reminded her, some verses from the past, off the cuff, even Nana's eyelids fluttered, there were nights, there had to be, she'd yearn for the sterile blanks her Mikés shot, no fireworks there, who always looked on the bright side and wouldn't have it otherwise.

More raki in their glasses, never a shortage of that in Katerina's house, sitting in the room's most uncomfortable chair with a snow-white cat in her lap, not ashamed to tell her visitors she missed love not at all, since her husband drowned she'd desired no other, a widow at fifteen, her body and her mouth remembered still, vaguely for sure, something of Vangelis, she licked her lips and his kiss was there, the delicate taste of cool saliva, not thick at all, perfumed with bitter almonds; a cook, not one complaint about his services aboard that ill-fated ship.

A silence fell that startled even the cat, who got to her feet and looked from guest to guest, and especially Marie sitting right beside her, flesh in goose bumps at the thought Katerina could have been telling the truth, jealous with it, she reached out to tickle her belly and preferred a different thought, that the teenage widow hadn't had time to feel husband and love, that's why she didn't crave it, though Katerina's tranquil face left no doubt the memory of Vangelis sufficed for her at least.

Nana forty-eight, Katerina forty, Hexadaktylou thirty-six, Orsa thirty-two, and Kiki, Marie, Katina, Mosca twenty-nine: a wild look in her sister's eyes, she'd secretly spread out and folded up her friend's two last embroideries in the next room, the wreck of the *Thrasyvoulos*, a delicate shade of grey for the Indian Ocean, a German U-boat, torpedoes away, an explosion amidships and twenty-six names and surnames in single file and the loss of the *Panachrantos*, just sea, waves, a deep-saddened mermaid with a banner, "Panachrantos," the ship nowhere in sight and the names drifting scattered on the brine.

Their menfolk and many more Andrians besides shared out among the oceans, sea and air battles from Midway to the Coral Sea, Madagascar to the North Atlantic, bloody and life-hungry, and the seven women had sworn not a word about the war on the way to Katerina's.

"Sing, Katerina, something Russian so we don't understand the words," said Mosca, no matter that the two sisters had not talked plainly of matters marital tonight, again, she got up, lit the oil lamp, because you couldn't trust the electricity for months now, and sat down again.

"Russian songs go well with cares and worries," Nana said.

"They're the best," Marie declared, "the best."

Katerina kissed the cat, swallowed once or twice, she knew exactly what her visitors wanted, the song best suited to the washed-out dusk, the endless song with the word *ljuba*, beloved, again and again.

So she started to sing, her voice broke and softened, Hexadaktylou thought, the women felt the birthday gathering in search of a suitable finale, and Mosca took her sister by the arm and lifted her to her feet, the pair twined arms round shoulders and waists and sought out steps half *syrtos* half tango, Kiki and Katina the couple next to follow suit as the rest hummed along to the tune and came out with "ljuba" at the right moments.

A little later, they left Katerina to poke and shake her presents, gloves, haberdashery, acacia eau de toilette, or musk the perfect pairing for a pansy in a small ornamental garden.

The three cats, the house's snow-white trinity, motionless on the terrace wall, languidly turning their heads to watch the visitors disappear into the distance, it was evening and a half hour back to town.

The distant whinnying, the smell of the parched fields, a startled bird, a skunk who shook his tail and disappeared behind some black-currant bushes; this was their home.

"Girls, Mina didn't give me the customary jar of blackberry jam this year," said Nana and linked arms with Orsa.

"She didn't make any," Mosca replied; her children had told her the blackberries were full of bird-shot, they preferred orange marmalade for the winter and mouth-melting apricot for the summer, those British novels their mothers so admired left them cold, with page after page dedicated to beautiful unwed blondes strolling wooded lanes for hours on end with baskets on their arms, picking every blackberry in the English countryside.

"Now you mention it," Kiki added, "the kids are absolutely right."

They dropped Nana off first and Hexadaktylou last, their elderly maid waiting for her on the doorstep, Orsa and Mosca bypassed the more central streets, deserted at this time of night, taking the pitch-black alley downhill instead; after all the hubbub, the revelations, and the sense of womanly complicity and solidarity, the night, the chill and the silence brought them back to the innermost affairs of their respective hearts.

A cold afternoon, skinny English kids, lots of them, maybe even a hundred, between six or seven and twelve, the boys in dark blue velvet caps and checked skirts on the girls, running towards the shore on the West coast of Britain, kneeling and licking the surf, the sea sweet, the waves syrupy, for off that very beach the *Dimitris Thermiotis*, laden with Cuban sugar, torpedoed, sent to the bottom with crew and cargo. It may not have been a dream exactly, what mattered for Maltambes was that reality had turned into a nightmare, war at full blast on land sea and air, all the ships playing their part as floating hospitals or divided between the Indian Ocean, Atlantic and Mediterranean convoys, where the mines and torpedoes were decimating the finest sailors and drowning fortunes in minutes when a ton of cargo could fetch thirty pounds, and that with sterling gone through the roof, months now, since October '42. With a lust for adventure on the high seas flowing in his veins since boyhood when he'd committed his grandfather's tales of past glories to heart, remembering them still like verses from school, feeding dreams of power and riches, he'd sail the *Little England* through the night, light his next cigarette with the butt of the last, and mess with his head, *Rodon Amaranton*, brig, 182 tons, *Nea Tychi*, bombarder, 61 tons, and schooners, sloops, caïques, not to mention ferries and trawlers, and it was December 7th, the day of his birth, his gift on the airwaves, the largest destroyer ever built, the *New Jersey*, launched in Philadelphia, but what else could he muse on but a procession of his forty years to be ready enough to meet his Maker at a moment's notice, like classmates, distant cousins and friends, Mansolas, Hionas, Georgalas, Laios, Karamouzis, Giannakoulas, Moustakas, Harharos, Perlourendzos, Karipoglou, Boukouvalas and the Palaiokrassas boys, all three of them.

Ten days earlier, Admiral Darland of the French navy had given the order to scuttle the fleet in Toulon harbor to keep it out of German hands, they'd burned and blown a quarter of a million tons that day, some captains hadn't wanted to see another, stayed on their bridges and gone to the bottom with their beloved ships; Maltambes had wept, and cursed too, as was fitting, he'd surveyed, caressed and kissed the *Little England*'s deck, her bulkheads and ventilators, "call the ship *Captain Mimis*, your father's name, bad luck not to follow tradition," his mother-in-law had struggled in vain to change his mind.

His thirty-first convoy, a small one, twenty-seven tankers and general cargo ships, he'd set sail from Boston and out into the North Atlantic, the Allies had improved their radar, warned them when U-boats were gathering for the kill, fast on his feet Maltambes executed some virtuoso maneuvers and picked up some survivors too, he'd lived a lot of death and wouldn't take any more, not a day went by without a familiar ship and face lost, with a crew of twenty-two aboard the *Little England*, all from seafaring families with kin afloat on other perilous sea lanes, mourning an everyday affair.

Enormous losses, dizzying figures. Spyros's head could take the big numbers, but there was no room for the little ones. He had to struggle to remember simple things, familiar images, lemon groves, the *meltemi*, the summer northerlies, making it hard to winnow grain, his children bored in church, Mosca drinking raki at his side, them nibbling on fried zucchini and eggplant, only Orsa—her alone—he would never forget, salvaging from the depths of memory all those hoarded details that brought with them pain and despair, a vaccination mark on her left arm, a tooth a touch crooked and smaller than the rest that lent her smile a little hauteur and spice, the silk coral dress the color of the August moon, her irregular breath, the girl ready to fizzle out or flare into an all-consuming conflagration . . . In his yearning, he even cast his mind in search of a future shared, a house in Kastela, a child of their own, a river of kisses and himself, a dog-tired Maltambes returning from the ocean to collapse on the bed and sleep atop her flowing hair and in her eyes so blue.

No news from the island, they heard of hunger and poverty in Greece, his Radio didn't know if his wife had borne him a boy or a girl, Leonardos the steward fretting over the blight that had ten of his most fruit-laden fig trees on their knees, the cook cursing his spirited daughter and a wife incapable of reining her in; everyone found something to worry them apart from the countless deaths and ruins of war.

They lost six ships on the first night.

Seven on the second, but as soon as Allied planes showed up and chased off the German wolves they were able to pull a few survivors out of the water, the *Little England* more than any, the Greek captain a legend yet again.

The third night, thankfully, was quiet.

They used their military dominance to swipe hens, the Italians made for suits, spats, and a slicked-back parting not fatigue, boots and lice, war didn't suit them like it did the Germans who shelled the island and flattened the shipowners' palaces and how many fine residences in Plakoura, piles of rubble, broken marble, smoke, and a pianola playing away to itself among the charred beams. The city changed overnight, a place whose every house was part of its body, a feature on its visage, the Hadoulises' mansion and next to it those of the Marideses, the Telemeses, Loukissas, Saltaferos, Mandarakas, the priest's silver-grey, Orginos's whiter than white, Vatokouzis' blue further up, and other well-to-do homes scattered among the public buildings with arcades, conservatories and French *parterres*, Nana's light green, the peeling pink of Nicephoros' widow's and Mouraina's yellow, canary yellow, the watchtower of the woman-mountain who'd hit fifty-five and lost herself, she didn't know whether to grow old as a tutor of dirty words and lewd tricks of the trade or as a virtuous abandonee.

Savvas Saltaferos and father Philippos with the backgammon board tucked under his arm, chased out of their homes, unwelcome, discussing all that with Emilios Balas, they'd gone round a-calling, drinking unsweetened sage and marjoram tea in his little kitchen and thank God not bored, because along with its monotonous misery and sadness, the war also supplied them with amazing changes in perspective and everyday life, take

Annezio, for instance, when the Germans besieging Stalingrad surrendered, she'd marched off into the rainy fields for poppy greens and white beet, treated both stories and some neighbors to fried wild green patties and wine two weeks after absent Antonis' name day, she'd fixed her thinning hair and accepted their congratulations, you'd think her son the Communist had vanquished von Paulus' hostile battalions single-handed, she wasn't fond of the Russians but reveled in the Germans' humiliation, in the future she wouldn't hate red, which she called bloody or bleeding or "the damn rash," she'd adopted this revulsion for a color many years since, just like Katerina blamed it all on blue, "a right good idea that," the old woman said, "taking it all out on a color."

What were folk to do? Luckily, they came up with countless ways of bearing the unbearable, of enduring the unendurable, of forgiving the unforgivable, of comprehending the incomprehensible, of uttering the unutterable, and all that so they wouldn't end up alone; it brought relief to winkle out a good word every now and again so as to live alongside different folk, whatever their beliefs.

Balas, all bones, a pair of huge brown eyes protruding from a face whose hollows and sockets had become holes and fissures, saddened by the destruction of Marseilles harbor, unconsoled by the devastation of Japanese convoys in the Pacific, fifteen thousand dead and twenty-two transports sunk in a single attack, much talk there of an American general, Macarthur, the Allies now gaining the upper hand overall, but those so distant seas did nothing for Balas, he had the Black Sea in his heart, the Danube, and above all the Mediterranean, whose harbors had taken bombs by the ton and were living bad times, flattened, dangerous and ugly.

The untraveled priest had only to hear the word harbors, "they've found the cure for syphilis," he said, he couldn't remember which, but he had a professional interest in the mat-

ter, "I knew why I absolved the sins of all the women that came
to confess, a child's home needs foundations more secure than a
parents' blessings," he said, Balas reached out and stroked
Saltaferos's neck and temples, the white tufts on his head and,
since they'd already discussed the discovery of a cure for syphilis
both straight and with innuendo, he brought the conversation
round to his pigeons, just two pairs left, he hadn't the heart to
cook them and other folk kept on stealing them, a thick layer of
droppings on the dovecote floor and, no longer so adept at
sweeping, his trouser legs got smeared in it, in fact Maritsa
opposite had tactfully offered to do his washing for him every
now and then.

"They're a nuisance and they eat into your corn flour, too,
why bother?" the priest wondered out loud.

"They circle round the valley come evening," Chora,
Paraporti, Livadia, Fallika, Livadia, Messaria, he watched
them and passed the time of day pleasantly, a liking shared by
great-grandfather, grandfather, father, son, and ending with
him; as a young man, Balas had failed twice in the matter of
marriage.

"Eat them before the Italians eat them for you, they've
stripped all the dovecotes bare," Saltaferos said, a fact Balas,
who was directly affected, had been aware of long before them,
the army of occupation would charge in and leave behind a
cloud of feathers and boot prints deep in the layers of pigeon
droppings.

Orsa hadn't shown up in a while either, another lover of those
flights and perhaps of the memories centering on his dovecote,
Balas, unintentionally and unplanned, because of course he
wasn't following her around, had happened upon her in the
cherry orchards roundabout of an afternoon or two, her eyes as
red as the fruit on the trees the moment she made him out
through the foliage, so many years gone by and no sign of her
forgetting his matchmaking failings, "I've been better off with-

out women and their cherries," he pondered the futility of love and set off home in low spirits.

Right on time, "there you are young Savvas," Mina and the priest's wife had dispatched him to search out their menfolk before the curfew and the evening damp descended, the kid brought Balas two pot-loads of macaroni, half a loaf, and a cake of soap wrapped in a towel.

A twelve-year-old boy can lift old men's spirits in an instant, they all livened up and couldn't have arranged it better if they'd been in cahoots, a bit more men's talk exchanged, his grandfather ruffled his curly head, *cabello rizado*, he shouted again and again without visible cause, he hadn't confessed his exploits in Argentina to anyone, not even the priest.

The two Savvases so close they were set to love each other till death did them part and beyond, often, on their walks along the island's lanes, quay, and beaches, Savvas Senior brushed off his ancient epigrams and Argentinean in what made for an entertaining hodgepodge, Junior would roll up his shirt sleeves and show him the black hairs sprouting in his armpits, like they were on his upper lip and elsewhere, winking at grandpa, the two free to talk about that sort of thing, but the black tufts and the fluff, not to mention the cigarette smoke he sometimes stank of, didn't spell impatience for a woman but impatience to escape to sea, and like the old-timers with it, signing on as deckhands at thirteen with a spoon, a fork and a blanket to their name, working twelve-hour shifts till 1930.

Old man Hadoulis found them on the road one afternoon and shepherded them into his new home, where they'd settled after their mansion was bombarded, him, the captain's wife and their two servants, they sat in the sitting room with the battered furniture and the shutters ajar and broke the news: having failed three times to make it to the Middle East, and seeing as how the British had already pushed the Axis out of El Alamein, his son and Vatokouzis had achieved the impossible, no one knew how, and were in New York, the news had made its way to an old friend with the utmost secrecy, one of the most powerful men in Piraeus, that was all he knew and was likely to find out, the important thing was that they were alive, and while we're at it, the ships-chandlers, travel agencies, shipping agents and hotels of America would be rolling in it after the war, clever Greek boys the pair of them, they wouldn't sit sucking their thumbs; the Hadoulises had already lost the *Minerva* and another two freighters and weren't the kind of people to sit around crying over spilt milk.

"But she'll lose her son that way," Saltaferos's thoughts for the old lady, with America so far away, deep down what troubled him was the thought of losing his grandson and Orsa, scared he couldn't hide his preference for their eldest from his body and soul, the sharp pain in his chest brought him out in a cold sweat, "hey, snap out of it, matey," he told himself, the boy was sitting quietly at the end of a sofa, tracing the pattern of the slightly charred upholstery with his finger, must have been broad dark green leaves against a cherry background in its heyday, he'd leapt with joy at the news his father was well, the rest beyond his ken, "fuck my funnel, pull yourself together," Saltaferos pushed himself, it was great news, he gulped down a couple of mouthfuls of water and felt himself again, his eyes moistened with relief, "daddy, Arta has the Big Dipper on her belly, just like me and you, give us a berth for a change of air, I swear I'll put up with your explosions, I won't get that sickness that makes them jump into the sea," he'd playfully written and enclosed a funny photograph, the newborn wearing his gift, the pink ballet slippers that were like hobnailed boots on her, Haralambis the acrobat had already ripped them to shreds. No one in the family had ever been to a ballet, not even Orsa, Saltaferos thought, I'll fry her some spuds myself and sit with her tonight and we'll talk, he decided and turning to Hadoulis, "you know, only the other day, the English radio said that at their annual flower show, I think it was in London, the Royal Rose Society awarded the gold medal to the El Alamein rose, a new variety, orange dappled with red."

"An El Alamein rose? Then I'll christen my parsley Gorgopotamos," the captain's wife replied dryly, she disdained all things British, her piercing narrow gaze had been fixed on young Vatokouzis for some time, whose good fortune it would soon be to be turned into an American.

Flannel, linen, denim nowhere to be found, not even strips to replace the torn ones on the kitchen shelves, the shops empty, Mina Saltaferou was having a hard time coming up with solutions for the household, Annezio useless, she'd go into the storeroom and stand staring at the silk gin, the bamboo loom, and the copper pipe of the raki still, a bit of cooking and lullabies all she was good for, as for the little maid, she'd eaten well with them, she'd drunk well, a great big thing she was now, you should see her, back in Vourkoti digging in the fields, wartime and strong men hard to find.

Saltaferaina wasn't one of those insensitive women who looked right through the totals of men dead and missing in action, her framed relations on the walls all shared that same melancholy expression the dead acquire over time, but her own total, of property owned, still a spoonful of honey. Hadoulaina counted the ships sunk, Katerina the men drowned, her mother-in-law the orphans made, Savvas comrades retired, Balas harbors bombed, the teacher deluxe hotels gutted, Nicephoros' widow flabby fannies sealed over, her daughters God knows what, and herself the five plots in Athens—Kifissia, Ambelokipoi—and Apikia, deeds signed over with Saint Kyriaki, Saint Varvara, Saint Anna, two flats on Stadiou Street, with the Anargyri, medical men those, under her signature, four shops on Stadiou again, she'd picked men saints for the commercial premises, Spyridon, Athanasios, Charalambos, and for the largest one apostles, Peter and Paul, now she was listless and prey to cold sweats, missed the cut and thrust, the money idle in the bank urgently needing putting to work, which is why she went to the Club, if Symbouras hadn't been singing his barcarolles for the thousandth time and *little schooner of mine* with it, and if Mina hadn't had her eye on his dairy shop in Athens, nice and central, there was no way she'd have attended the recital.

Mosca a bit sniffly, she'd stayed home with the gang of kids, Mersina sick and tired of the piano they'd hardly let her alone to practice, because there was always someone for her to annoy, Orsa in the middle until the intermission flanked by Saltaferaina and Bourada-Negropiperi, or rather Negropiperaina, for the second half Orsa put the teacher in the middle, she'd caught her mother quizzing the little ring with its green stone, now where might that have sprung from, the girl pulled her hand away, too late.

Vatokouzis would be taking her firstborn and their children to America, and that, Mina thought, would be a solution, not that she wanted it, just that things were getting beyond her, she stole a glance at her daughter's profile with profound guilt and a love she could not show, not daring to touch the hand with the mysterious ring, sentimentality something she'd unlearned.

In the second half, after the little ones, the Pertesi and Sarris sisters, it was Hexadaktylou's turn in full-length mustard crepe, this time she'd opted for an energetic, vibrant program of familiar pieces, no one left, no one dozed, for many present it was one of the recitals that justified the invention of the piano, the whole event aimed anyhow at keeping the islanders' spirits up, because the war had dealt the sailors' isle a heavy blow: the Athenians were dying of hunger, the Andrians drowning in battles at sea.

When the music came to an end, Saltaferaina, wearing an elegant shift, beset Symbouras with insincere compliments and a profitable proposal, business, the crowd well-groomed and dig-

nified, a calm Hexadaktylou accepting their formulaic congratulations, in small societies everyone sets off together for the
church, the fair, the event secular or religious, the lack of new
faces and venues tiresome but also bringing a sense of security
with it, whatever happens, we're all here, all known quantities.

When Saltaferaina got home with Orsa, they climbed up to
the first floor to scoop up children and bid their goodnights,
great orchestras from abroad playing on the radio, always quietly on, Mosca on her feet stirring the rice pudding to stop it
sticking, Annezio at the kitchen table with Arta asleep in her
arms, shelling broad beans with a knife.

Orsa, pausing from tiredness, still managed to put together a
long phrase to describe the recital gossip to her sister, Marie
twisting her ankle, Katina forgetting her high-school zeros, spotted once again in the company of *kyria* Hazapi the history
teacher, Symbouras wearing a two-tone suit, the Italians well-
behaved and keeping their distance, Hexadaktylou dedicating
Mendelssohn's *Songs without Words* to her with a nod.

Their day already over when the radio headlines started up:
the usual stuff, the Pacific again, didn't really take in where,
probably never heard of the place, the Americans bombed and
destroyed a lot of Axis ships and planes, they didn't note how
many exactly, hundreds, by the in-depth reports the women
weren't listening any more, the drone of words of war constantly in their ears, anyhow, the Allied broadcasts only ever
mentioned enemy losses, the rest they'd hush up, for obvious
reasons.

The news the BBC had kept quiet Kiki Bousoula delivered,
bursting in, waxen. She'd stumbled on the way, on a step, who
knows, her heel had come off and she was limping. She leaned
against the kitchen cupboard, took off her right shoe, clutched
it to her chest and couldn't master the flood of tears that
flowed, wetted, confused and spoiled the flow of syllables and
words, through the white noise of her sobs and tied tongue the

black news came together, somehow, via her brother-in-law stranded in England, his partner from before the war with the offices in Piraeus, Liverpool and elsewhere, and chiefly though the British Red Cross, word was out, the *Little England* sunk off the Irish coast on March 11, 1943, the British had picked up three crewmembers who'd provided the relevant information, no one else.

They could not breathe.

Orsa, out of control in front of them all for the first time in her life, leapt to her feet like a wounded lioness, kicked children, cats, stools out of her way, sent the rice pudding flying with the white pumps in her hands and half climbed half fell down the outside steps, Mosca, a pillar of salt, not wanting to believe either what she'd heard or what she'd seen, the racket had the houses on either side on their feet in an instant, neighbors in slippers with napkins in hand from their dinner, others in pajamas running into the white house, "tell us, for God's sake, what's happened," some asked, out of their minds, menfolk of their own on Maltambes' ship, but who could explain, no way Mosca could, or Annezio, Mersina, Christina, little Dimitris and Arta all in tears, and Mina Saltaferaina, still in her good dress and pearl necklace, banging her head on the wall until she passed out.

When Savvas senior and junior turned up home, the downstairs home, the news had found them fishing on the quay and they'd come back as fast as their feet would carry them, the youngster afraid for his grandfather's heart, Annezio wouldn't let them in, dispatching them upstairs and following in their wake, the kitchen in a state, pots, chairs, stools, walls dripping, olives walked into the floor, dried broad beans scattered here and there and Mina with all four grandchildren in her arms, snow-white, downstairs in uproar, "Nikos, Nikos, my poor lad, my poor boy," the old nurse chanted, the only one sparing a role for Vatokouzis in the drama right then.

The moment Mosca realized that the loss of husband and boat were not the end of her troubles, she charged downstairs, elder sister in her kitchen in floods of tears, she hadn't the strength, or the will, to stop her little sister wrenching open cupboards, drawers, cabinets, jewelry boxes, hatboxes and hurling their contents to the floor, upturning mattresses in search of evidence, ripping letters and postcards kept filed in boxes cases handbags by subject matter or continent, delving for notes between the pages of books then smashing them against the wall, upsetting the saints on the iconostasis, pulling pictures off their hooks, unscrewing globes, lifting the lids off milk jugs, sugar jars, soup tureens from the good dinner service, scrutinizing gifts and souvenirs Spyros had brought back for Orsa, two baby elephants in silk, a wooden alligator, the geishas, the American lemon squeezer, the green gloves and the peacock feathers, searching for some coded message, a word, a date, initials, something; when she'd turned the whole house upside-down, beside herself, Mosca laid into Orsa with kicks and punches, bloodying temples, chin, throat, knees, hauling and yanking at that never-cut, honey-colored hair until, a physical and mental wreck, she paused and lit a cigarette, "tell me," she asked through her tears, "who's Mersina's father: Nikos or my husband?"

Part Three

THEM THAT DROWN DON'T LIVE TO REGRET IT

Many months after the Liberation, a bright and frigid Sunday late in 1945, the square in front of the town hall filled with people who one way or another had heard, streaming from their villages and far-flung market gardens on mules in carts on foot; as for their clothes, doubt there too, those in mourning hoping against hope for some magical reversal of fate, those not wondering might our menfolk, too, be drowned and darting guilty glances at their grays, their greens, their browns.

But life had a way of righting itself, in Palaioupoli's temporary shelters the scouts held a memorial service for the American president, Franklin Delano Roosevelt, in Strapourgia they repaired the graves and built an ossuary, they sprayed Paraporti marsh over and over with that new pesticide DDT, the pig farmers and beekeepers haltingly busied themselves again with herds and hives, but the shipping shattered, the official reports spoke of fourteen hundred Andrian sailors unemployed, and the support offered their families shameful, compared, say, with Piraeus, where it was more than respectable, so it was "no to foreign crews" and the slogan "Andrian ships for Andrian sailors" emblazoned front-page in the *Voice of the Aegean* and all the local newssheets and stirring workers' rallies, seafaring folk still paying a high price for the war.

Kostas Karyotakis from Zaganiari, greaser, missing since his ship went down, straits of Madagascar 1944, prisoner of war in Japan then the Philippines, one of the five thousand men liber-

ated by general Macarthur when he announced the fall of
Manila in February 1945, had finally made it back to the island,
answering wives' and parents' anguished questions as best he
could up high on town hall balcony, if in the Pacific he'd happened across any of those with names still absent from the lists
of the dead and survivors.

Mosca with father and nephew, never missed one of these
but to no avail. The war at an end, most of the crew of the *Little
England* had returned from every sort of confinement, the ship
torpedoed on Thursday March 11, 1943, the convoy's fourth
night, just short of the Irish coast, dead calm, the lucky ones
picked up by the British, some other poor souls taken prisoner
by a German troop-carrier later sunk by Allied fire then picked
up by Germans again, what with all the ships sunk and prison-
ers taken, who was saved and who was not, not a single one sure
of their captain's fate.

In his aunt's living room, young Savvas had moved the family
photographs from above the sofa, replacing them with framed
medals for bravery, laudatory letters and expressions of gratitude from Allied ministers, ambassadors, shipping companies,
international syndicates and individual tars from foreign lands
rescued by fearless Maltambes, "Captain Phantom" the foreign
press had dubbed him, a spirit who had still to reveal itself. The
boy sat studying the foreign seals, the signatures, the elegant
scripts in the world's alphabets for hours on end, nothing he
didn't know about the whys and wherefores of the family feud,
kept his distance from aunt and mother alike but adamant, he
would not condemn the hero; anyhow all of Andros, distilling
the whole Saltaferos affair in kitchens, pantries, washrooms and
al fresco cookhouses, enamored with the scent of Spyros' glory,
for children and adolescents especially, him and Theseus,
Odysseus, Saint George one and the same, and as certain news
of his fate remained elusive, the legend grew well beyond the
bounds of reason.

Men sat together recounting and reworking Maltambes' daring and patriotic exploits since, aged five he'd wriggled out of an old aunt's grasp and made his own way down from mountainous Vourkoti to Chora, when he was seven and did for a nest of adders, eight when he spent a whole summer long with a school of dolphins that went wild with joy at the sight of his splashing, at eleven when he saved a relative from certain drowning, September '22, on leave between voyages, when he'd strode onto another man's caïque and sailed across to Asia Minor and rescued many a Greek from certain death, his later exploits on the high seas, taming whirlwinds, calming storms, cutting days off voyages, steering clear of mines, tricking the Germans.

Captain Phantom had stood to attention on the bridge of his flame-licked *Little England* and gone with her to the bottom, Kostas Karyotakis had heard the news in the camp from two Russian officers, reliable men, like every ship the *Little England*'s nameplate kept covered right through the war, but the description of the general cargo, the date and location a perfect match, and no other reports of a similar loss, their submarine had located him, but he was adamant: he would not abandon his ship.

Not a peep out of Mosca, she just stared at her dark red knitted top, felt some kind of spasm inside and wet herself, her face taut with the tension of release from near three years of agonizing, over all sorts, not just her husband's fate, supported by the two Savvases she slowly set off along the road back, to the white two-storeys. A solemn procession formed behind her, Kiki Bousoula first—Panagiotis, her husband, had often told friends and journalists from the national and international press the tale of how that fateful night it hadn't seemed right to obey the order to abandon ship and leave him behind, how Spyros had kicked and cursed and punched him twice to get him in the lifeboat—followed by Zanaki and Maistrou, whose menfolk, crew on Spyros' ship, had made it too, Emilios Balas looking dreadful, a bird with a broken wing, Katerina Basandi, even Archontia Sarri, the second cousin, who'd lost her Zannis to another convoy and sewed her widow's weeds herself, blinded by the freezing gusts, they headed down to Riva, while the news of Maltambes' brave and traditional end raced from mouth to mouth, supplanting every other topic in cafes, Club, and printer's alike.

Looking older than her years, Mina Saltafführer, as some now called her, hadn't dared accompany her daughter into the square, she'd stood well over to one side, excuse at the ready, a caïque just in from Mykonos laden with fine turkeys, its captain parading them round the streets on a pole fishing for customers, but he wanted fifteen thousand an *oka*, and the townsfolk didn't have it, when the news of her son-in-law reached her she sat down heavily on a wall, windy up there, she missed the lilac tree in the square, the sick bastards had cut it down.

"How could you?" her husband had asked her in '43, the night everything came out.

Mina had no reply for the man she'd married without loving, and who hadn't allowed her to love him even in retrospect, she had the strength, there on the wall, consciously and not out of habit, to mourn not just the man, her unhappy girls and orphaned grandchildren, but the beautiful lost ship too, as it deserved, the ship none of them had ever laid eyes on. It would fall to her to seek out the dead man and the *Little England*'s dues, deposited in an English bank; the others were in mourning, heavy mourning thanks to Mina who secured them their daily and their morrow's bread, and the luxury of grief and of melancholy.

Till then she'd proved there was nothing she could not take, that she was as resilient as a wild pear tree, but look at her now without the guts to go home, the gobbling turkeys made the city small and provincial again, a mote in the universe's eye, Saltaferaina shrank in on herself accordingly, a black cinder, one with the wall, so she wouldn't be there when Orsa heard the final, irrevocable news.

She still wished for Spyros to be alive, that alone, with her dark green knitted dress and honey hair, the colors of autumn gardens, glancing out the window every now and then at the somber monk-like mountains at the Eye of God, picking the bugs out of tomorrow's lentils, so tense her face was frozen and white, "he'll be alive," she thought, word to that effect coming through from time to time, it was just that sometimes sailors swore they'd sighted Captain Phantom in Vera Cruz, Brisbane and the Cape all in a single week, maybe that Kostas Karyotakis had borne witness to one version of many, Orsa thought, just let him be alive, she didn't want to think beyond that, to all the rest.

The revelation of her feelings that day a bomb which had shaken the two-storeys to its foundations, the next two months had witnessed many an episode the equal of any melodrama when it came to milking a tear, all islanders with a streak of fatalism and romanticism, a thicker one in this case, "the blue-green shirt," Mosca suddenly shrieked and hurtled downstairs, Spyros with a weakness for them, and she, struggling and wrestling with her memory then struggling some more, always unearthing some incriminating detail or other, years before, in Paraporti, one rare, breathless, windless noon behind the swaying reeds her eye settling on something blue-green and a little later there she'd been, big sister, flushed and running to catch her up so they could walk home together.

And the initials S+O=O+S carved deep into the prickly pears, ancient but untouched by time, Mersina and Christina, suspecting, had found those, eleven years old and though neither'd blurted it out to the other, thinking they might not just be cousins but sisters, too, they'd overheard their mothers quarreling, Mosca madly exploring months and dates and Orsa sitting in silence, dawn the following day she'd left for Apatouria, suitcase in hand and five-year-old Arta, grandma Orsa with health problems, too many to count, and her granddaughter wouldn't be budging an inch from her side; it was a solution of sorts.

The old woman hadn't come out with the usual, not once, foolish, seductress, infatuated, no, because deprived herself, "blessed are they," she'd mutter to herself, "who love and are madly loved," casting withering looks at Christ and husband to take the wind out of the sails of possible objections; an explosion of life between poison-dripping walls, a flabby grey and foul-breathed corpse capering on her divan, reaching out its hand to caress and love unbounded.

Orsa's eldest two would come up too, to play with Arta for a while, to sit on the little terrace and watch the hawks aloft above the ravine's dense vegetation, looking askance at their mother, but they loved her, just lacked the strength and the nerve to ask her those five questions straight out, did you ever love dad, did you see uncle in secret after you were married, what sort of parents are the old folk who caused this mess, do you still love them, and since you didn't marry the man you wanted, why didn't you become a spinster?

Orsa stole glances at her children, she adored them and couldn't rub Mersina's tummy any more, tickle testy Savvas, spread them slices of raisin honey, show them reams of post-cards, anyhow, she didn't feel like arranging the five continents' mountain snowscapes anymore so it was like you were slowly climbing the foothills of a single enormous mountain, the World Mountain she called it, passing villages scattered on slopes to east and west, mountain ranges interspersed with untrodden mountain peaks, and from one strategic point, a view of the whole world or something like that.

In May, she returned to the two-storeys for good, grand-mother Saltaferou, her soul bleeding, lightning bolts shooting from her eyes at son and daughter-in-law for the last time and in the presence of all, it didn't seem she forgave them, a step away from death her anger raging unabated, Father Philippos, old and tired himself, chanted something vague and fell silent, the dying women kept the upper hand till the end.

Orsa felt alone without her grandma, her own children had never tasted of that heady honey, a granny who conspired with her grandchildren, who laughed and giggled and cared about feelings, who'd fight for them, even intrigue.

Time refusing to go by in the once-white two-storeys; what with one thing and another no one had a mind for whitewashing and Savvas ashamed of the state of the house, but without the heart, either, to have round-brushed painters in, "as if they didn't have more to worry about than giving their walls a fresh coat" they'd say, those folk who live to coin the phrase of the day, who add a caption to an event so it can do the rounds in a jiffy.

Orsa, Mosca, avoiding each other, the house a range for practicing the avoidance of head-on collisions; so one would be cleaning lentils and have her antennae out for footfalls and news, and yes, the crowd at Mosca's side did stay in the distance, her high heels rang heavy on the marble of the outside staircase, the upstairs door, the shedding of shoes in the porch, the pad of feet in the hall, in the identical downstairs house Orsa copying her sister's route step by step, who'd reached the bedroom and crashing like a sack of potatoes, clearly fully dressed, onto the right-hand strip of double bed; "so he's dead," Orsa said to herself, imagining his black eyes breaking, his eyelids coming undone and nothing left but staring at the ceiling, the single partition, the plain cypress boards sagging slightly and in need of a coat or two of gloss.

She shut herself up in her room too, to spare her parents and her children the difficult situation they were in, they'd sent her nieces and nephews round to Marie and there was stew in the pot. She didn't come out, not in the afternoon and not for dinner when her father begged her to, only late at night with everyone deep in exhausted sleep, only then did Orsa throw a cardigan round her shoulders, go out and climb the twelve steps one at a time, the key in the kitchen door as always, the flickering lamp lit by her mother on the iconostasis guided her soundless feet towards the bedroom, barefoot, she touched the walls with her palm and the back of her hand, pressed her finger against the mirror's carving, the curves of the Viennese chair, inhaled the room's scent, caressed the curtain, the sheets on the empty left-hand side, the left pillow, sat on the edge of the bed, twisting her calves, rolling the rug into a ball under the bed with the soles of her feet and tracing the floor's straight joints, peered down or guessed at the floor here and there, "cypress boards break in a storm and drown our men, but in a home too, thin and unbacked, they can prove just as fatal" she thought, she made out the vial of laudanum on the dresser in the dim flickering light, took in the little shelf with their wedding crowns and the photograph, the couple on their New York honeymoon, "he's gone, gone forever" she said under her breath, "gone, gone," and suddenly felt she could face life no more, leaned towards Mosca asleep on her back, unmatting locks brittle with snot and tears, she kissed her on the cheek.

*O*ur *Smokers on Edge*, the headline in the local paper, not one ship landed in ten days now due to storms, the two Savvases, who smoked on the sly, the older one with heart problems and the younger one just young, had run dry during the ten-day drought, more than that it was mostly the illicit smoking that kept them close still, the grandson's trust shattered by all that had happened, he pitied his grandfather, the worst thing, partners no more in secrets and truancies, "never mind," he told him, "I'm not that interested, anyway," they wouldn't be sailing to Syros together to see the captain's last ship off, the well-traveled *Marousio Bebi*, sold for scrap.

Syros just a hop and a skip away, they'd hardly wet their feet.

Since '38 when he'd laid up for good, Saltaferos traveling a lot more than before, though in his head, sometimes to slip away from the present and sometimes to castigate himself for mooching round in slippers, farting fancy-free round the Argentine's place—hear a fart in the morning, heed the warn-ing—while an ancient tragedy was being played out in his home, an insane state of affairs, caused by love, *for men commit senseless acts of every kind under the goddess's influence; rightly does her name of Aphrodite begin the word for senselessness,* Euripides probably, by way of his immortal teacher Fokas Rallias, a confirmed bachelor, lucky man.

And the waves in no mind to calm, the moment Spyros's death made freshly official with ministerial stamps and the Bronze Cross for fallen sailors, off they went, telegrams of commiseration, patriotic eulogies in the papers and things getting worse all over again.

Saltaferos grief-stricken, like any real sailor he loved the female sex, no displeasure there when his wife had borne him three daughters one after the other, the first baby, christened Orsoula with air not water then and there, she'd only lasted a few hours, "perhaps for the best," the captain thought, so intensely aware of his paternal inadequacies and without mitigating circumstances he'd crossed swords with his angina on purpose; up and about since seven, frying potatoes for Orsa like a mad thing or mushrooms, and her not even looking at them, refusing to put food in her mouth, she couldn't swallow, they watered her with thin soups laced with tonic without her knowing, her husband had brought multivitamins from the States, and not just that, a mountain of related correspondence with doctors and professors from Athens, and right beside it the herbs and the potions, Hadoulaina, Mouraina, Nicephoros' widow, Tasa, the priest's wife, and, of course, Nana had made it their sacred duty to set Orsa back to rights, something about the girl, no one spoke ill of her, the legitimate widow, Mosca, they felt close to, but Orsa wielding another quantity, that which cannot be understood.

Everything else they could take. A disease blinding cattle in Gaureio, another blighting the poultry, the cereals yielding next to naught, just a dram and a half per dram all told, a shortage of tomcats in Kapparia, the Italian guards had cooked them up, quadrilles at the Club dance and ten tons of English coal in the smithies sent by British Military Liaison, an expiry date on the exchange of army sovereigns, a hundred drachmas for an *oka* of meat and the same all over Greece, one difference only, the state of siege not lifted in the Cyclades, a military zone, as the Government Representative and Senior Allied Military Commander in the Aegean reminded its inhabitants by decree.

Saltaferos would awake lyrical before daybreak.

He'd gaze at the clouds over the Eye of God, the clouds the miller saw as bags of flower, the draper as unironed calico, the confectioner as baked meringue, old Katina the spinster as a bridal veil and Madame Nana as an extension of her climbing rose, while Savvas admired them fulsomely as just clouds, one of those who held nature in special regard, who spoke with it, sweet talked the Dawn, had words with the snow, sent the humidity to hell, and placed his trust a hundred percent in the ace up his sleeve, the Cyclades' fine, pellucid, lukewarm light.

Early afternoon he'd traipse round the printer's, Maritime House, newly-founded, and the cafes, whose regulars compared the doings of every village Foods Commission and at 7:15 took in the latest news from Nuremberg, their particular interest the fate of the German admiral, Karl Donitz, commander of the Nazi U-boat fleet.

After school, the grandchildren couldn't find a single adult with time for them, all of them rendered useless by guilt. The captain would sometimes watch Maltambes' twelve-year-old orphan, Christina, from afar, dressed in black, black too the ribbon in her pony tail, playing in the damp sand of Nimborió and gawping at the little wooden bridge, a miniature of the one in Brooklyn and her and Mersina's meeting point, his two grand-daughters inseparable till then and fated to share their parents' every pointless thoughtless deed, set to lose that too, sure letter-writing's fine, but can't compare with hot tears shed on the shoulder of a friend.

February, a Thursday, nine in the evening, sleet falling on a deserted Athenian square, Marousi, a vast family taverna, a frayed Carnival garland, few customers, the waiter, eyelids weighing heavy from the inactivity watching the headlights as the occasional car drove round the dimly lit square. When the glass door opened, he didn't even turn to see the couple who sneaked in hurriedly, him round thirty her thereabouts too, twenty-eight rather, dressed in black__not fashion, mourning—they didn't look around, just dived at the first table they found and ordered right away, fumbling for each others' fingers, especially the woman, looking each other straight in the eye, again the woman more, her head inclined a touch to the left then to the right, her hair flowing free and full from the wet rebounding off her shoulders, her gestures, carefully posed, their recent acquaintance proclaiming itself to the rooftops, this man, who was clearly not even going to unbutton his car coat, meant everything to her. They were hungry and set about their food, but the woman, as though she regretted the *kokoretsi*, didn't keep it up, a *bonne viveuse* with an obvious weakness for spleen, heart, liver, innards in general, but that wasn't food for a romantic date now was it, she touched the crispy intestines with her fingertips, caressing and scratching them with as much grace and elegance as she could muster, like the strings of a mandolin, taking delicate bites from the very edge with lips half-closed as though nibbling Belgian chocolate, raising the *tzatziki* to the side of her mouth and tasting the garlicky yoghurt like crème patisserie, dunking her roll like communion bread, transported, in heaven, not with the dead man who'd dipped her in black, with her curly-haired companion who was calmly and pleasantly stripping his food from the bones like a cat, the girl took in his split ends, her eyes descending slowly to his pale forehead, to his eyebrows, his dark eyes, sliding down his nose to his mouth, the greasy fingers and moustache and coming to rest with unadulterated adoration on the lamb chop, lingering along its length.

At the other end of the room, Nikos Vatokouzis had pushed his plate to one side after a single mouthful, riveted to the sight, to the woman, so madly in love and sensual, shooting off sparks, his wife had never sparkled like that for him, he wanted to lavish erotic caresses on Orsa, caresses never seen before, but her always holding back, she loved another, and Vatokouzis wept onto his half-eaten chop.

Germany had collapsed in May '45, Nikos, who'd long known how the land lay, that liberation was a matter of course, returned that Christmas, a battle lost without a shot fired, as they say, the sight of Orsa haggard and weak, the color of lemon and ash, enough, the words hadn't come; it was futile to insist on carting them all off to America.

But Savvas and Mersina, fifteen and twelve, young kids, up to here with the sick state of affairs in the two-storeys, he had to get them out of the house and Andros and Greece, lucky they were too young to imagine what forever meant, Hadoulis junior in America, New Jersey, like a brother acquired at forty, he'd care for them like his own, he'd picked up something years before, foreseen the outcome of erotic rivalry and sided in time with the vanquished, left middle-aged and unmarried by a series of mysterious romantic disappointments, he'd picked Vatokouzis and stood by him, voyeuristically weathering the storms of a great love from up close, something that more than sufficed for his needs.

Mersina's world had collapsed, when she asked if it was right that she be separated from her mother, Nikos leaving no room for argument.

"Are you punishing her?" she said, and he rolled his eyes, he'd never expected a question like that from a little girl still in primary school.

Annezio didn't hate Orsa either, the emotion's raw material quite absent from the girl's gaze, not the slightest hint of empathy, she made no bones about it, she laid the blame at Nikos's mother-in-law's door, she'd never thought of the lad as her employer, the poor man a piece of her; so she'd moved alone to the blue two-storey to let a little air in, to renew the annual bulbs in the terraces, to prune the lavender in the French garden to the right geometry.

With old age as her alibi, which she equated with bad eyes, bad ears, bad legs, she went round Orsa's but just to iron, because the house made her sad, she thought it a sin for a fine young woman to give in like that, a beauty divine to waste away, vainly searching the sunken cheeks, the blue eyes, the shriveled breasts, the vanished hips; she didn't eat, they said.

And now she was to lose her children too, a harsh punishment.

Vatokouzis getting their passports ready in Athens, taking his pre-war Desoto on long lonesome rides to distant neighborhoods, he'd loved the Greeks of Asia Minor since his student days and first months at sea, so he'd head for the refugee quarters, Leftist hotbeds, Kaisariani and Byronas, which Byron's fellow countryman, major-general Scobie of the British army, had shown less pity than even the Germans; the marks of war still fresh, pulverized walls, plasterless ceilings, black-clad residents, political passions a world apart from the Americans', the passion of Christ, of parents, of all mankind, a different neighborhood every day, as though weighing the place and its people to gauge how heavy this homeland weighed on his soul, this strange land that had only really occupied his thoughts since the day he abandoned it, since he decided to deprive his children of Greece, too, a land he'd served with a sense of duty, while Maltambes, how could he avoid the comparison, had learned life's lesson, no, Maltambes wouldn't miss another opportunity, he offered Greece his passion, he loved her madly and without limits, like them that weigh in through thick and thin and get their girl in the end.

March 31st, a huge flock of cranes aloft over Andros, Emilios Balas half walking half stumbling along the paths round Livadia, watching his pigeons fly low over fields of broad beans and wild artichoke, the hairs stood up on the back of his neck at the sight of the full horizon, "now that's something I've never seen in all my seventy-five years," he thought; with Spyros dead he had no more reason to live, the birds feather-light, filler, no more, and him never shallow enough to be satisfied with that.

She was going to Chora, to Saint George's, Spyros's orphan Christina to baptize Kiki Bousoula's twins, her Panagiotis a survivor of the *Little England* and the whole town on their way there, in the end there really was no escaping fate on this accursed isle, Mosca thought, assuming a role she'd reviled since adolescence, the captain's widow, invulnerable and dutiful in her black suit, standing to one side with the two expensive christening coats from London in her arms and not letting her dark-haired daughter out of her sight, her first period on the way any time now, she calculated, examining the pointy little breasts and more the face on its way to becoming a woman's, anticipating the trials and tribulations to come.

The church packed with Christina's classmates, the new generation already entering the game, for, though the twins, at two months, were merry and the service as bright as the Sunday afternoon, Maltambes' irrevocable absence was everywhere, Maltambes the symbol incarnate of all lost sailors. Those that didn't drown there to a man in the church, a fair few of them alive thanks to the courage and ability of the captain who'd fought the oceans for twenty-three years and won.

Which was why *the black sea moans and the narrows boil and my heart weeps and sighs* and why *how handsome the sea dog when he dresses all in white and takes the helm*; Vangelakis with his lute, little Vangelis sixty years old if he was a day and heavy with it, ran through his maritime repertoire at the christening feast and they raised the roof.

Captain Savvas, as the family representative, looked after his gaggle of six grandchildren and sat with ancient Hadoulis, Balas, and others not up to the *ballos*, discussing the route of the Gavrio-Chora road, up and rolling again in light of the elections.

Mosca had gone back home after the church. Downstairs, a light on in Saltaferaina's room, and in Orsa's.

She climbed up the marble stairs and sat on the little balcony without a jacket, without a light despite the cold, she lit a cigarette, "Good God, I'm just like Mouraina," she thought and remembered her adolescent severity, back then when she'd reviled the flabby cunts and hung round the teacher, foreign he alone who could prize her out of this familiar landscape.

She hadn't married the coward, she'd married the hero, so there!

Her daughter who was shooting up at a rate of knots brought her back to ages, to effort, and to the essence of relationships, Saltaführer, for example, her mother, morale low, would raid her daughters and steal theirs.

Dark blue, black, distant lights around her, something like the nighttime Valparaiso painted by that Whistler; the neighborhood and whole town preparing for more bloodletting, the American embassy having recently issued a notice to all American nationals advising their immediate return to the U.S., the men with dual nationality rounding up their women and children, Marie had already trunked up dowries and heirlooms,

I humbly pray that you'll right away get monks and priests and bishops at feasts to fix a magic ditty for New York City she'd written in the farewell card she'd handed her along with her christening earrings, as for Katina, she'd gone away too, her father finally laid to rest she'd met a Massimo in the baker's on a visit to Piraeus aunts who could help her work as a nurse, the Italian mesmerized by her huge, firm breasts, mermaid figurehead they'd called her when they were girls, but if that soul from Genoa hadn't happened to be there, the mermaid figurehead, thirty-seven years old, would have fallen prey to termites and silverfish on the shelf; so that was the end of the sisterhood of four. Its time had come, Mosca lit another cigarette then another and a fifth a seventh a tenth, realized the toing and froing of her thoughts was just a pretext, a prolonged wait for her ears to seize upon a cough, a saucepan lid, the radio, any sound at all from Orsa, but in vain, barricaded up in her room she'd have missed the storks too. "A good omen" some toothless old grandmothers gummed at the christening and Balas with them, master ornithologist, himself the spitting image of an ancient crane, who fed all the feathered folk with lightly mashed corn, and whose soul pitied crows and their kind, "wanted" at three thousand drachmas a head.

Three days later his neighbor Mardissa Antonoglou found him in the dovecote, face down in a foot of droppings. The forty days mourning up, Mosca, setting his bachelor household in order, burning old junk, throwing rubbish, decimating souvenirs and tear-dampened clippings, found seventeen envelopes Spyros posted to his uncle, no letters inside but on the little triangle of paper the sender licks and folds down like a cover, on the inside, the phrase, "for my dearest Orsoula."

The weather mild and the children running free in Paraporti, Nimborió and Gyalià, lying on the sand and pebbles in twos and threes, bickering and bitching.

Resvanis GP, possessor of the worst case of sciatica on the island, deprived of his springtime strolls, robbed of the tranquility the Lenten liturgies brought, housebound and a sitting duck for Saltaferaina who bugged him constantly to find a miraculous tonic for her daughter. "Manos Sotiriades, microbiologist, Institut Pasteur, Paris, behold, too his telephone number," little use considering Andros was still unconnected. "Mina," he later explained, "an analysis of gastric juices employing the Winter method followed by a detailed fecal examination in order to diagnose complaints of the stomach and intestines." But how were they to get the feces fresh to Athens? The steamer took twelve hours to Piraeus, and Orsa, so what if her stomach had sealed so she could barely swallow, wouldn't submit to the discomforts of the journey and the examinations; she just didn't care about her health at all.

Eftychis the electrician, who put all his earnings into shot for woodcocks and scrawny turtledoves, would give Saltaferos a share, Louis, Nonas, Lavdas, Skordas sent weevers, rockfish, and those ones with the nice names that glimmer broad and silver like ancient jewelry, Nana's description of all fish unknown en masse, and then there were the medlars from Apatouria, Orsa didn't willfully refuse food, she'd lost her appetite for life and the whole backdrop of cooking and baking an irritation, in the end she threw the pills out the window, too.

No one in the household went to the trouble to put themselves in Mina's soul, they noticed other things, that she didn't
celebrate the monarchy's landslide referendum victory, didn't
lament the leveling of Japan's palaces by American bombers,
just shook out some sloppily-made cushions for cat hairs then
back to stare at the radio. Truth was she was repenting, suffering, and worrying herself sick from a distance, the thousand
clumsy attempts to reestablish her relationship with her eldest
abandoned, their words never matched, their meanings never
coincided, one's question the other's answer never met, Orsa
used strange words, as though they were intended for her own
ears only and her own head, that head, that mind which
Saltaferos, too, so feared, for he'd lost a brother long ago to the
sickness that has men leap into the sea.

"Give me the letters. All seventeen of them."

Mosca entered her sister's room after so long, she'd closed
the door behind her and so much played out in so few seconds,
anger in the one over the secret correspondence, surprise at
the sight of Orsa up close, indifference in the other at the
reproach and something like a sigh of relief at her sister's reap-
pearance.

"Moscoula . . . "

"Give me the letters," Mosca repeated, her voice imperative,
threatening, screeching, she jolted Orsa, kicked the stool at her
feet, sought retreat in cigarettes and smoker's cough, and when
the other rose out of the rocking chair and put on thin stock-
ings and a sweater, she followed her as they headed down
towards the little bridge, lashed by the North wind and the desperation they shared.

They did the Maltambes circle. For almost all the second half
Mosca supporting her sister who hadn't the strength, but
unhesitatingly shed the load of five six phrases, dripping drop
by drop, knot by knot, onto the relevant locations, little bridge,
Wednesday July ninth, 1929, Saint Dimitrios's church,

Thursday July seventeenth 1929, rocky cave, Monday July twenty-first 1929, the site of grandmother's victory, dispensation won for extraordinary burial high on the hill, the cemetery of the Anargyri, Sunday July twenty-seventh 1929, reed thicket in Paraporti, Friday August first 1929, dovecote, Saturday August second 1929, despite all that "the letters" Mosca demanded, terse, "the letters," Orsa's calm reply "only when you believe me, only then."

Night falling, the dirt track's few passers by standing to one side in surprise, the cattle lowing, myrtles all around, broom, blackberries, wicker, "cut a wicker twig for luck" the priest would say back then, seeking reinforcements beyond heaven.

Informed of the joint departure, Nana Bourada-Negropiperi had run down to Orsa's and sat in the rocking chair, smoking, waiting, brushing off her entire arsenal of alliteration and similes for some time now to ignite a spark of interest in her favorite, but all for nothing.

That night, when Orsa returned and crumpled gasping on the bed, Nana offered her the petit beurre she favored for visitors, seizing upon another irrelevance in her fright, plants, her trump card since Mikés, God rest him, had teased her in public about her housekeeping, Nana's dishes may lack flavor, he'd say, but her gardening skills quite enough to keep a marriage going without children but with four flower beds whose color combinations kept a smile on her husband's lips, "we, my little mountain girl, married for the pansies" he'd tell her, and no trace of irony.

"Please stop," Orsa interrupted her, all this she'd heard before; she noted the half-empty liqueur bottle out of the corner of her eye, on the booze again, the teacher often came around the white two-storeys, for her goddaughter she said, but mainly because there she could muse on wild passions past, she considered Orsa's room something like an altar to lost loves.

Except that Orsa, tonight of all nights, wanted her out, needed to think of Maltambes, her two children she was losing because of him but bore no grudge, the image of him sinking into the ocean driving her mad, sailor's coat swelling in the water, bubbles escaping from his mouth, hat soaked but staying afloat on the surface for the longest time.

Saltaferos seized his chance and had a new angina attack to cement the truce and bring his daughters closer. Present in the same room, even just for moments at a time, they gave him his pills, Mosca read to him from the paper, the news they all already knew, because columnists Stamatoudis, publisher-printer Papadopoulos, headmaster Salonikis, captain retd., and Lefentarios of the local Panhellenic Naval Federation branch all lived hereabouts and knew what the others knew, when the *Voice of the Aegean* announced that the *Brotherhood*, the Greek War Aid cruiser, had taken eighteen horses on board, cargo from the USA, the beasts had already grazed up half the valley's milkwort, trefoil and dandelion greens.

Mosca read whether she felt like it or not, *Mosca, Moscoula, Moscaki, a thousand moles on your back so white for Maltambes to kiss all night*, Saltaferos remembered her newlywed, full of life and a dirty stopout, those crazy friends of hers bombarding her ears with doggerel, my little girl, he said to himself and tried to love her as much, but how was he to show it, he didn't fancy the role of repentant Magdalene and left things as they were, he put things off.

The teacher visited, too, and for the first time showed she liked him that much, just before leaving she plucked up the courage to say something, as though she'd been thinking about it for years, he brushed off his old self, as he saw it necessary or unavoidable in view of his visitor's profession, and Nana who'd been expecting it repeated herself slowly, almost reciting three or four sayings, the captain's bread and butter.

"But Mr. Savvas, you're not signing and sealing a thing with those, you're evading, let's say you're mounting a motto and riding away on it."

"But you quote them, too . . . "

"In full knowledge of what I do."

He respected her, though, no matter that his ear had caught an indiscretion, years ago, one afternoon, her telling his eldest "the only thing your parents have in common is the shuss, loquacious and malicious."

And the youngest grandchildren would stick their head round the door to see granddad with their own eyes, Arta, Mimis, Mina in their beige and light blue primary school smocks, young Maltambes with the kestrel's eyes pining for something more, he'd squeeze under the sick man's bed, to stare the cat in the eye he said, to see who'd hypnotize who first, and forget himself under there for hours on end, but granddad, an old man now, no appetite for new relationships serious and demanding, after a certain age people do feel the weight of their years, stop following the exploits of the young, only take an interest in existing acquaintances, they'll do for what's left.

Savvas junior, the last meaningful friendship in his life, nowhere about, adolescent doubts and love at first sight, Archontia Sarri's daughter, away all day and for good as soon as school was out, him and Mersina would be going to America.

"You're fine, go on, up you get," old Resvanis announced one afternoon.

Mina and Annezio there, panic-stricken at the doctor's exhortation, Orsa and Mosca in the same room, their only solace in years.

Spring well underway, the Americans, UNRRA, handing out antipyrin and other anti-malarial drugs, bolts of cloth, pullovers and shoes still being distributed through the village committees, not enough of the cheap magazines sent by the British Intelligence Service to go round, a troupe of traveling magicians performing in Loukissas's café and Mr. Dinos, a lover of fine acting he said, of pretty actresses they said, inconsolable that diarrhea had robbed him once again of Sophia Vembo's Cairo–Khartoum–Addis Ababa tour.

Saltaferos reentered town life with his new cup, red and enamel as always, purchased on his recovery and in the care of his cholera, wrapped in his thick sailor's coat.

He walked as far as the mole, stood staring at the *Farouk* unloading grease, ground beans and powdered milk and, little by little, won back his sea-borne looks.

"Let's go home, my son's sent you a letter from New York, highly personal it says," old man Hadoulis, at eighty, out and about too, to move around and get the blood flowing in his legs.

Saltaferos afraid the America missive would be Vatokouzis' decision to take Orsa's third child, and how was he to break it to her he thought, "Lord have mercy, who knows what fresh disaster's on the way," he said turning round to the elderly ship owner fit to burst, but this no a fresh twist in Orsa's tragedy.

Entering Hadoulis's place, they went into the office with the silver icon of Saint Nicholas, the outsize portraits, the varnished charts and leather-bound tomes that had consumed junior's youth, the old man took a manila envelope out of his desk and discretely left Savvas alone, "I'll get them to bring us some lemonade," he said and took his time returning, walked to the kitchen, ordered, helped himself to a couple of spoonfuls of leek pilaf from the pot, stroked the cats asleep on a rug atop the yard wall, his old lady had missed the monks so bought new pots, pans and skillets for the monastery, a train of thirty mules or so had set off bright and early for Kavkara.

Strong-boned Hadoulaina mounted and dismounted like a man. Both times they'd lost a ship, the *Hydroussa* in '21 and the *Aegean* in '23, she'd ridden to Syneti, Menites, Zaganiari, and Aprovatou to deliver the bad news in person.

Hadoulis came back into his office and found his company's

chief captain of old somber, with the expression you see on the faces of folk surrendering after one broadside too many. A letter had arrived to the New York office from the Greek consul in Buenos Aires, informing them that the search was on for Savvas Saltaferos, a retired captain formerly of Gabriel Hadoulis & Son Sea Transportation, heir to a flat in the Argentine capital and a certain amount of cash.

Just a formality, but then Savvas and the consul, the Hadoulises too sometimes, had got together in the old days for professional transactions and high jinks outside office hours—and we're not just talking once or twice—beer, *asado* and Merdita, Carmencita, Lolita, Teresita, Negrita, and Chicita; sailors know about all that. So Angelita Rodriguez San Pedro, Ita, and handsome Odysseus, Odysseus their son, killed in an overturned bus, the captain their inheritor.

"First of all, she leaves a handful of jasmine on her bedside table every night, just like her old grandmother the child never met. That's not copied, it's inherited. Second, the two Mersinas the spitting image of one another, the girl transparent too, an open book. Third, when she weeps, she takes to the streets. Next. She won't eat rabbit. And something else they have in common, no talent for the piano, none whatsoever, the Vatokouzises tone-deaf and all left feet. Want another? She loves white, snow, wave caps, sugared almonds, calico and sea gulls."

"I've something important to tell you," Annezio had told Mosca; Mersina had dreamt a lady in white urgently requesting a pot with a carnation, that white too, no doubt about it, the woman was her grandmother, Nikos's mother, the old nurse had racked her brains for incontrovertible proof of Mersina's patrimony and emptied the drawer with the unframed photographs on the table.

"Come on, we turned out untalented on the piano too, and it's not just the dates that sow doubts, there are the seventeen letters, too," Mosca dropped the empty envelopes in her lap, the old woman didn't deign to pick through them, yellowed papers, nothing more, illegible stamps and scissored backs, Balas gave the stamps to the woman opposite.

They were sitting in the kitchen, the girl swiveling on her stool, the view from on high, the Aegean above the bread-bin and Paraporti's golden sands above a bowl with a pot full of green beans, "green beans split with a sigh," like Orsa used to say, "green beans split with a sigh."

She fought back the tears, realized how trapped she was in her hollow arguments.

What on earth had made her hurt Annezio so, who'd settled the smallest room in the huge blue two-storeys, eternal hand-maid to invisible masters, who kept their mansion as it was and the plants exactly as the mistress had once wanted them, a French frontage, ferns, fennel and hyssop in the shady hall through to the backyard, and pot plants in the conservatory, apothecary's rose, calendula, primula, columbine, cuckoo flow-ers, eglantine and the white carnation, a little worse for wear after a visit from Saltaferaina's tomcat.

"Why don't you go to America, too, to Antonis or Nikos to help him and the children?" Mosca asked.

"That was Orsa's job, but how? Anyhow, he's never asked me to. Deep down, he wants me to keep an eye on your sister, though there's no getting near her no more," Annezio paused then announced, ever so proud, that though America had taken both her boys away, Andros was more interesting, an entire city of two and a half thousand souls to pick from, half of whom, at seventy-five, she knew, name and surname, father and mother's names, beliefs, and as for the other half, face and gait alone enough for her to work out from which stock each had sprung.

America was over and done with for her, she had no wish to see it again, she'd already been in the Museum, seen a woman boss in a furniture factory, a black eating baklava, and three Chinese women having a perm that didn't suit them, scolding her son for letting his customers delude themselves. The only thing she'd liked was riding round in the automobile. Everyone knew that every Sunday at noon, after the memorial services, she'd pay the island's only taxi driver to drive her to Three Churches and back in his cab.

"Kippers and cod at Gavrio at last," she declared, not that that interested her at times like this, her mind constantly on Nikos, sometimes like this and sometimes like that, a schoolboy and then plying the Black Sea where he'd spoil her with spicy tidbits, salted tuna, roach, cheese from Roquefort and salami from Prague. And the island's old piano teacher, Kelly, with five grandchildren, an enormous behind, faint whiskers, wire-wool hair and dripping with gold teaching Nikos Tchaikovsky with a plate of anchovies and pickles on top of the piano, no great artist's looks or tastes for her, unlike Hexadaktylou who'd succeeded her to general relief, unworldly and unlucky in life, perfect for a pianist.

Mosca scanned the photographs, Madame Kelly, all blubber and cheer, embracing the child, the piano by itself, various ships, the captain bolt upright beside statues you'd swear envied him, sights and casinos, Mersina, who hadn't lived long enough to benefit from penicillin, fine and photogenic, her eyes and cheeks, the waves in her hair shooting off criss-crossing sheens, like the game with sunrays and mirrors. Her sister had the same photograph in her drawing room, she hadn't set foot down there in a while.

"So. I'm with Vatokouzis not Maltambes, and I'm telling you you're being unfair to them all, to your husband, God bless his soul, and to your sister and brother-in-law. There's little Mersina, put the two photographs side by side, same mush, same black fate."

"And the letters?"

"That poor devil Balas never put the cat among the pigeons alive and pulls it off dead. Forget them. Dig a hole in the ground and throw them in. There are six kids and they come first, don't let them suffer from their mothers what the two of you did from yours."

"Was it her put you up to this?"

"No, on the bones of poor dead Mersina, I might have been

born a servant, but I don't take orders from Saltaferaina, she's done enough damage."

All this time Mosca avoiding looking ahead to where all this would lead, stubbornly awaiting answers on the sidelines, wouldn't believe Orsa had loved Spyros desperately and silently for seventeen long years, that theirs was a childhood bond, like hers with the Englishman, who she'd got over completely and forgotten, a little blurred and cheekless face.

"Let her give me the letters to read, I need to see them, it's not just that there was a lot happening, maybe, behind my back, I want to know if and how much my husband loved me, Annezio, you compare photographs to reach your conclusions, I'll compare words, those he wrote to her and those he spoke to me."

The windows closed because of the west wind and the kitchen with that special smell old folk's kitchens have, a covered plate with the leftovers from lunch, the brown cracks in the porcelain, pots and pans on the shelf not used for years, the soap dissolved in the sink's trough, down to the size of a bean, and the water that smelt as though it, too, were old; with nothing else to say Mosca stood up and wandered a little round the house her sister had repeatedly rejected, valuable furniture, heirlooms adorned with wondrous unused gifts, ice skates, golf clubs, rods and fly-winged hooks for tricking highland trout and salmon, a pith helmet, and above the piano on a wooden base, an African antelope's horns, "horns for the cuckold, now we're getting somewhere," she thought and stood at the corridor's end gazing absentmindedly towards the kitchen where well-practiced Annezio was attending to the photographs like a poker player to his cards.

The most suitable place for what they had in mind was out at Piso Gyalià, far from prying eyes, a landscape that takes hold of the heart and the soul and leaves neither the same. A yellow beach, five hundred meters long a hundred and fifty wide, dried grass mattresses steaming in the midday heat, mini-dunes that settle on balconies and fill the hills ranged all around to their very peaks. And since the sand rises up to heaven why shouldn't the waves break there, too?

He half shut her eyelids, heavy and sticky with dried salt, the colors flickering, the sun nailed him with a thousand blades and he saw white caps streaked with seaweed finely chopped like lettuce salad welling briny from the mountain top and splashing all around the aluminum afternoon.

He heard the sizzling evaporation, went numb and turned onto his other side, no mountains simmering now, just the blue water, a chill color by nature, and the cool swept down from his eyes to his whole body. He shivered.

They'd just made love for the first time, Marina in a shirt, Savvas too, it was that they'd been kissing endlessly and staring into each others' eyes, those four coal black eyes, and hadn't felt so shy in their shirts though they were completely in the raw beneath, they were stuck together like writhing magnets. Their clothes thrown to one side, Marina's knickers soaked and floating, some tinily studious lizards inspecting the two school bags.

The last day of term, Nikos Vatokouzis, whom business commitments had kept in Piraeus for five months and since Orsa wouldn't change her mind how he'd dragged them out, had everything in order and come to take his two eldest to America.

The town watched on with bated breath, as though they couldn't condone or at least imagine mild-mannered Vatokouzis taking the children from their mother, and himself wondering why he went on with this mess he hadn't started in a vengeful state of mind, though he'd been someone else for a long time now, perhaps it was a ruse, the children as bait, to wrench Orsa away from the island, to save her, to make a new start far away. The plan now well underway, a flat rented in New York, schools found, a housekeeper, shipping-supply contracts, they needed him urgently, a one-way journey and so many obligations and emotional complications that could only lead to wrong decisions, one after the other. Not that Annezio didn't point them out to him, "think it through again," or Orsa shame him, the state he found her in, skin flaking, nails breaking, hair coming out in tufts on pillows and sofa arms, everywhere, four-foot hairs all tangled and matted, changing the design and colors of fabrics and embroidery.

The last night before their departure, when the relations and the rest had gone, she asked for her children to be brought to her in bed, they lay down, Mersina to her right and Savvas on her left, "I'm weak and cannot follow, maybe later, as soon as Arta finishes primary school," she told them, they knew it was impossible, but, so brave all three, they kept up the lies till morning and the tears at bay.

For Savvas, Orsa had prepared a notebook depicting land-scapes, each on a separate page; spring, summer, windswept . . . Andrian landscapes all. "I'm not as observant as your father and you." "That's the truth," Savvas thought bitterly, but his mother always saw something no one else would ever notice, he opened the notebook and flicked through it, Gerakones, Dipotamata, Mouvela Tower, Lamyron, Tourlitis, Lidi, Pithara, Piso Gyalià. Marina Sarri, the finest landscape on Andros, wasn't there; he was seventeen, an age quite unsuited to admitting how definitively attached he was to the land of his birth, inside he even made fun of his mother for her saccharine souvenir and read the final description a second time, of post-war Gavrio, "a half-derelict windmill on watch, a hero's tomb with railings down, a deserted tannery on the beach and the half-burnt ship at rest in the shallows."

Her body another ruined Gavrio, he felt her pressed against him and was filled with despair, at everyone, without a single exception, sitting back and watching his mother waste away until the end, till there was nothing left, it scared him, but he wanted to touch her, to feel her shoulders her knees her chest, to figure out how much of her was missing, most of his mother gone, so little left.

Compass card, full steam ahead, narrows, mainmast, binnacle, bulkhead, sea lane, dog watch, bosun, words the boy slipped into phrases he cooked up for the purpose, his mother hoarded beloved fine-sounding nautical words on slips of paper, exercise books and postcard backs, and Savvas clumsily and poignantly presented Orsa with his gifts.

For Mersina, Annezio and Mina had prepared a trunk with silks, during the wretched occupation Saltaferaina had lain in wait for the youths who trudged eighteen hours at a time up to the Arvaniti villages to exchange dowries for peas, picking out the finest lace and most intricate embroidery and palming second-rate stuff off on them; so there they were, three overflowing trunks for her granddaughter, you'd have thought they were packing her off straight to the groom, Nana the editor of an album with dedications from all the girl's schoolmates, Orsa had written her out the fairy tales, legends and riddles with which she'd once sung her to sleep or gotten her to eat her egg, the Loungatides, local sprites, Gigaina the witch, the *Palatinos* with its Dutchmen under sail, what's got four legs in the morning, two in the afternoon, and three in the evening, she asked her daughter again feeling foolish and uncomfortable, not that Mersina was even listening, flapping round like a sea bream in a caïque, she opened her mother's bag and hey prestoed the three brine-encrusted spoons without asking what they were doing in there or if perhaps they were lucky charms, as though she'd stolen glances and touches many times before, she pointed at the one with the bent handle.

"Can I have it?" she asked.

"Of course, my love," Orsa replied, "of course."

*D*ear godmother,
  *On the peak of Olympus, two thousand six hundred and
  fifty meters above sea level, the lot of us staring at the
severed heads of some anarcho-communists, capetans they dare
call themselves, the postman handed me your check and you can't
imagine how immensely grateful I am, Herakles Bonis, 912
Regiment.*

Mosca asked Nana for the letter and read it over a couple of
times to herself, engrossed in household business she'd lost
touch with the business of the world, which could go anything
but unnoticed, Greece living something unprecedented, a civil
war, brothers in opposing political camps at each other's
throats, Alekos, her old man's godson, fallen in with the notori-
ous Abatielos, turned into a gutsy trade unionist who did much
as he pleased with the ships in foreign harbors though he'd
never had so much as a six-foot rowboat to his name, the folk
from the printer's, Christina's math teacher, Eftychis the electrician and second cousin Archontia had the Leftists in the
right, Dr. and Mrs. Resvanis, Saravanos the pediatrician, Aristos
the grocer, the barber and Tasa opposite, who could wrap you
around her little finger, in the wrong, Nicephoros's widow and
Mouraina, an old soak by now, the same, though the moment
she heard her nephew, little brother to that poor Takis who'd
broken down at sea, poor sod, was to be tried as a spy,
"Giannios a spy!" she'd pulled her crippled knees together and
shot straight to Athens like a banshee, to support the silly bug-

ger at his court martial, and she pulled something off, she moved heaven and earth, she managed something.

And then that depressing wee lad they'd gone and christened Herakles, who had teachers of literature for godmothers but was thick as a brick, twenty-one years old and writing stuff like that; they'd convened round Hexadaktylou's home this time, the preliminaries out of the way, exclamations of wonder at the ivy, a flood of green across the dining room walls and ceiling, for the forty or so begonias in the hothouse and the cages with finches and canaries set amongst their fragile stalks, brought down to earth with a bump by the young man's letter that had devastated Nana, not because she sympathized with the Left, no that never, "lucky we women don't have the vote," she often said, but because childless, she was reckoning on leaving everything to that distant cousin and godson, an illusion of an heir, and she may not have given a damn for her bureau, but the postcard collections with their elegantly scripted captions and verses, an entire world, totally wasted in Herakles's hands.

Hexadaktylou did not entertain often, senility and the depression of old age had made her bedridden mother aggressive, she sent them all to the devil that day, "Portuguese whores," some business left unfinished and unforgiven, they supposed, with the old womanizer long since dead, the maid too a decrepit old woman famed once for the snowdrift perfection of her icing-sugared *kourabiedes*, she forgot things too, thrice serving coffee and syruped black cherries. They didn't stick to one subject, blurting out news as it came to them sat in a circle, the pianist, Mosca, Nana, and Katerina, who the sinking of the *Chimara* the other day, January 20th, with the loss of so many lives, had shaken to the core, she felt trapped among the countless wrecks, "give it up" Mosca had said and she did want to stop embroidering them but saddened by the thought of abandoning tormented souls, "one more, the last," she'd say each time, and behold the *Chimara*, filling the straits of Kafirea and the

Euboian gulf with corpses, the ebb and flow carrying the drowned in and out and up and down, the ships fishing out bloated bodies for days on end.

"What will you play at the fundraiser for the troops?" Nana asked Hexadaktylou, all of them going crazy with dance after dance and Greek Welfare collections for the brave boys at the front, half the nation being cut to pieces on Greece's rugged mountain peaks, the other half singing and dancing for the fighting men. Madness.

Mosca resting her head on Katerina's shoulder, in no mood, that afternoon especially, for deciding if she was a monarchist, a democrat or red to the core; that bruiser Herakles had broken her chest with a blow from his spade, as though they didn't have a civil war of their own round the two-storeys, Orsa and her laying ambushes upstairs and down.

She bade them goodnight, the first to leave, back home in her kitchen Arta climbed the stairs and gave her something "from mother," a cigar box, now where did she find that, Mosca wondered, but it seemed that Friday was mail day; inside the wooden box Maltambes's seventeen letters to Orsa. She was scared, unsure if she could stand to read them. And what if reading them make things even worse, she wondered. The paper thin and age-yellowed, the ink gone brown, her eye made contact with a few isolated words, Surabaya, copra, coconut husks, my little mermaid, the sea too blue, the brine too salty, a few more further down, dead calm, kiss, cigarettes, Mosca lit one too, turning sheet after sheet, and towards the end "my little Orsa" all over the place. What do we do now, she struggled to think, her insides all knotted up, stealing words that were not hers, she cleared the big table of fruit bowl, ashtrays and the vase of winter flowers and carefully laid out the seventeen letters in chronological order. She looked again at the dates Spyros had written on the notepaper, top right, Chitagong September 27 1929, at sea October 1 1929, Calcutta October 7 1929, Surabaya October 17

1929, at sea October 25 1929, Vasora October 26 1929, Vasora October 28 1929, at sea November 7 1929, at sea November 11 1929, Lorenzo Marquez November 21 1929, at sea November 23 1929, at sea December 7 1929, his birthday, Bengo December 25 1929, Suerte January 5 1930, at sea January 24 1930, at sea February 22 1930, Surabaya March 20 1930. All seventeen letters posted before her engagement and marriage to Spyros, something that had never even occurred to her, the blood pounded in her veins, "Surabaya," she whispered and again, "Surabaya Surabaya," many times, maybe ten, and though she should have returned the box right away she sat up all night deciphering Spyros's scrawl with the accents in all the wrong places, the worst schoolboy that ever sat at an Andrian desk, he'd broken half of them and his exercise books all grease spots; so nothing reprehensible there, nothing to show there'd been anything extraordinary between Spyros and Orsa back then, she even recognized a couple of phrases he'd written her as well, almost identical, passionate phrases, "I miss your smell and your fresh-washed hair" and elsewhere, "I'll bite your lips and teach you a lesson" followed by the addressee, Orsoula and Orsaki like Moscoula and Moscaki, and of course half and more of the letters full of anger and quashed male pride over her marriage to Vatokouzis, inviting her sister to leave him and elope together to the other side of the world, throwing tantrums when married Orsa didn't even reply, "does that syphilitic kiss better than me?" he asked, and "pray his seed doesn't take." Of course, that sort of thing more fitting the spoilt malicious womanizer than the hero, poor Spyros doing a much better job in the paragraphs about the sea, his inventiveness and poetic verve translating into something sublime, "I sometimes weep like a baby as the sun sets over the Yellow River," he wrote, "even the mud a-sparkle and the darkness leaping in on fire," or "no way a man who's seen the moon on a white night over the Coral Sea will ever surrender his sailor's jacket, a prisoner of the ocean, enraptured for life."

So who loved him more, Orsa or me, she wondered for the first time of the man who had refused rescue with such hauteur and gone down with his ship. Perhaps he loved the sea more than any of them? Or perhaps he'd died to spare himself the peacetime choice? Mosca knew she could never have certain answers to all these questions, that's life, not everything comes clear in the end, people get by and move on to chapters new.

With the word of the evening, Surabaya, slipping steadily and silently from her lips for company, she stowed the letters neatly in the cigar box and sat for another cigarette or two staring at the wall, the framed letters of thanks from sailor navigators and gunners and petty officer signalmen, Captain Phantom had rescued two hundred of them and more, something like that is never forgotten, Mosca thought, her stomach stabbed, her mouth awash with bitterness, and Spyros, handsome and distant, with something of the wanderer and of Apollo about him, sitting without a care in the world in his frame, alone and seemingly in need of no one.

When his patients died, old Resvanis had all the time in the world afterwards, till the forty days were out, to make a correct diagnosis, in his youth, only after he'd buried Vatokouzis's youthful mother did he realize it was hypoglycemic shock that got her, because he hadn't prescribed an intravenous hypertonic glucose solution, unlike the middle-aged diabetic in Koureli he'd gone visiting and brought cakes, he'd done for her, too, and that boatman from Nimborió with all the kids he'd sent to heaven, a knee injury all he had, Saltaferaina had long since despaired of an improvement to the vitamin drinks and disgusting Norwegian cod liver oil, in the meantime bothering every doctor, obstetrician, ENT specialist and dermatologist that came to the island to offer his services for a week or so, and so she'd ended up networking with saints Greek and Roman, the Anargyri, the doctor-saints from Asia Minor on November 1st, their Roman brethren July 1st, Saint Barbara with the herb that cools a fevered brow and wards off rashes, Saint Spyridon, an ear specialist, Saint Paraskevi for the eyes, Saint Antypas for dental problems, and Saint Panteleimon GP.

Orsa rocking in the Viennese chair Nana had given her, propped up on two three cushions for comfort, looking at a light blue rectangle, less broad than high, sky and Aegean, from her window, telling Arta a tale or two, though the girl usually stayed away, two spoonfuls of mashed potato, two sips of chicory broth or a cup of watery soup and that was all.

There'd been a time the whole island agreed she was three

inches short of being a spot-on Aphrodite of Milo, now she was a scarecrow. The radio never off in her bedroom, volume low, she'd listen to songs, whatever, news, whatever, and the local bulletins Annezio issued in her febrile attempts to give her mistress life and cable Vatokouzis waiting in the wings.

The second bell arrived for the Assumption of the Virgin, they'd sent it to Athens for repair, damaged in the bombardment, the poultry dying but the market full of cheap lobsters, twenty two thousand drachmas an *oka*, Gaitanakis's Athenian troupe performing the *Lady of Pera* in the café, the scouts' dance in aid of the Troops, the shipowners getting lost fleets back with the liberty freighters, a gift from America, thirty British women got their seaman's papers and were serving on a pair of steamers with unpronounceable names, she talked and talked, rubbed knots out of calves and neck with a dab of cologne and Orsa surrendered to her love, paying her back with a flurry of kisses to her old woman's hands.

Which is how Mosca found them one afternoon, entering the room with a plate of custard in her hand and a different hue in her eyes, not black, her own. Annezio changed the water in the glass and left them alone.

Without words or much ado Mosca bent down and took her sister in her arms, she so needed to touch the other body, to feel the gelatin skin, smell the hair, a ton of it now, an unentanglable knot, to synchronize the beating of their hearts.

A start of sorts made, they talked all night long, a relay of confessions de profundis and commonplaces they'd stifled and deprived themselves of in equal measure, the two sisters had lost a lot of time and hurt each other without meaning to.

"Mother didn't want to undo us, either," said Mosca.

"Father loved another before they married."

"He had obligations in his wake and the dowry, the postal vessel, there right in front of him; the little white boat with the red and blue stripes their mother called lucky and had excelled in its day in the lemon and melon trade, from the Asia Minor coast to the Aegean islands and the City."

"Poor uncle Panagiotis, roast beef, moussaka, they say he was quite a cook."

"The sickness that makes men leap into the sea," Orsa said, ironically wondering if there ever was such a thing, she'd once or twice heard words to that effect behind her back and teased in an angelic sing-song voice, "but me, I'm not a boatswain," though it seems her put-on voice made some less hesitant when it came to foreseeing a bad end while the girl shut herself up in her room and wept with laughter.

"Father and mother weren't in love, not even for a moon," Mosca said and lit a cig.

"Though she did bake him tomato pilaf yesterday, she avoids it herself because it blocks her up, but he likes it."

"Tomato pilaf . . . "

"She wouldn't be a snake, not if she'd been loved."

"Or if she'd loved," Mosca added, realizing with a start she'd never wondered or asked about her mother young.

"She did." She, too, had loved; up in Apatouria grandma had entrusted the complete chart of the island's loves to her, just like a satanic and mirthful artist would have drawn it, of the last century, of course, because the old woman couldn't be bothered keeping the doings of the twentieth up to date and in depth, the family's extremes unprecedented and quite enough for her.

"Ah, dear old gran," Orsa said, and the invocation of the dead and the questioning and answering may not have been in keeping with women close to forty, they were girlish, wry and clumsy, but how else could they have covered so much not said before, when it should have been, maybe there are matters that, overburdened in themselves, cry out for clichés and stereotypes, lucky Nana was absent tonight, she'd often high-handedly impose mannered philosophical and literary expressions on the conversation.

"Mother'd sent me off on an errand when Balas came in his best suit to seek your hand for Spyros, so I wouldn't cotton on. I asked her afterwards, 'came to sell the dovecote,' she said, 'but squabs don't interest me, I invest elsewhere.'"

"If you weren't jealous of the cloth and lace pa sent me, if we'd been closer, I'd have told you, we wouldn't have ended up like this."

With all this and that, an enormous misunderstanding had settled over the white two-storeys, everyone thinking something else what with the silences and conversations left half-finished, their minds working overtime, Saltaferaina, for instance, had forced each of them into a mold since they were little and refused to see the truth, her eldest introverted, a loner, ironic, faithful and austere, the younger robust, hard-working and sociable, and mother grumbling Orsa seemed snobbish, aristocratic and willful, Mosca a tomboy and a leader.

"Spyros had forgotten you. We were happy those first years."

Orsa had leaned her head back and closed her eyes, no worth in lies.

"It was the *monopatosia* wouldn't let me forget him, when he came home on leave I wouldn't budge from the house, it became a sick habit, straining my ears, now he's emptying his pockets, now he's searching the hangers for something to wear, now he's closing the shutters against the glare, cackling watch-words and curses, his hoarse breath"; Orsa listed slowly, staring ceilingwards as though it were all happening there and then, fully in control, fully aware of what she was saying and to whom and not going to stop, she described sleepless nights, the sound of fresh-shod shoes on cypress boards, clumsy fatherly lullabies whose whale wheezings had the children wide awake, ancient conversations with just-married Mosca winking and to tease him over not taking after Balas when it came to birds, "my daft young chick" she'd call him and ask for a present of a Padua hen, one of those with the golden feathers in the ninth-grade school book, and she described other sounds, spoon on glass at two in the morning, Maltambes always craved a tablespoon of syruped blackberry after lovemaking, and spoke of habits, moments and images, his, she'd loved in secret, his gurgling and gentle snores, the way he licked the head off his beer, the inexplicable white tuft on his chest, his manly pigheadedness, old-fashioned and arousing, the favors, his prowess, the promises he made to all with unfailing generosity, and above all his all-embracing love for the sea, whose eyes, when you got down to it, he'd never once pulled the wool over, to her he'd surrendered unconditionally in the end.

Mosca laying down her own remembrances side by side with all she heard, the endless stream of carpenters in vain, for the *monopatosia* and their mother's downstairs fury, on bad terms with sleep she'd known from the start, banishing children and Annezio to the other end of the house, she remembered Nikos's fruitless appeals to move to his father's house and right on cue her children converging upstairs, shoes off she could hear them spinning round the rooms like tops, dropping their pencils and arguing in hushed tones over fresh almonds and a comb, she kept her head tilted back for the rest, eyes fixed on the single partition, twenty-four cypress boards, plain with the stamp of maternal stinginess, painted magnolia, an elegant ceiling that had done her so much harm.

"It sometimes crossed my mind you might not be asleep. Now we're speaking plainly, I think it was only in Piraeus, a few days here and there in the hotel, three times in all I think, that I enjoyed my husband freely."

Orsa started but not a sound.

"And Nikos?" Mosca asked.

"I didn't manage to love him enough, always patient and backing down, too good and too tolerant, a made match, and me seeing the wreckage round at Mouraina's and Nicephoraina's, Orsa's oath to marry for love or not at all."

When Saltaferaina's sleight of hand turned her life upside down, not a word, no resistance at all, however futile, she realized it was beyond her powers to sail against the tide, and Maltambes hitting her hard in his letters, you should have put up a fight, he wrote, the fight he didn't put up either in the end, him otherwise the reckless, the untamable, the fearless, the international lionheart.

Why had she loved Maltambes for twenty years at such cost to herself? Orsa still had no answer, she had no need of one, Spyros had a thousand good points but a thousand faults too, and it seems the combination drove her wild, she just loved him, she'd learned to think of him and to love him when still a little girl, she'd learned to remember him, and her feelings, repressed, remained and swelled, torching all the rest, everything permissible in the light of day and the small island community.

A girl still, she'd searched Mina's eyes for a hint of warmth for Savvas, her parents' lack of love pained her, that and the "I'm up to here!" and "I've had it with you" writ plain on their faces. And when at twelve she fell in love with Spyros, she swore she'd never give him a sour glance, that sort of look she renounced in perpetuity.

And Mosca?

The sheer bulk of Orsa's love pained her, it seemed her sister was made to love madly, like something out of a novel, that was what, deep down, Nana and all of them so envied for themselves; she shot sideways glances at the little body thrown over the armchair like an unstuffed cushion, she couldn't bear it, comparing how much they'd loved, Orsa had won the race that ultimately cost her all she had and more.

"If we'd had jobs . . . If we'd been out of the house, not poking around inside it, if we hadn't had the time to live a different life in our heads," the older woman, barely audible.

"I see the orange tree on the terrace every day, every day for years, in the end it comes up and reveals its secret, that one night beneath its branches illicit kisses were exchanged"; Mosca hadn't heard anything like that because it had never happened, but Orsa didn't protest, one of those things that doesn't suit denial, ideas like that not mad at all, but brought on by familiarity and interdependence with the unchanged and unchanging of everyday life in their little city, ten, fifteen in all, that's what happens when everything and everyone is known, their good side and their bad and feel something eating away at them, pilfering their private moments.

"If we'd worked," Orsa repeated.

"Or if we'd gone on to study. Why didn't we study, Orsa?"

"I was always a mediocre student, you could have become a teacher or interpreter."

"A nurse would have been fine, during the war I'd sit there where I do my sewing, on the little green sofa, with Christina on my knees untangling her hair for hours on end my conscience heavy. 'Kleisoura taken amidst a snowstorm,' remember?"

"Kleisoura taken amidst a snowstorm," Orsa repeated; she agreed with her sister on everything, but they were confessing all this after the seahorse had bolted, little help that at this stage in the game, but the night had brought it up, Kiki Bousoula calling round earlier, twins left a while with Mina and young godmother, and in this very room, apropos of nothing but her timing perfect, "Spyros saved our menfolk, he's our hero and that's the end of it."

It was late, Mosca stood at the window magnetized by the dark, whenever she cast her mind back in search of her first childhood image, it wasn't her mosquito net, Markos the house-cat then who'd slept on her slippers or desk, or that Stratakis, the teacher who was always clearing and feeling his throat to make sure his Adam's apple hadn't upped and left, no her first memory the view from the window in the gold-blue light of afternoon, Aegean, Saint Ermolaos, Paraporti, sand, with three six- or seven-year-olds dripping and running as though their little bottoms were on fire, shrieking delirious and blinding each other with handfuls of sand.

Orsa had put a spoonful of custard in her mouth, she didn't want her pills, "don't torture me" she'd begged and drifted off to sleep, the strain of today's meeting with all that was said and implied would have exhausted a bull; even Mosca, who was as strong as one, had to summon all she had to get to her feet for the climb upstairs.

She pulled the light summer bedspread over Orsa and took the brimming ashtray to empty outside; lately, she'd been opening a second packet.

As the two sisters began to spend their afternoons together, the neighbors, the women especially, initially breathed a sigh of relief, but were a little shocked when they thought it over, even the parents who weren't completely in the picture were bewildered that jasmine and moonflowers were breaking out in the bedroom instead of war, no change on the food front, though, and Mosca no longer pressing her sister who had muscle pain, diarrhea, a low-grade fever that wouldn't break but neither moaned nor groaned.

Arta averse to her mother, she blamed her for daddy leaving, and Savvas and Mersina, "regards to little Arta" or "floods of kisses" at best and that was it, they still hadn't sent her a letter of her own, not one, just boxes of toys she quickly grew to hate as well.

The most serious charge she laid at her mother's door her pitiable appearance, a ma all skin and bones.

Orsa wasn't punishing herself with starvation, wasn't punishing the others for their interventions in her life, wasn't trying to burden her family with guilt, she didn't feel like that anyhow, even if she was watching her youngest grow up deprived of brother and sister, even if she hadn't put her foot down, either, to keep Savvas and Mersina at her side; the fabric of history, complex, things all knotted and slowly unsnagging of their own accord, portioning folk anew among the cities, transforming friendships and loves, carving out routes and sea lanes, molding the backdrop afresh for the new batch, the six

Maltambes and Vatokouzis children who had to stop to catch a breath at last.

Annezio's four-square mind pleased, it was something, but dedicated body and soul to preparing the house, not expecting Nikos this time but her Antonis, an American citizen with an American wife, a manicurist, permission received to sleep them in the master bedroom and drape it with all the City silks that had made it through the war, before the moths finished them off.

The little town much impressed by the foreigner's long orange nails, her heavy make-up, Antonakis the communist had suc-cumbed to luxury and a chill in his mother's heart, "there," she told him and handed him the *Voice of the Aegean*, about his schoolmate Manos, "Manouil Tsoumezis of the Royal Engineers, 3rd Battalion, 5th Company, 902 Unit condemns communism and declares himself ready to return to the service of his nation," and if the nation didn't want the stutterer, his mum wanted him back, Annezio keeping her company on days like this, so as not to stay at home and watch her son's bride staring in the mirror, acting the big shot and making her a servant again.

Everyone concerned with Antonis, with the tragedies in Agrafa, on Grammos and Vitsi's peaks and ridges, the fratricide that had Mina murmuring "deliver thy children from civil strife, immaculate Mother of God," as she stared at the Eye of God, fed up to the back teeth with it all, as though admonish-ing Him up there, "what is it you're up to exactly, do some-thing," and apart from that all attention on that superlative achievement of the Krios shipyards, sailing Turkey-Greece-New York and moored off Chora to drop off a stowaway and wow the sailors' isle with its gyro-compass, direction finder, sonar bathometer, and gadget for automatically calculating Greenwich time, with so much to discuss, Orsa and Mosca left in peace in the downstairs room to examine their faith and love each other one more time.

"I want to go to church, on Saint Nicholas's day."

It wasn't only Resvanis and the Athenian doctors, Father Philippos, too, had given up; he'd come to the house to hear her confession and the younger priest who'd taken up his post, they'd struggled in vain, defeated by the emaciated woman, "I admire your persistence, you just don't give up," she'd told them, the devil.

"Orsa, why did you let him fall in love with you again?" Mosca talking to herself, her appetite for interrogations sated, but there was still something gnawing away inside sometimes, how grand it would be if they led a normal life, far from the medals, the rare loves and ancient tragedies.

Even Marie, her peevish and unsatisfied friend who found everyone insipid, dopey and hollow and mocked them with rhyming barbs, the sharpest-shooting verse-monger of the four, took the women by surprise writing from America, finally captivated by her husband in the eleventh year of their marriage, she'd just found out Takis had been rescued from a shipwreck in the Pacific, the crew leaping into the foaming sea and him afraid of the waves clinging to the half-sunk prow, all hands lost, the *Estoril*, nineteen men, and Takis picked up two days later by a Russian coastal steamer perched like a seagull on the ship's tip, trousers terror-soiled, Marie so moved he'd dared feel a child's fear.

So Orsa didn't know how and when Maltambes had fallen in love with her again, they'd stolen a few moments together, their hearts in their mouths, so few times, she didn't care why, she just stuck to the fact that they had.

Just before the outbreak of war, nothing could wait, everything had seemed urgent, a final chance.

When old man Saltaferos entered the room, he thought about asking Mosca to leave for a while but came to his senses right away and avoided the gaffe. He closed the door behind him, even though Saltaferaina was in Apatouria seeing to some business, sat down heavily on the edge of the bed, laid some photographs on the blanket along with the buff envelope and took a cigarette from his daughter, all the while explaining the existence and the loss of a son and the Argentine, he didn't mention the woman's profession, that forgotten long ago, he'd kept the whole thing silent so long, a thorn in his conscience, his daughters ought to know.

They'd suffered so much, confessed and forgiven one another, they took their father's lapse in their stride. All part of the sailor's life, a year before, Christakis Tezas, former cook aboard the *Theomitor* and the *Marousio Bebi*, had retired and instead of returning to Vourkoti had hung his hat in Chile with Froso, Tasoula, Vaggelio, Chilean wife and daughters, the family a carbon copy of his first in the village, they'd found out from their little pre-war maid, Eleni, the niece of the ship's cook who'd turned out a master when it came to cooking the books of life.

So there you had it, father had loved another before his marriage and loved another during it, and if he'd lost Angelita-Ita he was left with Asimina-Mina; Mosca brewed him some coffee and they stayed to look at the photographs, hot foreign Angelita and mostly their adopted brother, so handsome so ill-fated, *vanidad de vanidades, todo vanidad*, never a truer word, futility and all that.

"Don't say anything to Mina."

"Don't worry, pa," Mosca replied and buried herself in his embrace, how many people have to die to breathe new life into a few relationships, she thought angry and bitter, spying on her father's irregular heartbeat and the warmth of his body, she'd missed him but didn't want to keep him all for herself, if only that Argentinean boy were alive, she might ask him more in time.

Orsa envied neither the son nor the hug, it was time for those two to make up, only she was ashamed to catch her father looking at her hair, old man Saltaferos pretended not to see the terrible state his daughter was in, "poor poor hair," he'd say every now and then, "poor poor hair," once *cabello largo e rizado no more*.

Each new day found Anton more at home and in love with the island, he'd leave his wife in Plakoura amidst all her fuss and rediscover pastures old, his boyhood love from Aladinou and her fun-loving husband, the grocer who interpreted dreams, and Cosmas the refugee from Asia Minor who'd taught him how to catch mullet with a thrown net, he asked after all those who were missing, and charged headlong into christenings, engagements, funerals and memorials. He had the language and accent back in a fortnight, his old taste buds, some carefully camouflaged Leftist friendships, and the rhythm of the island's day; Annezio scared out of her wits, couldn't face the responsibility for bringing him back to the island in a time of civil war and separated at that, because his wife, Barbara, wasn't comfortable and didn't look like a woman who'd take it all meekly or mildly. But she'd still asked him a favor: "never tell Orsa to cut her hair again," and before going back to Chicago to sit down and patiently tend to her head, America way ahead when it came to hairdressing and with Orsa not wanting to disappoint Annezio, the sessions began, experienced Antonis massaging in olive oil and something aromatic from foreign-looking tubes, patiently untangling and brushing.

On Saint Nicholas's day the city saw her honey-colored tresses again.

Wintry sun after three days of rain, the streets well-washed, the bells, flags, drums, the countless figures clad in black, seaborne toil bane and boon alike for this community.

Orsa couldn't make it to the church on foot, Savvas Saltaferos, Gialaros and Takis, classmates of her son, and Eftychis the electrician hoisting the rocking chair aloft two at a time in relays.

Mosca talked them up the endless steps, so they wouldn't stumble, people rushing to their windows or moving aside in the narrow streets, staring at Orsa in awe, Mouraina crossing herself on her balcony, schoolgirls silently praying, the delicate creature beneath the tartan blanket rendered holy by a surfeit of love.

Orsa wanted to see the townsfolk in church once more surrendering to the authority of the patron saint who saw to crews and their fate, *him who now and forever stills the winds, calms the waves, brings storms to an end and stirs the good and fitting winds and climes, be forever commander and mate to Your servants, and guide them to safe havens*, she'd learned it by heart in high school, for a sketch about the fire-ship captains of the Greek Revolution, all the men in her life, father, uncles, husband, son, beloved, His.

She took communion, saw the young priest tending to her with respect, gently blinked or nodded her head in good morning to the old schoolmates, shopkeepers and neighbors she had not seen for so long, eyes searching out her father's erstwhile bosom buddy Father Philippos, but he was nowhere to be seen, not since his wife's sudden unconscionable death gulping down her milk, backgammon seemed lukewarm without her nagging, the house cold without her clutter, church monotonous without her superstitions.

Orsa's eyes had glazed over once or twice during the service, sinking into a void of exhaustion, emotion and thoughts that would not focus.

The return even more spectacular, word was out and all the men came running to lay eyes on the woman once hailed the town's most beautiful, now a burnt-down candle wrapped in unshorn hair, Orsa's procession at times as emotive as that of the sacred icon and no one thought it blasphemy, indeed Nana explained to two young female colleagues that this was a triumph of love that softened the fire and brimstone of the Christian faith and its doctrinal excesses. Whatever the case, it was a morning that those who lived it were never to forget.

Marina got engaged to the teacher in Stenies, twenty-four years old, Peloponnesian with amazing eyes like coal and a tongue that twinkled even more, he wouldn't leave her in peace, and the truth was the flow of letters with America had slowed to a trickle, Savvas replying to one of her five and the seamstress's proud daughter had no intention of sniffling and imploring, not with so many others beseeching her.

Mersina-Christina also tailing away, different continents, a different life, an age at which the young can sometimes wipe their old selves away. Who knows, the two might rediscover each other in a decade or two and take it from there, what had united them in childhood not the stuff that time erases, Nana was banking on that.

"Women's necks are more flexible because they're made to look back too, female friendships are based in trust, self-sacrifice and self-denial," and one fine morning Mersina and Christina would stride ahead arm in arm.

And Christina Maltambes might be wearing that ring with the green stone, her namesake grandmother's. Following her sister's instructions, Mosca had unearthed it among the countless boxes in her chest of drawers.

"How come I didn't find it when I turned your whole house upside down?"

"I had it in my cardigan pocket," Orsa replied, her condition much worsened in the last two weeks, often losing touch with the world around her and Nana Hexadaktylou and Katerina, second cousin Archontia had gone all cold on her, coming round for half-hour visits or to give Mosca a break, so many obligations, the paperwork for the fortune she'd entrusted to Vatokouzis to keep up with, the children to mind and teach English, more intensively to her niece, she'd taken on another two or three, confidence in her proficiency in the foreign tongue the only one left standing.

Annezio sighing deeply and losing heart and Saltaferaina doing what her husband did when the house wasn't big enough for him, she'd leave, with her unused sailor's papers in her handbag to finger from time to time, to curse, in spring she'd wander the fields and chase away the Mediterranean fly that blotched the fruit trees, with the cold came visits to the MP's office to let fly at the Minister for Agriculture who wouldn't let the eighteen cows, twelve mules and two bulls come from America to Andros and, as always, she'd help out with the *kolyva* of strangers and the clearance of the homes of the dead, many couldn't take the tasks and Mina justifying her reputation with actions. All hope of reconciliation gone, proud, she'd stood the isolation and her whole life falling to pieces around her.

Midwinter, fierce cold, as cold as '41, with snow covering the whole island all the way down to the sea, and the place packed with wild geese on the run from central Greece, frightened off by the cold and the barrage of war.

The Cyclades, those little scattered islands, lived events in miniature, Andros's few Leftists, not wanting to rouse suspicion, couldn't even organize a collection with real money, they'd secretly sent two barrels of oil to the central Communist Party cell on Syros, impossible for battles to be fought, their echoes alone reached this place, the occasional declaration of repentance in the *Voice of the Aegean*, and now the wild geese, five *oka* a piece, and a run on powder and birdshot.

So that Thursday, Nana sitting goddaughter on lap at bedbound Orsa's side worried the starch would come out of her pleats, because she'd parted with most of her skirts during the war for a few bags of flour, chattering away about the freshly-printed postcards of the Acropolis with the too bright colors and casting her vote in favor of the old ones, sepia shades with a Doric silence about them entirely in keeping with antiquity's prestige. The collection destined for little Arta, who in years to come, if curiosity tickled, could in an evening learn where half of Andros had honeymooned, and had only to turn the cards over to enjoy near-indiscreet details related in a romantic and literary style.

The Brooklyn-Battery bridge, the largest in the world, still a couple of years away from service, turned into a postcard and, as the hundredth, bringing to a close the cherry velvet album Nana had years since tired of.

"My age is advancing faster than technology, I'll not live to see the Cavo d'Oro bridge, the one I've dreamed of all my life, no nipping off to Paris and London for me, no clapping eyes on my hometown again."

With two pitiless furrows, time's, in her blue cheeks, a face whose eras past existed layered one on top of the other, childhood and youth visible in the pianist's most recent version, with its musing childish expression and slightly protuberant lower lip pouting in longing for a kiss, an erotic kiss no longer, the kiss of a child, because Hexadaktylou had claimed the little one for her own; the piano always there, and resorting to tricks to tempt her, picking out the meowing of the cat on its keys, the sound of water dripping in the sink and of Saltaferos breaking wind, the Mandolinata School, too, already with fifty pupils, boys and girls, and at the Musical Circle's soiree for the New School Year all the girls dressed in white, a sight for sore eyes. Andros's musical life, always provincial, on the up and up and the Philharmonic approaching full strength, nearly all the Italian swag replaced, three cornets, three clarinets, two flutes, a kettledrum, the bass drum's bits and bobs.

Nine-year-old Arta had been counting and recounting Hexadaktylou fingers for months now, and as she kept finding only five, the same number as her and everyone else who wasn't a pianist, she'd stopped sneaking glances and bothering with her, not overly keen on these women fit to burst with ideas and interests, and it was true that the years, the loneliness and the war had left them with a touch of egotism and hysteria, she watched Katerina, always quiet, turning her mother over carefully, as though she were made of glass, rubbing her back and legs gently with alcohol and thought how small her mother had got, she could easily have fit into one of her little skirts.

Something happens to you when you stop being a child, she thought, the adults around her all proof of that.

But she didn't stay out to escape them like her younger cousin Mina, a wild thing the earth would swallow up for hours at a time.

Relative quiet had just settled over the upstairs home, a pause in the trampling feet and slamming doors, "Katerina, sing us a song," Orsa asked; she felt relieved and happy, they'd twice lifted her up to look out the window at the snow she so loved, and when she fumbled for Arta's hand the little girl had not refused.

Saravanos had tried to do something, too, every two months when he came to the island for a week or so, he'd wind up his surgery and leave Orsa's house call till last, stare methodically and silently at the little bottles and then, evening already, climb upstairs to Mosca's children, dallying over little Mina, seven going on eight, looking for herself in the mirror and whispering secrets and nonsense in his ear, "won't you stay for dinner?" Mosca's invitation, she'd take his jacket and there'd soon be just the two of them, the plates pushed away, the pediatrician slowly peeling an apple or two and offering her them slice by slice on the tip of a knife, neither of them hoping for anything more.

Their footfalls upstairs again tonight, familiar, high heels and squeaky leather soles, and when he'd walked down the hall and the front door had closed behind him, with a bang due to the draft, he climbed down the entrance marble and Mosca the kitchen stone, powdered, a hint of lipstick, "I'm so tired," she sighed, settling on the edge of the bed and fighting back the yawns.

Katerina was ready, no music she didn't love thanks to the records Vangelis had sent her, clueless, he'd fallen for the covers and bought something of everything, popular songs, national anthems, symphonic works and operas, the girl bold in her choices, Hexadaktylou thought, not knowing the special importance some things have. So she quietly struck up Filippo's aria from *Don Carlos*, Verdi, she could pick out the words a little better with the men, the tenors and basses.

There were no halcyon days in 1948. The sun appeared in early March, spring right off. The islanders needed to shake off the confinement of the long hard winter, folk of all ages with errands to run and without, strolling down the streets, to the barber's for a trim, to the Club and the cafés for a chat, to the mole for a walk in the company of their thoughts.

Saturday morning, the children still at school, Archontia sewing round Loukissas', Nana had Bey down from Livadia pruning her famous white rose, Hexadaktylou on her way to Athens to look into her circulation and attend a recital by an acquaintance in the Parnassos Hall, Annezio and Katerina off at the grave lighting lamps and burning incense, and Capt. and Mrs. Saltaferos with the Hadoulises and other upstanding members of society visiting Chora's hospital, to be present for the delivery of the electric refrigerator Hadoulis Junior had sent from New York for the penicillin.

The young monk from the Panachrantos Monastery dismounted, oil lantern in hand, unhooked a canvas bag from his mule's saddle, and entered the Saltaferoses' yard where Mosca was waiting for him. One of the buttons on his overcoat didn't match and his robes were worn. He was hungry and willingly sat at table with Mosca, brought round by salt cod, beetroots with a garlic dip and a little wine, and Spyros Maltambes's widow no ordinary woman, kept current with world affairs by the BBC and blessed with the virtues of forgiveness and fortitude.

They spoke mostly of Epirus, chance had never brought Mosca there, but the monk, Symeon, who heard others' problems, needing to share his own from time to time, childhood friends, his grandfather and his dog.

After coffee he picked up the bag and climbed down the kitchen stairs, Mosca threw a couple of logs into the range and they went through into Orsa's bedroom. She was calm and smelt of cologne, but nothing about her recalled the angelic beauty they'd described to Symeon, he looked for and found in the photographs on the walls.

He sat close to her, pulled open the bag he was carrying and took out the pearly box with Saint Panteleimon's skull; all winter long, because he was good with the mule and seemingly immune to the flu, it was him they sent to the far-flung sick and dying. Mina Saltaferaina had sent the abbot a very sizeable gift.

Symeon regretted the garlic, blushed, opening his mouth for the blessing against all disease a torment, *O Lord Almighty, healer of souls and bodies*; Orsa mouthed the words along with him, she really had nothing to answer the monk's inquiring gaze, the blame not hers that some thought her a fool to die so young or mad like uncle Panagiotis, lost to the sickness that makes men leap into the sea.

"Cast out of this woman every wound, every ache, every scourge, every fever or chill and all sins and trespasses, comfort, pardon, forgive in your mercy. Lord, spare your creation."

With Mosca's help, Orsa raised herself and kissed the sacred relic, eyes tight shut, the idea repulsed her, she'd never had much truck with all of that, but lacking the strength to reject the rituals prescribed, all this just a detail.

Symeon closed the book of prayers, the box too, the woman before him was dying of earthly love, of eros, very young, he could not bear her closeness for too long, he pulled the drawstring closed once more, picked up his lantern and hurried out, he had to pass by Aristos's shop too, for the abbot's salami and hard cheese before it was time for Lenten fare.

When Annezio found out about the visit, she could have kicked herself, she wouldn't have sent the dip if she'd known, she'd have sent soup.

The following afternoon, Sunday, with a sweet light turning the clouds over the Eye of God to tulle and the people on the mole or glued at Chora's windows with binoculars watching the Andrian freighter *Katina Marie*, under captain Georgios Falaggas of Stenies, sailing by out to sea and blowing repeated greetings to the families of its crew, Mosca took something out of the drawer and went downstairs, her watch, Saltaferos had just taken his grandchildren out for cakes, their mother there, with the cat and her door shut.

She entered the bedroom, Orsa's eyelids fluttering from sleep and exhaustion, unfolded the sheet she was holding and covered her sister, grey and blue, embroidered by hand, Katerina Basandi's work, the sinking of the *Little England*, a fluttering banner in the sky declared the date, March 11 1943, the grey sea, the ship in flames and half-sunk and captain Spyridon D. Maltambes on the bridge. Katerina had given it her eighteen months before, "for your children, at least," she'd said and Mosca hated her that noon for her devotion to duty, not knowing if she wanted that terrible cloth, and no idea where to hide it to forget, and after days of stowing it away, moving it from the trunk with the needlework to the bottom of her nightdress drawer and from the sideboard with his shirts to the top of the wardrobe, in the end she'd stuck it in an out-of-the-way trunk with the souvenirs and journals of her seafaring family, mouse-nibbled captain's logs from ships that were no more, broken bric-a-brac, an African woman who'd lost her head, an elephant without its trunk, some kangaroos bereft of young, pouches empty.

"My Christina's, when the time comes," she told Orsa whose

eyes had livened up, she'd never seen its like before, Katerina had lain a veil of silence across her work all these years; she was moved by the desperation and the faith that emanated from the sewing basket and the embroiderer's weak points, in the figure of Spyros particularly, with his large out-of-proportion head, the head with the curly black hair, the black eyes sometimes restless and supercilious, sometimes fixed on the horizon with the glazed expression of one-up-manship and of pride slowly cracking and betraying his sadness and loneliness.

"Them that drown don't live to regret it," she remembered the phrase he liked to turn out before raki or to put an end to conversations about shipwrecks and her heart was beating again, irregular and violent, she'd struggled to erase the images of the night of March 11 1943 from her imagination, Spyros's face amongst them, for her his loss was contained in a captain's hat, without insignia in time of war, afloat, alone, in Irish waters.

"We never did see that ship up close," Mosca said, Katerina had imagined it long, faintly yellow, with three black funnels, it wasn't like that but what matter the mistake? The years made some more sorrowful and sour, others it softened, Katerina of the latter sort, in her needlework she'd found purpose and salvation in routine.

Mosca made some coffee, she'd spend all afternoon with Orsa.

"Give me a spoonful, for the aroma."

"I'm thinking of getting my driving license when I go to Athens in October."

"Don't forget Nana, to take her for a ride, too."

They could hear the cheerful bustle outside thanks to the *Katina Marie*, conversations shouted across opposite windows, running in the alleys and, later, the three whistles of departure and the slow road home.

Not one of them still a captain's wife, Hadoulis junior, a member of the Greek Shipowners' Union of New York, had got three liberty freighters on the usual favorable terms, and Nikos with a thirty percent share in their offices night and day, dispatching cargo from America for Haifa, to the fresh-formed Jewish state, the mathematics he'd half studied at the age of twenty more than useful. Mosca kept him up to date with the situation and other family matters, writing letters on Orsa and Annezio's behalf, a brief account of her own news tacked on as a postscript, she didn't want her news sailing too far from the island and with little time to spare, the life assurance she'd turned into plots in Athens, Ambelokipoi and Kallithea, and from Mina's drawer downstairs the briefcase with the deeds, fencing bills, tax paid and estate agents' cards had found a new home on the first floor, in the oak desk of her schooldays, vacant as her untidy children did their homework on all fours on the kitchen floor or in the porch. The Vatokouzis family would be arriving at the end of the school year, they hoped they'd be in time, but still would have nothing to say, they'd suddenly find themselves faced with something they thought strange but which Mosca and other patient souls had come to respect and accept.

Orsa, though, wanted to die before that.

The same old questions again, the despairing glances, Nikos with blond hair now almost white and glasses with thin wire frames sitting facing her for hours, his strange hands crossed on his chest, the hundreds of veins, rivers and rivulets breaking the banks of turned-up sleeves and throbbing with the anguish that consumed him, it wouldn't change a thing, just cost her children yet more dear.

"They'll never forgive me."

"Since we're sitting here drinking coffee together, it'll be easier for the others, we've forced them to follow suit, sooner or later."

"And your son?"

"Mimis is the hardest."

"He doesn't even speak to me."

"Nor to me."

And that was the truth of it, Maltambes's only son, with a couple of urchins in tow round other folks' homes all day and night, on the rocks and in Balas's dovecote, his command post, not opened a book once since the cinema arrived in town last year, Nana pressing the teacher to turn a blind eye.

"And him starting high school next year."

"Marine school," Mosca clarified, it almost went without saying but she said it again, "the marine high school," on his request, she'd enrolled him as a boarder in Piraeus.

It was getting dark and Orsa staring out the window as lights and lamps came on one by one in neighbors' homes and the street, brushing her palm across the long and slender banner proclaiming *Little England* on the sheet and in a weak and intermittent voice began to tell her sister of their last meeting, her and Spyros.

"The day he was to leave and you were having us round to dinner, we met in secret in Apatouria, in the ravine. I'd gone to fetch grandma."

Mosca didn't interrupt, just listened, moistening Orsa's lips now and then with a drop of water.

"He caressed me like he had the very first time, quietly intoning his every move, tracing the oval of my face with the back of his hand, the triangle of my chin, the wings of my nose, the full stop of the little mole on my right temple, three dots for my eyelids, the half-moons of my eyebrows, the half-moons of my ears, that's the sort of things he said, the man who knew so little of poetry, I'd read him poems once and he remembered, he sniffed ravenously at my hair and I gave myself to him there among the myrtles, on his jacket. I knew his movements and his sighs, the *monopatosia* had revealed them to me on so many occasions, eleven years of torture, a pleasure whose sounds I'd garner and let my body ache."

I'll burn this house one day, Mosca thought, and squeezed

her sister's hand, by rights she was madder than Orsa, to be sitting here listening to a confession like this.

"I haven't kept anything from you."

The relief was plain to see that the whole truth and not half truths brings, as for Mosca, her precise emotions weren't dissimilar from those that flood the soul when we put down a lengthy novel, the story not left unfinished, they had made love, even if it was just once, her husband Spyros before he died in the war, and her sister Orsa before her passion melted her away, she loved those two and when, left alone, she had to close the mouths that remained, she could draw strength from this mad passion, it seemed she and Nikos were made to stand aside.

"Mosca, are you crying?"

"No, see my eyes, they're not shining," Mosca thinking all the same, how could Orsa stay all alone in the darkness, four feet under the earth and stones, she'd heard Emilios, near the end, tell his pigeons, "I can't bear the thought of being down there all alone."

In the days that followed, the doctors coming and going, serving a lost cause, Savvas and Mina at the kitchen table in their little home next door, internal partition, suffering in silence, "let me see Smyrna too," he asked and touched her hesitantly on the elbow, a few photos had found their way to her via metropolitans and priests, mostly of the house in which she'd spent her carefree childhood, destined to be her life's only happy time, she didn't recognize a thing, the wisteria missing from the entrance, not even sure about the lamp on the sitting-room ceiling, but in one of them a little Turkish urchin with a tomcat in his arms, ashen whiskers to half-tail, the other half pure white, just like their cats back then, half a century before, Turkan Hatun and Panagiota his distant forebears, no doubts there.

"Fancy that," said Savvas.

Mina remembered the old days when her husband had shown her that for him the last word in satisfaction was sucking the meat off a blackfish head and cursing the government, and her contempt of him inside; if only something like that would happen now, she'd look upon it with sympathy, to be honest, she'd really like that sort of thing to happen, she wanted none of the rest.

She raised her head and searched high for the Eye of God through the half-open window, so they could stare each other down, but it seemed he spurned her in the way conspirators admit their guilt and failure, "my precious girl, you're going to meet him," she admitted, and then, no tears, nibbled at crumbs, one by one from the branches on the waterproof tablecloth.

The printer had the notice of death ready, the town looking for it on the front door of the white two-storeys, impatient at Orsa's soul so slow to depart, some annoyed at the protraction, perhaps because no one was jealous of a woman at death's door, many though did not avoid the comparison, how much love had they lived in their lives?

Anyhow, Orsa died in her sister's arms on the afternoon of Friday April 16 1948, aged thirty-nine, as the idlers and the children, a whole swarm of them, were rushing to the central square where restaurateurs and confectioners were replacing the old chairs of wood and straw, en masse, with two hundred and fifty modern models in lime green.

ABOUT THE AUTHOR

Ioanna Karystiani was born on the island of Crete, Greece, in the town of Chania and now lives in Athens. She made her literary debut with *I kyria Kataki* (*Mrs. Kataki*). She has since written three novels, all of which have been translated into several languages. She wrote the screenplay for *The Brides*, directed by Pandelis Vulgaris and produced by Martin Scorsese, and *Estrella mi vida*, directed by Costa Gavras. She has received the Greek state prize for literature, the Athenian Academy prize for her first novel, and the Diavaso literature prize for her second.

AVAILABLE NOW from EUROPA EDITIONS

The Days of Abandonment
by Elena Ferrante
translated by Ann Goldstein

"Stunning . . . The raging, torrential voice of the author
is something rare." —Janet Maslin, *The New York Times*

"I could not put this novel down. Elena Ferrante will blow
you away." —Alice Sebold, author of *The Lovely Bones*

AVAILABLE NOW from EUROPA EDITIONS

Cooking with Fernet Branca

by James Hamilton-Paterson

Gerald Samper, an effete English snob, has his own private
hilltop in Tuscany where he wiles away his time working
as a ghostwriter for celebrities and inventing wholly original
culinary concoctions—including ice-cream made with garlic
and the bitter, herb-based liqueur of the book's title.
Gerald's idyll is shattered by the arrival of Marta, on the run
from a crime-riddled former soviet republic. A series of hilarious
misunderstands brings this odd couple into ever closer and more
disastrous proximity. "A work of comic genius." —*The Independent*

AVAILABLE NOW from EUROPA EDITIONS

Minotaur

by Benjamin Tammuz

translated by Kim Parfitt and Mildred Budny

An Israeli secret agent falls hopelessly in love with
a young English girl. Using his network of shady contacts
and his professional expertise, he takes control of her life without
ever revealing his identity. Minotaur, named "Book of the Year"
by Graham Greene, is a complex and utterly original story about
a solitary man driven from one side of Europe to the other
by his obsession. "A novel about the expectations and compromises
that humans create for themselves . . . Very much in the manner
of William Faulkner and Lawrence Durrell." —*The New York Times*

AVAILABLE NOW from EUROPA EDITIONS

Total Chaos
by Jean-Claude Izzo

translated by Howard Curtis

"Jean-Claude Izzo's [...] growing literary renown and huge sales
are leading to a recognizable new trend in continental fiction:
the rise of the sophisticated Mediterranean thriller . . .
Caught between pride and crime, racism and fraternity,
tragedy and light, messy urbanization and generous beauty,
the city for [detective Fabio Montale] is a Utopia, an ultimate port
of call for exiles. There, he is torn between fatalism
and revolt, despair and sensualism." —*The Economist*

This first installment in the legendary Marseilles Trilogy
sees Fabio Montale turning his back on a police force
marred by corruption and racism and taking
the fight against the mafia into his own hands.

AVAILABLE NOW from EUROPA EDITIONS

I Loved You For Your Voice

by Sélim Nassib

translated by Alison Anderson

Love, desire, and song set against the colorful backdrop
of modern Egypt. The story of the Arab world's greatest
and most popular singer, Umm Kalthum, told through
the eyes of the poet Ahmad Rami, who wrote her lyrics
and loved her in vain all his life. Spanning over five decades
in the history of modern Egypt, this passionate tale of love
and longing provides a key to understanding the soul,
the aspirations and the disappointments of the Arab world.
"A total immersion into the Arab world's magic and charm."
—*Avvenimenti*